AUNTIE BEERS

A book of connected short stories

CATHERINE ASTOLFO

Auntie Beers

A book of connected short stories

Catherine Astolfo

Paperback ISBN 13: 978-1-77242-181-1

CARRICK PUBLISHING

Carrick Publishing

Catherine Astolfo is a two-time winner
of the Crime Writers of Canada Award
for Best Short Crime Story.

Reminiscent of Alice Munro--these stories are heart-wrenching, authentic, and luminous.
~ *Ginger Bolton, author of the Deputy Donut Mysteries*

Dedication

To my granddaughters, Catey, Sydney and Livi,
who embody the strong, intelligent, powerful females of the
present and future.

To my grandmothers, mother, mother-in-law, and aunts,
who embodied the strong, intelligent, powerful females of
the past and who gave me these stories.

Clare's Family Tree

Name: Fionn (Fiona)
O'Sullivan
born: 1874
place: Ireland
died in Ireland

Name: Padhraig
(Patrick) O'Sullivan
born: 1876
place: Ireland
died in Ireland

Great Aunts/Grandmother

Name: Bairbre
(Barbara) O'Sullivan
[Auntie Beers]
born: 1894
place: Ireland
died in Canada

Name: Gráinne (Grace)
Murphy
born: 1899
place: Ireland
married: Brendan
Murphy
Children: Anne, Sean

Name: Maighread
(Maggie) O'Sullivan
born: 1900
place: Ireland
married: Seamus
O'Sullivan
died in Canada

Children of Maggie and Seamus O'Sullivan

Name: Eoin (John)
born: 1920
place: Ireland
married: Carol
died in Canada

Name: Eammon
(Edward)
born: 1921
place: Ireland
married: Jennifer
died in Canada

Name: Daniail (Daniel)
born: 1922
place: Ireland
married: Colleen
died in Canada

Name: Maighread
(Peggy)
born: 1923
place: Ireland
married: Marco Fallaci
died in Canada

Name: Micheal
(Michael)
born: 1924
place: Ireland
married: No
died in Canada

Name: Caitlin
(Kathleen): Clare's
mother
born: 1925
place: Ireland
married: Steven Doyle:
Clare's father
died in Canada

```
Name: Brigid                        Name: Liam
born: 1929                          born: 1936
place: Canada                       place: Canada
married: Alan Watson                married: No
died in Canada                      died in Canada
```

Clare's Aunts and Uncles with Cousins

```
Name: John O'Sullivan      Name: Eddie                Name: Daniel
Born in Ireland, 1920      O'Sullivan                 O'Sullivan
Married Carol              Born in Ireland 1921       Born in Ireland, 1922
No children               Married Jennifer           Married Colleen
                          Children: Timothy,         Children: Grace,
                          Helen and Joan             Theresa, Mary,
                                                     Seamus, Peter
```

```
Name: Peggy O'            Name: Michael              Clare's family unit
Sullivan                  O'Sullivan                 Name: Kathleen
Born in Ireland, 1923     Born in Ireland, 1924      O'Sullivan
Married Marco Fallaci     Married Raeni, no          Born in Ireland, 1925
Children: Mario,          children.                  Married Steven Doyle
Francis, Rose                                        Children: Clare, Fiona
```

```
Name: Brigid                        Name: Liam
O'Sullivan                          Born in Canada, 1937
Born in Canada, 1931                Never married, no
Married Alan Watson                 children
Children: Robert,
Patrick, Lisa, Christine
```

She Died as She Lived

Auntie Beers 1960-1965
Urbston (near Toronto, Ontario)

If only the bullet had veered to the left just a smidge, our great-aunt would have been awarded the "longest-to-have-been-a-resident-of-the-Queen's-Hotel."

The very next week, Stu Burnside received the honor instead. It included a case of beer and a gift certificate to Perk's Family Restaurant, both of which Auntie Beers would have appreciated.

Sitting here at my desk, I realize now that my great-aunt died the way she lived. Auntie Beers always stood in the middle of "if only/when" and "then." Constantly revising the past in hopes for a different future.

"If only I had been born rich instead of the ravishing beauty that I am," she cackled, tossing a cigarette butt over the porch.

"When I get that job, I plan to lord it over the rest of you," she declared, dressed in a business suit destined to hang in her closet from that day forth.

"When my mother dies, sorry to say but then I'll be free." A pause and a wink. "But not sorry."

"If only the lads had had a brain, we'd've been landowners instead of farmhands," was her critique of male choices in our family.

If only the bullet had veered to the left. When she got involved in a shooting match. Then she would have been Queen for A Day of the Queen's Hotel.

During Auntie Beers' residency, the hotel sat beside a clock tower that housed the Post Office.

"The day they put up the clock tower, we stared at the feckin' thing in wonderment. That post office was the tallest building we had ever seen. How they did it is still a mystery," Auntie Beers told us. "Those stone bricks must be full of broim, not cement."

We all studied her face to see if we were supposed to laugh at a joke. Even in 1960, the clock tower barely reached the middle of most of the apartment buildings around. But she was dead serious. She thought it the tallest building in the world and the only way to accomplish that was to have bricks made of broim—farts. Of course, the boys thought this was a statement worth repeating.

That tower remains an instant reminder of the difference between her experiences and those of her great-nieces-and-nephews.

Auntie Beers had a way of telling a story that compelled my cousins and me to sit at her feet for hours. Ironic, sarcastic, oddly humorous. She told us about life. Her own in particular. Her view of the world in general. Tales that I, a dreamy imaginative child, thought were colorful and exciting, even as Auntie Beers spoke of poverty, despair, and war.

We lived in Urbston, a thriving smaller city northwest of Toronto, Ontario, in Canada. As young Canadians, we were anti-monarchist (a sentiment we probably got from our Irish Catholic immigrant parents), proud of our country, determined to make a difference in the world. It didn't quite turn out that way, of course.

As children, I imagine the top of our heads as my great-aunt would have seen them from her chair: a cross-section of dark, curly, straight, and blond. We sat cross-legged on the floor, hands in our laps, listening intently.

"Yer a well-fed bunch, I'll give you that," was her only comment on our appearance.

My cousins and I were a quartet. Similar ages. A mix of European heritage. All privileged and, yes, well fed. It was a time of relative prosperity and heady visions of the future. Released from a childhood of want, our parents partied through their adulthood. Pampered their own children in ways they only dreamed about as kids.

The first time we sat and listened to her stories, Auntie Beers invited us to return. She was convinced she had a lot to teach us.

"Ye can come back next Sunday, too," she said. "Skip the catechism and come see yer old auntie for the real story."

Skipping the classes held after Mass in the basement of the church was incentive enough. Not to mention the treats that Auntie Beers always provided. It took three years for our parents to catch on. My mother learned that the catechism classes had been cancelled the previous year, yet off we happily went every Sunday.

Despite some of our parents' disapproval—including my own father's—my mother convinced her siblings that Auntie Beers was lonely and needed us. I think they didn't mind a couple of hours minus one child.

I couldn't get enough of our great-aunt's narrative. The way she told a story. Dramatized. Held onto the ending. Drew out the words. She was a master.

Some of her great-nieces-and-nephews would drink in the tales and, as adults, repeat them either in print or on a canvas. Others would miss the underlying message and go straight to the drink.

Auntie Beers was baptized Bairbre, which, my mother explained, is Irish for Barbara. Bear-bree was, everyone admitted, difficult for a small child to say. One of the kids, as a toddler, mispronounced the name. Since we never saw her without a beer in hand, Beers seemed to make sense. She was an Irish expat, one of thousands who migrated to Canada.

In the early 1960s, when my cousins and I formed our circle with her, Auntie Beers was considered an old maid—a term we never use anymore. She was technically our great-aunt, older sister to our grandmother. We didn't really know the difference at the time and no one, as far as we knew, ever referred to Bairbre as great.

"Part old maid and part wild child," Auntie Beers said about herself. "Never been married but often been screwed."

Bairbre had slim, long legs, a narrow waist and full breasts. By the time we were old enough to remember, her lovely red hair was threaded with silver. Add flashing green eyes and, even in her elder years, Auntie Beers was beautiful.

From my viewpoint as we sat on the floor listening to her tales, she resembled a tree. Lean and strong, waving slightly in the breeze of her own fixations.

Before we existed, Bairbre taught our mothers, her nieces, to be fearless. To behave in ways that were authentic, not simply fashionable or expected. She taught our fathers, her nephews, that they were not invincible. That it was okay to be vulnerable; it wouldn't destroy you to cry.

Thirty years later, she taught another generation with her voluble nature when she released unashamed revelations of her truth through story. Unapologetic opinions that she never censored.

She may not have been demonstratively affectionate nor conciliatory. Often intolerant. But she was witty and honest. Encircled her family with connections to the past. To history. To the present and, in many ways, the future. We learned to expect the best but be prepared for the worst.

Some of my cousins pretend those days at her feet didn't happen. Ashamed that they spent any time in the

Queen's Hotel with people our neighbors and friends call "rubbies."

I'm sure we had no idea what rubbies meant back then, but I do know that Auntie Beers would have laughed at some of the definitions I've researched. Alcoholics with no money. People who drink rubbing alcohol. A way to relieve sexual tension with your clothes on.

The Queen's Hotel likely housed all three.

As for me, I took my great-aunt's stories and gave them lives of their own. I became an author of mystery, crime and fiction.

In my own work, I embellish the settings. Ignore the historical facts. Manipulate time frames. I tell tales that are distanced from her yet enmeshed. Accounts that often veer far from the truth. Stories exaggerated and twisted or idealized and fantasized.

My stories reflect her wicked side. Her tender side. Her.

Before long, the tales bumped up against my life and have become legends of my own.

The Broom

Near Bantry, Ireland, 1920
By Clare O'Sullivan Doyle

Brendan adjusted the green cap, feeling around for the fuzzy ball that was supposed to stand up from the center. No one was looking, but he felt embarrassed anyway. He wondered if he should remove the hat—or at any rate, the ridiculous pom-pom (who had dreamt up that as part of the uniform?)—before she saw him. He wanted to see pride reflected in her beautiful hazel eyes.

He slipped and slid over the moss-covered stones, making somewhat of a crash landing up against the solid wall of the shed. The sturdy hut had been made of rock, mud and wood and would defy any flood or windstorm that might be invented. Brendan knew this, because he had helped build it. He'd also encouraged Mr. O'Sullivan to engage in a side business of selling peat. Not to mention a variety of crops, some pigs, and dried fish.

Brendan had listened to a speech from some Irish politician who warned farmers to adopt "diversified farming," instead of focusing solely on potatoes. In the speaker's opinion, relying on only one crop could lead to disaster. And so it had. One tiny little spot on one small potato had led to famine and loss that could barely be described.

It was the reason Brendan now had to wear a pom-pom on his head.

He saw Grace in profile from the side of the shed. Even the smell of the peat couldn't spoil the moment.

Her hair lifted in the breeze. Wrapped around her thin shoulders. Webbed her face with strands of red. Hid the creamy color of her skin. The mixed green and blue of her eyes. He could imagine the scent of her. The feel of her. Soft and satiny beneath his touch. He hated to see her so tiny. Bones protruded from her waist and her arms were stick thin. Brendan moved around the shed and opened the door. A nice solid shed, if he did say so himself, made from stone, mud and bits of foundling wood, but strong as a fortress. The latch hung open, no doubt waiting for Grace to add her morning's pickings. Brendan had found a nice lock, just in case, but he knew Grace and Fiona rarely used it.

The door swung a bit in the breeze. It opened outward to avoid the piles of peat bricks. The smell was powerful. Nevertheless, he stayed where he was, holding it slightly ajar, nice and hidden from Fiona's sharp eyes. He longed to leap out from his hiding spot and wrap Grace in his arms. But he had to wait until she turned to see him. Not yet sure that she was alone. She suited her name so perfectly he often wondered if her mother looked into the infant's face and saw the future. Grace. His amazing Grace.

Though Grace was never "anyone's." Never his. She reminded him often that she was her own person. Made her own decisions.

"If we become partners, mo ghra..."

"If we come partners, my love? You mean when, don't you now?"

"You can't say 'when' until it's fixed in everyone's mind," she said. "If we become partners, we are equal partners. We make decisions together when it affects us as a couple. We are free to make decisions on our own, too. You see, Brendan, I won't need you. I will want you."

Brendan found the difference confusing, though Grace had explained it a few times. He didn't really care what words she wanted to use to describe the fact that he would do anything to be near her. Forever. Need, want. Love. All of it. The whole thing. A woman who made her own decisions or made them with him. Just as long as the woman was Grace.

Lately his heart twisted whenever she spoke of her sister Maggie. Grace, Bairbre and Maggie were like no siblings he'd ever encountered. His brothers and one sister were distant and cool. Like strangers or even further apart than that. They'd all scattered to England, Canada and France. He, being the youngest, was left alone with their parents.

The O'Sullivan sisters, though, were attached by a rope that had been strengthened with threads of love, shared life experience, kindness and empathy. They were fiercely protective of each other. Though they would tolerate no criticism from anyone else, they were good at giving advice to a sister who'd wandered off the path. In comparison, their brothers were weak, both in mind and body, as though they knew from a young age that they were destined not to live long in this world. Three males had died at birth; the other two were presently consumed by fever and not likely to see their teens.

Most of Brendan's family farm had been appropriated by an English landlord. They were left with a patch even smaller than the O'Sullivan's. But at least they owned their patches, which was better than what had happened to many of their neighbors who were forced to be renters.

Once again, Brendan applied his creativity, so the two families were able to subsist. He tamed the old Irish goats. The animals procreated, provided milk and, eventually, they would give the family meat. Their fierce black faces and curled horns had become familiar to him, even beautiful.

He'd stolen a couple of pigs from a fair in Cork. He scouted and sneaked around until he found a pair from an

Englishman who'd usurped a farm and couldn't be bothered actually working it. Bragged about it to anyone who'd listen.

The feckless Irish don't deserve the land, have no clue what to do, put these filthy animals on perfectly good soil.

In the dead of night, Brendan relieved him of his burden. The pigs were so ill-treated they didn't make a sound as he loaded them into his wagon.

Now they had several piglets. The piglets' oul wans would soon feed Brendan's oul wans. Though he kept delaying butchering the four original animals of whom he'd become quite fond.

Grace thought he was brilliant and always told him so. She pointed out that most of their neighbors and many of their friends had given up. Hitched a ride on a ship to North America. Went to England, which Grace's Ma called the land of the enemy. Some stayed in France after the war. Worst of all, again according to Fiona, some went to work for the armed forces who held the Irish in check.

Brendan touched the tassel on his hat. He hadn't officially signed up yet, but he was ready. He'd found an old green hat in a dumpster. The tassel at a county fair. Brown jacket and khaki pants discarded by the side of the road. It seemed a sign. All he needed were some boots, which he figured he could steal or find on the trek to Dublin. If he worked alongside the Royal Irish Constabulary for a couple of years, he'd actually make real money.

He could not imagine leaving Ireland. His body itched to build, dig, pet, lift, fish, heal. And walk the hills. Each morning he watched the sun rise and breathed in the ocean air. Every evening he watched the sun set and let the scent of wet grass seep through every pore. When he had a few coins, he loved sitting in the local pub listening to music and the chatter of his neighbors. Enjoyed it more with Grace at his side.

Brendan was certain he could stay here and support his family with his farming ideas. He could help with Grace's too if they would let him. But they had an abiding fear that he would steal their daughter away from the land. Just as Séamus had taken Maggie to Dublin and was now threatening to move her across the sea.

Even Bairbre was considering going to Canada. Taking the whole family over. She was already an old maid since losing her lover in a rebellion skirmish. Grace, however, had him.

During the two years he planned to spend in the Black and Tans, Brendan knew he would barely see Grace. That seemed impossible to contemplate, but he had figured out the amount of money he would make. It seemed enormous. Perhaps she'd visit Maggie in Dublin more often because Brendan would be there quite a bit. In the center of the fight.

Eventually he could save enough to return to their land near Bantry. Apply even more ideas to the farming and fishing he envisioned. Stop Grace from going to Canada with Bairbre, Maggie and Séamus if she knew the future here was hopeful.

He watched as Grace walked slowly through the green clover. The moss-covered walls to her right, ancient property dividers, led almost to the sea. These days both neighboring farms were deserted. One lot over, lay the Murphy land. Different in its needs and qualities. Combined they were beautiful, perfect. Bhí se go halainn. Just like Grace and him.

The O'Sullivan cows drifted along the edge of the wall, munching on grass and clover. Now and then, Grace bent down to pick up decayed moss and weeds to shove into the bag around her thin shoulders. More fodder for the peat shed. Beyond her, the sea crashed around the cliff and danced over the rocks.

Brendan couldn't see anyone else in the field. In the past, her two young brothers would be hovering about, especially on a Sunday afternoon. Back from Mass, fed as much as they could spare for the mid-day meal, they'd wrestle and roll in the grass. Nowadays, they were curled up in their beds most of the day.

He kept his eyes on his beloved as he decided to cautiously step from behind the shed and meet her in the field. Which explains why he didn't see the broom as it swept through the air and struck him in the forehead, sending him off balance.

His assailant pushed the wooden door against him, causing him to fall backwards into the shed. He landed on the hard ground with a painful thud. The door shut solidly. He heard the sound of the latch sliding into place. The key in the lock affirmed its finality.

Rolling over, he ended up in the pile of peat. Almost choked until he forced himself to a sitting position. His head pounded. He'd landed on a hard brick or two.

In the smelly darkness, a sliver of sunlight pierced through where the mud and stone had crumbled. I must fix those holes, he thought. Brendan laid back and allowed his body to rest. The shriek in his head lulled somewhat. He closed his eyes.

Grace turned to see her mother uncharacteristically hurrying through the field in her direction. Her first thought was that one of her brothers had succumbed to the mysterious fever that had gripped the young boys and wouldn't let go. Fiona had lost three male babies at birth and was now in danger of losing two more sons before they reached teenage.

Grace hated to see her proud ma shrunken with bones at angles up and down her body. Bent over with unrelenting grief.

Quickly she realized that her mother was actually alit with excitement. Not anguish or illness or hunger as usual. Instead, exhilaration. Her lined face pulled back in a satisfied grin.

"What's the craic, Ma?"

"I got one of them. I got one of them bastards and I'm going to feckin' teach him a big lesson."

Grace stared at her mother in confusion.

"One of who? And what do you mean, you got him?"

"One of those Black and Tans. Standing as proud as you will in front of our peat shed. Ridiculous bobble on his head. I got him."

"How? Where is he?"

Grace surveyed the field, glancing over at their low stone house. At the shed and pens that Brendan had built. Their farm looked busy and profitable. An oasis in the midst of desertion and neglect.

"First I hit him with my broom, didn't I? Pushed in the peat shed door where he was leaning and he fell right in. I locked him up."

Grace shivered at the thought of anyone being locked in that stinking structure.

"Oh, Ma, what are we going to do with him? You should have just shooed him away."

Her mother folded her arms across her chest. Fiona stood straighter than she had in months. Perhaps years. Her face was still lit up with the thrill of imprisoning a man she considered her worst enemy.

"Those Black and Tans are evil. They've been causing terrible havoc since they were dumped on our fair soil. He might have wanted to rob and violate us."

"I've heard that some of them are our own lads. Trying to make some money."

"Most of them are British."

Ma spat on the ground by her feet.

"No good for anything but fighting. Haven't got a skill to use since the war ended."

"Still, we shouldn't become this one's jailor. It's not right, Ma."

"He will no doubt learn a lesson after a couple of days in a stinky hole. Then I will let him go. He'll think twice before he crosses an Irish woman again."

"What if he dies?"

"That pile is as natural as Ireland, mo daor. He will emerge from that shed with clear nostrils, sure he will."

When they reached the shed, there was no sound inside the little stone and wood hut. Grace pressed her ear against the door. Nothing. What if her mother had already killed the fellow?

Grace had no love for the British, including the Black and Tans. They had been sent a year ago by the British government to assist the Royal Irish Constabulary. The Irish Republican Army had carried out numerous attacks on the RIC, wounding and even killing some of the constables.

However, the British men appeared to have no order among themselves. Once "trained," they moved into small towns and caused all manner of trouble, some of it extremely violent. Burned homes. Beat and brutalized or even shot villagers. The IRA became even more vengeful and ruthless, which resulted in RIC retaliation in kind. All of them drunk and out of control, psychologically and physically damaged and ready to treat their fellow humans as though they were scum from the earth. Women left at home were raped and assaulted.

Grace was appalled by the lack of humanity, by the brutality on both sides. What caused men to set aside their consciences and moral compasses and allow rage to fuel their actions?

Grace spent a few weeks with her sister Maggie after she gave birth to little Johnny. She was already pregnant with a second wee one. Dublin was currently the center of the fighting, burning, and killing. She worried every minute for her sister and family's safety. Some day they planned to go off to Canada, where free housing and jobs were on offer. Maggie wanted the whole family to come with them.

Da spent most of his time smoking beside the fireplace. He had no motivation to plant or tend or weed. Ma's energy, such as it was, came only from anger. Grace's two younger brothers were physically weak and were slowly and miserably succumbing to illness. There was no way they would survive on a ship across the ocean.

Grace leaned her head against the door of the peat house. Had the man locked here committed terrible offenses? If he was already dead, could Grace bring herself to drag his body into the field and bury it? Could she justify all her actions and those of her mother's by picturing the twisted corpses left in the city streets or at the side of the road, victims of the ridiculous anger and stupidity caused by government rules? By people who thought only one way and refused to compromise or change?

As the sun went to light up other places in the world, and darkness moved swiftly over the cottage, Grace went inside to scrounge up some dinner. It wasn't as difficult these days, ever since Brendan had expanded their selections with various crops and animals. Fortunately, no political or military eyes were looking in on them, perched as they were on a cliff above the ocean between Bantry and Ballylickey. Since the neighbors had flown, they were deserted, the closest farm being Brendan's family acreage a few minutes' walk away. Her lover, with his creative and skilled hand at farming and fishing, had saved them all from starvation. If only her parents recognized his abilities and truly partnered with him on all his ventures.

Fiona sat grinning in the corner, rocking back and forth in her chair, as though she were a cat with a mouse to torture.

Grace considered herself a potential rebel. If she allowed her deep disgust with the current situation to fill her veins, she could scream and protest in Dublin too. She could shake her fists and even point a rifle. Shoot someone? Maybe not. But maybe.

Yet when she glanced over the silver green land, wispy with long natural grasses, or stubby stones, dirt and weed, past the cliff to the rolling sea, Grace felt a calm like no other. Her heart steadied, her fists unclenched. Inside, her whole body rocked with the ocean, back and forth, as much a part of the land and water as anyone could be. Her love for this country, for this patch of living such as it currently was, almost matched her love for Brendan. Perhaps it did match, though she would never tell him so. She could no more leave Ireland than give away her ability to speak.

Grace knew she had to tell Maggie and Bairbre very soon that she was not leaving. Not only could she never part from this dear country, Ma and Da needed her. She knew her brothers had very little time left.

She had to make it clear to her sisters that she was not giving up her life to care for others, nor did she want them to feel any guilt whatsoever. Grace had a different attachment to the countryside, to this farm and this land, than Bairbre and Maggie ever did. She suspected that, even if she had children to protect, Grace would do everything she could to remain here.

Bairbre had not been the same since her lover had disappeared. She was listless and detached, only brightening when she was with Maggie's little one. She needed to leave with them.

As she cooked up some mash over the fire, Grace wondered if the soldier had water.

She needn't have worried about her mother's captive. Along with the jacket and pants for his uniform, Brendan had acquired a belt, a handkerchief and a water container. Which he had filled on a whim, even though he hadn't planned to leave for Dublin until next week. Now he sipped carefully, uncertain of how long he'd be left here. He also didn't know who had clocked him with the broom, but he had a strong suspicion that it had been his future mother-in-law. This did not bode well for his formal proposal to Grace.

He pictured the lovely ring he would buy her once he'd worked for the RIC for two years. How stupidly gorgeous it would look on her slender finger.

He lay down on his jacket, nose pressed against the bottom of the door. Obviously, they hadn't enough wood to reach the ground and left a long gap. Although that would keep it from scraping, so maybe he and Grace's Da had done it on purpose...he drifted off to sleep. Sucking the cool night air through the opening under the door. Dreaming of chores he could do around his fiancée's farm.

He awoke sometime in the very early morning, before the sun had risen. Stiff, chilled, and almost adjusted to the peat smell. A small trickle of water dripped from the rock face that reached behind the shed and up to a spring that eventually fell headlong into the sea. There was nothing else to do but get to work.

Grace rarely argued with her mother, but she awoke that morning in a bad mood. Sleep had mostly evaded her as she imagined the soldier stuck in the shed without water or food. Suffocated by the decaying moss and vegetation that was breaking down into excrement of the earth. Ready to be formed from water and mud into bricks. Most Irish people in their area used these lumps for heat and cooking.

Brendan had begun to make more peat units than they could use. He'd haul them around in a wagon behind the one horse who'd survived pretty much everything. Sales were surprisingly strong. Often, instead of money—since most people had none—he'd take various types of food. This kept his family and hers in good supply.

Grace wondered where her fiancé was. He'd promised to stop by yesterday, but perhaps the presence of her mother had deterred him. All day Fiona had hovered more than usual because of the soldier.

Grace was determined never to let Brendan know about the imprisonment. The man had to be released today before Brendan came over. Somehow, she needed to check that the Black and Tan had no weaponry. She'd warn him to get back on the road. Maybe she'd tell him there was a whole army of women like Fiona.

Even if they had to give him some food and water, they had to get rid of him.

The sun's rays were still only a filter of light with no warmth. Grace threw a shawl over her shoulders. She grabbed the key from the hiding spot Fiona had used once too often. Tiptoed through the silent cottage. She would open the shed door and allow the captive to get on his way. Before Ma got up and invented another torture.

When she reached the peat hut, however, Fiona was right behind her. Brandishing her broom as a weapon, she stood stiff and red faced, legs apart to anchor herself. If a live person wasn't trapped in their shed, Grace would have found the situation comical. As it was, she felt a flush of anger at the little woman whose hatred had compelled her to be cruel. Just like the people of whom she was so critical.

"I'm letting him out, Ma. I'll just open the door and we can go back into the house. Allow him to get on his way."

"I plan to give him a piece of my mind first, so. Let him know he should rid himself of the uniform and get on back to enemy island where he belongs."

"This is not a good idea," Grace protested. "As you told me yourself, he could be violent."

Brendan could hear the two women clearly, but he said nothing. Prayed that Grace would convince her mother to open the door and return to the house. How could she ever forgive him if she saw that he was the one in the Black and Tan uniform? He hadn't had time to explain his plan. Fiona would place him into a category with the evil violators that roamed around looking for trouble. A place from which he wasn't certain he could return.

His prayers were not answered. Grace unlocked the door. Her mother, her tiny frame able to slide nimbly around her daughter, pulled on the door just as the latch let go. The heavy wood fell against the outside stone wall, opening up the peat shed to the air.

At first all they could see was a dark hole. All they could smell was rotting vegetation.

Slowly a man's shape appeared, sitting straight-backed on the ground. There was a moment of silence as dawn's fingers outlined Brendan's face. He didn't move until Fiona spoke.

"Brendan Murphy!" she intoned, shock forcing her voice several octaves higher than usual.

Brendan unfolded his legs slowly, muscles pinching him in protest. He had to use his hands to push himself upright. He stood inside the shed, head bowed, as though awaiting permission to step forward.

"Yer a bloody Black and Tan?" his future mother-in-law hissed. "Y've gone over to that side? Given up all morals and love of country?"

She was screeching by now, beside herself with anger. Her small body jumped up and down, around in a circle. Out of control.

"Fiona," he said in a calm, low voice. "You know that's not me. Can I explain to you, Mathair daor?"

"Do not call me Mathair," Fiona hurled at him, but she stopped spinning.

At last Brendan raised his eyes to meet Grace's. Terrified to see rejection, anger, disgust. Instead, he thought he saw understanding, so he plowed ahead.

"Fiona," he said politely. "Listen, will you? I'm considering joining the Royal Irish Constabulary. I wouldn't be one of those Black and Tan thugs, would I? I'd be someone trying to keep the peace. Protecting people, like. But I'd make some money. Enough to keep Grace and all of you, and my oul wans too, from starving. Enough to get my beloved that ring I want to put on her finger and ask her to be with me forever. Enough to keep Grace from going to Canada with Maggie and Bairbre."

Grace's mother opened her mouth widely, showing the places where rotted teeth had left gaps. Even so, her laugh was infectious and almost beautiful.

"Grace will never leave Ireland, ye langer," she barked. "I begged her to, but she's got the love of the land deep inside her. Just like her father. And her mother, sure tis the truth. Likely love for you as well, Brendan Murphy, though God knows why."

"I love her too, Fiona. As much as I love this country."

Brendan's wide thin shoulders sunk forward as his head bowed with fatigue and frustration.

Grace had not spoken a word during the exchange between her lover and her mother. Brendan's heart pounded in fear that he had let her down too far to climb back up. He thought there was still a glimpse of understanding in her eyes, despite the fact that she kept her arms folded across her chest in a gesture of disapproval.

"I want to marry him, Ma," she finally said.

Brendan looked up in surprise. Fiona coughed and laughed at the same time.

"In fact, I want to marry him as soon as we can. I don't want a ring, Brendan. It'll just get dirty in the soil and I'll have to keep taking it off. I'd probably lose it. I don't need a ring to remind me that I love you. I know that with every beat of my heart."

He stepped toward her, his face alight with joy, but she stopped him with a raised hand.

"Ma, sure you can convince Da to partner with Brendan. Do what he plans. Follow his ideas. It will give Da a purpose for getting out of the house. We're in a perfect position to survive until the fighting stops. It's got to stop so."

This time Fiona got the hand. She remained quiet.

"When the war is over, we will do more than survive. Brendan's plans will make our farms a business. We will be able to afford more than the necessities. We might even be able to afford grandchildren."

"Where will you live?" Fiona demanded.

"We'll live in the cottage at the end of the Murphy property," Grace told her. "It's big enough for two. We'll be close to both our families and our work on the farms."

They were silent for a long moment while the breeze sighed. Sunlight lit up the ground at their feet. In the background came the insistent hammering of the sea.

"Father Peter will perform the marriage," Fiona said.

Both Brendan and Grace uttered an oh of surprise. Their eyes finally met and they smiled. Private, intimate energy flowed between them.

"Father Peter?" Grace asked doubtfully.

"Sure look, he owes me at least this one thing," Fiona said. "A small favor given the circumstances, isn't it?"

"War changes a great deal," Brendan said. "I am truly sorry for thinking of joining the fight. Don't believe in war, do I? Desperation drove me."

Grace stepped forward this time. He leaned over and wrapped her small body in his arms. Despite her thinness, he could feel the strength in her and knew they would win.

"No more desperate decisions," she told him.

Fiona cleared her throat. "Sure now. I will speak to your father, Grace. You're going to be a success, Brendan? Maybe the oul wan will even come out of his fog to help."

Grace and Brendan parted and faced her. Squaring their shoulders as though ready to begin at the moment.

"I already got a start on the peat," Brendan offered.

All three of them looked into the shed. Lit up by the sun, the bricks that Brendan had haphazardly fashioned during the night lay piled in crooked bunches inside.

Grace laughed.

"You're a slim one," Fiona said.

And she placed her broom against the wall.

The Brit

Dublin, Ireland, 1921
by Clare O'Sullivan Doyle

"Maggie."

His voice is soft and urgent in her ear. She sits up. Feels her heart in tune with the baby's, fast and insistent.

"Séamus." Her whisper is a statement heavy with fear. She already knows what he will say.

"I have to go, love. There are fires everywhere."

He rubs her enormous belly, feels the life move underneath her skin. He leans over and kisses her tenderly. Puts his hand over his child.

"Don't ye dare arrive today, boy or girlie. That won't be a way to start with your Da."

"Or your Ma," Maggie says. "Ah, Séamus. If only you hadn't taken that job."

"Only one there was. Fire means they need firemen."

He pulls up his pants from the floor, hooks his belt and leans over to fasten his bootlaces. He turns once more to kiss her.

"Ye was brilliant to get Bairbre here. In case little Derry or Kathleen here decides to disobey. I hope not to be long. Once the fires they set at dawn are out, sure we'll be let off."

His blue eyes are lit with the adrenalin of the job ahead, his square handsome jaw resolute. He stretches his long body. Wide shoulders ripple with the kind of strength that comes from heavy lifting and unflinching work. Even in her extreme pregnant state, Maggie feels a tingle at his magnificence.

"You're sure about the name Derry then?"

"As long as you are."

"And still all right with John instead of Séamus? It's not too English? When we go to Canada, I think it will be easier for him."

He gives one of his beautiful smiles.

"Everything is all right with me, Maggie. As long as you are with me."

She lies back when Séamus has closed the front door. Looking over at the handmade crib to her left, as sturdy as hands could fashion, she smiles at John, who is fast asleep on his side, little fingers pushing at his mouth. Not even a year old and destined to be a big brother. Yet in her heart she admits she would not lose a minute in her husband's embrace. Despite babies as the curse and the promise of their love.

When she reawakens, she can hear pop, pop, in the distance. The narrow row house shivers in domino fashion. Maggie rolls her big self out of the bed just as Bairbre's lovely, worried face appears in the doorway.

"Did ye hear that?" Bairbre asks. "Gunfire?"

Her older sister knows the answer but she looks for another explanation anyway. Maggie can't give one.

"Séamus said there were fires everywhere."

She moves to the crib and rubs John's back. He's stirring, his fist still crammed into his mouth.

"He told me they were set at dawn and that he'll be able to come right back when they're out."

She wants to repeat every word he said because perhaps the repetition will make it so.

John rolls onto his back and blinks. He rubs his eyes and smiles up at his mother.

"Oh, you'll charm the pants off all the girls, my lad," Maggie whispers before gathering him in her arms.

"He's far too handsome, that one," Bairbre agrees as though being good-looking is a curse. Which perhaps for her, it has been.

Maggie puts the little boy down on his chubby legs before whipping off his jumper and diaper. Bairbre takes the wet clothing and dumps it unceremoniously into the hamper. Her sister will be out in the back shed later, Maggie knows, scrubbing everything down in the old washer tub.

John toddles down the stairs, holding his aunt's hand. Behind them, Maggie steadies her clumsy frame on the wall, tipped over sideways like a giant ship in a rough ocean.

The sisters are shocked when they reach the main floor level. The noise, dust and smoke have drifted in through the cracks in the window frames and under the door. Many feet pound the pavement, up and down the narrow road.

When Bairbre pulls the curtain aside, they glimpse the crowds. Moving in a stampede, shouting and red-faced, they carry guns or pitchforks or clubs over their shoulders. Men and women. Young and old. United in their cause of freedom for Ireland. Smoke funnels through the street from a violent destination in the city centre.

Maggie stares at her sister in shock and fright. Living in Dublin, they've become accustomed to rumbles and protests. They've witnessed fights and arguments. But never have they felt the pressure of this movement of people, their anger hanging in the air long after they march past.

"We'll stay in the kitchen, back of the house," Maggie says. "We'll wait for Séamus."

Bairbre nods mutely. She takes John's hand and leads him through the door to the kitchen, murmuring comfort words about food.

Maggie stands in the front room a while longer. She peeks through the curtains once more. The marchers are gone. Only the smoke and dust are left to fill the space. Pop, pop, echoes down the row. Blood and water leak down Maggie's legs. She toddles to the kitchen and sits heavily. The first pain crushes her in its vise.

As Bairbre turns toward the table with a plate of bread and fruit for John, she catches her sister's eye.

"No," she says.

Maggie nods, unable for a moment to find the breath for a response. She smiles weakly.

"My water broke. I made a mess in the front room."

"Don't worry about that, love. Don't worry about anything. We'll set ye up here nice and comfy and wait for Séamus."

Bairbre rumbles around. Brings a bunched-up hassock in for Maggie's feet. Places a pillow at her back. Shoves a cup of tea into her hands. Maggie gives her sister a nod of gratitude.

Once again, she wishes Bairbre had been able to have children. She is tender, kind and patient with her nephew. If only she'd been able to love another man after her Michael disappeared.

John plays with a prized toy truck and hums as he eats. He's propped up in the wooden highchair. More of Séamus's creations. Fashioned from found wood and the rudimentary tools he has gathered in the old shed at the back.

Maggie feels dread and longing in her stomach. She wants her husband here with her. Safe. Steady.

The contraction squeezes and releases. Leaves her dizzy. They are about five minutes apart, she thinks. She needs to get to the hospital.

Maggie has a horror of giving birth on the kitchen floor. From her own mother, she has heard terrible stories of babies who turn blue and women who bleed to death. She realizes that Fiona often exaggerates, but both Maggie and Séamus have faith in professionals.

"Bairbre, now listen to me. I want to go to the hospital. If I go right away, I can do the walk. If I wait for Séamus, I might be too knackered."

Maggie anticipates the look of terror on her sister's face.

"It's all right then. No one's going to hurt a pregnant woman in the street."

"I'll come with ye."

"No." Maggie is emphatic. "I won't have John out there. He'd be so frightened of all those angry people."

She stands up and looks down at her baby's head. He smiles and babbles at his mother.

"What if you wait a bit longer? Please? See if Séamus comes back."

Maggie puts her arms around Bairbre. She speaks in a low urgent tone in her sister's ear.

"If I wait longer, even if Séamus arrives, I'll be giving birth on this floor and I'm terrified to do that."

Bairbre holds onto Maggie fiercely for a moment, strengthening into the decision. Knowing what's needed of her. When they part, she is the older sister once more. She takes charge. Packs Maggie a small bag.

"John and I will stay in the back of the house. Don't you worry about us. When Séamus comes, I'll send him off, right enough."

Big tears run down Bairbre's cheeks. John fusses in his aunt's arms as Maggie slowly closes the front door on them.

Their street is deserted and silent. The ghost of anxiety and anger drifts in an eerie cloud of smoke rising higher by the minute. Maggie is able to make her way along the walk without coughing. She stops several times to lean, to breathe, into the pain. Sweat dots her forehead. The contractions are coming faster, more quickly, than she anticipated.

Though the hospital is only two streets away, even the distance up their own small road seems insurmountable. As Maggie creeps along, using the rough walls as her railing, she begins to hear the noise.

The main cross street ahead is shrouded in a fog of violence. If the pain were not so pronounced, Maggie thinks she might have turned back. She has no choice but to move toward what she hopes is a lesser danger than the terror of giving birth in the street. Shouts, screams, the firework pop of guns. Hundreds of feet create the sound of thunder. Maggie's heart hammers. The baby moves forward reluctantly, squeezed by an inconsiderate womb.

She stumbles into the crowded high street, immediately surrounded by protesters as they march toward the city centre. In their fervor they don't notice Maggie as she slides along the building walls. She knows the hospital is straight ahead, across the street. So close. At the moment all she can see is dust and smoke.

Maggie is doubled over in a prolonged contraction when someone prods her roughly from behind. The muscles in her back react to the blow and her womb reverberates. Remaining doubled over she turns her head as far as she can and stares.

The man is young in every way other than his eyes. Those are ancient with hatred and fear. He's dressed in the light brown jacket and dark pants of the Black and Tans.

"Move along ye stupid cow," he hisses.

Stooped as she is, breath hard and noisy, Maggie feels like cattle. She feels stupid and helpless. She studies the sneer on his face and lets out a long shudder. Her body stutters forward, step-by-step like a stiff wind-up toy. She is angry when uncontrollable tears flow down. She doesn't want him to see so she keeps her head high and forward.

The ruffian marches up to her, shoulder to shoulder. When he looks down and sees her swollen belly, he gives a terrible sneer. He spits at her feet as he barrels past to find a more challenging foe.

Maggie keeps walking, legs apart to ease the pain of insistent pressure. She wants to wail but she's too frightened. Terror blocks her throat.

Ahead of her she sees a dozen fires. Flames pierce the smoke. Determinedly lick at buildings. Windows. Homes. The stink of melting detritus is overwhelming. Pop, pop, echoes loudly.

The blockage in her throat loosens when the soldier walks in front of her. Becomes one long screech of shock and fright. My baby, my baby, brainstorms her lips.

This fighter is older than the other one. He's perhaps late twenties, around Séamus's age. His reddish eyebrows and hair give him a softer look. The straps of the round tin helmet pull his chin into an unnatural tightness, but his mouth can still show grief. Covered by dust and grime his red coat looks brown.

"Oh, lady, oh I'm so sorry I frightened you."

He grasps her by the elbow to steady her. Maggie has no trouble understanding this English. His accent is clear and round.

He shifts the rifle so that it rests behind his back. Away. Safer. He looks into her blue eyes with a blue of his own that is genuine and troubled.

"I can take you to the hospital. You'll be safe with me."

For a moment Maggie is unable to speak. She leans over once more under the fist that squeezes her womb muscles into a mass of agony.

"Will you let me?" he asks, as though he is the one who needs a favor.

Her mind races. She has been trained to fear the British soldiers almost as much as the Black and Tans. But beyond anything she fears the damage that might be done to her baby if she doesn't reach the hospital.

She raises her head to study his face once more. He smiles amid the mud and smoke caked across his cheeks. Somehow his look contains concern and sympathy despite the remnants of war that stain his skin.

Maggie nods. "Yes. Please," she manages to say.

He crooks his arm and invites her to hang onto him. She lets go, both in her head and in her body, and clings heavily to his strong frame. He leads her slowly yet determinedly through smoke and around rubble. Skirts the many fires and pounding feet.

Maggie keeps her eyes on her shoes to avoid tripping over debris. The clouds of violence swirl around them. Occasionally explode too close by. She draws from her companion's strength. Walks through the contractions, not allowing her body to stoop under its power. This baby will be born in safety. Just a few more steps. Just a few more steps.

They reach the front door of the hospital before Maggie realizes they have arrived. She is aware of faces and hands behind the glass, ready to reach out for her. Professionals. People who will take care of her.

Once she is steady at the door, the soldier turns to make for the street. She calls after him and miraculously, he hears. He stops. Looks back at her, a sad smile touching his lips.

"What is your name?" she asks.

"Edward," he says. "But everyone calls me Eddie."

He touches his helmet as though it is a top hat and she a grand dame. The light of his gaze touches his eyes.

"Thank you, Eddie," Maggie says. "Thank you for saving us."

"My pleasure, ma'am," he answers. "I wish your baby a safe and happy life."

Maggie allows the hospital staff to draw her in. Later, when she cuddles her tiny son in her arms, when Séamus arrives breathless and worried, still covered in soot, when she looks at the baby's perfect little face, she decides.

"His name is Edward," she tells Séamus. "But we'll call him Eddie. And he will be a good person no matter what the rest of the world does."

Three Sisters

Auntie Beers 1920s
Dublin, Ireland, 1926

They stand at the end of a line which snakes around and around, over the pathway, along the dock, and finally up the gangway to the ship. The gazes they share suggest doubts about whether they will make it before the ship sails.

The enormous boat puffs as though impatient. Towers so far above them that at first the children are frozen in awe and terror.

As third-class passengers, the sisters have no power. Tickets—the cheaper ones—were sent by the receiving country or provided by the country that wished them gone (in this case, Ireland). For Maggie and Bairbre and the children, it is the former. Canada offered jobs and homes to farmhands. After working for a year, Maggie's husband Séamus was able to send for them.

Maggie's six-five-and four-year-old children, John, Eddie and Daniel, race up and down the gangway, never going out of sight of their aunt and mother. They've been warned in no uncertain terms that their freedom will be curtailed if they do.

Peggy, the three-year-old, stands beside her Ma, watching everything with keen eyes. Bairbre holds two-year-old Michael in her arms and Maggie, one-year-old Kathleen.

In 1926, in line with all the poor, five children do not even earn a sideways look. There are lots of families with many more. At least a thousand people line up for the lower deck.

Grace and Brendan help with the cartons and suitcases—cardboard affairs, strapped closed—which they are forced to drag along the ground. They keep checking for holes in the scraped cardboard.

Occasionally Grace will take one of the babies in her own arms, relentlessly kissing their cheeks.

Bairbre amuses herself by scanning the first-class passengers as they skirt around the third-class lines and mount their own gangway. Mostly couples, dressed as though they are about to attend a ball. Single, portly men, also wearing suits and bow ties to accentuate their importance. Once, she glimpses a priest accompanied by a brother and considers this peculiar. Obviously the church has provided him with the first-class ticket. Perhaps he's being sent to Canada to convince the natives that his god is the only god.

Maggie can think of nothing but the children and the voyage ahead. She is distracted, frozen by fear and fatigue. Her emotions are torn in two. Heartbroken to leave. Excited to have Séamus in her arms again.

Grace quietly allows the tears to slide down her cheeks. She swipes at them now and then to keep from getting her dress wet. Her grief flows soundlessly. Unashamedly.

Hours later, after devouring all the food and drink that Grace and Brendan brought, they finally are within sight of the inspectors who will check their identification and health papers. Now Grace and Brendan must exit the gangway.

Brendan hugs all of them. His gentle eyes fill with tears but he doesn't allow them to fall. He discreetly goes ahead, pushing his way through the line-up to the dockside.

John holds hands with Peggy and Michael. Eddie wraps Kathleen in his arms, as though someone might try to steal her.

The three sisters form a huddle. Maggie can't help but sob. Grace cries in silence. Bairbre holds her emotions back, but her eyes are full.

"I love you so much," they whisper in turn.

Only the looming presence of the inspector forces them apart. Grace nearly runs down the gangway, the crowd having dissipated. Toward Brendan. Ireland. Away from the sisters who have been part of her soul and being her whole life.

Maggie and Bairbre force themselves to concentrate on the paperwork. The children are tired and confused, but at least this keeps them quiet and hovering around their mother and aunt.

Once they reach the deck, they turn and look toward the dock. Tiny figures, surrounded by other tiny figures, wave at them.

One of them stands with her beloved husband. Solid on the land that she loves, despite its difficult, subsistence life.

The two on the ship turn toward hope. They sail away from the known to the foreign, their emotions tangled but determined. They believe that a new life will be better than this one. Despite being separated from the only family they've ever known, especially their beloved sister. They believe they will escape the hatred, the violence, the risk of starvation.

They are crowded into the lower deck, where the air has less oxygen and even the hull sweats. The crash of waves is like fists pounding against the ship, threatening to come in. The two women and the children are piled onto bunks with thin mattresses and one small blanket. At least they have their own alcove against a wall. Perhaps a transformed storage closet. After a few days, they become used to the smell and the noise, and live for their time on the top deck. Fresh sea air keeps them from despair.

Although the tables at meals are crowded, and sometimes the children sit on the floor, the food is nutritious. Stews and soups with real meat.

At some point, Bairbe disappears for hours and even whole nights at a time. Guiltily, Maggie can't help but be grateful that they have more room on the bunks.

One day, and all the days afterward, they are offered more food, removed from the second-class dining room by a steward named Colum. He also arranges for more time in the fresh air, when there are fewer people. The children are able to run a bit, though their strength wanes as the days go by. Three times through the sailing, Colum takes them to a second-class facility where they are able to take a bath.

Maggie, exhausted and stressed, grateful beyond thought for these extras, takes a long time to realize what her sister has done in order to get them.

If Maggie and Bairbre had known what the future held, they still would not have turned away. Their shared love for the children, and Maggie's love for her husband, convinced them that life would be better in Canada.

The future holds generations of smart, successful, strong people. Leaders and change agents. They will do their best to make the world a better place. In lots of ways, they will succeed.

Nothing is Free

Auntie Beers 1960-1965
Ontario, Canada, 1920s-1930

When Auntie Beers told her stories, her version of history—herstory as I've come to know it—her presentations had several layers. She'd begin with her Canadian accent and slowly drift to a southwestern Irish one. If partying with our parents, our great-aunt would graduate from beer to whiskey and the Irish would gush from her.

By the time I was sitting at her feet to listen, Auntie Beers had outlived her youngest sister Maggie and her beloved brother-in-law, Séamus. Our parents, their children, cared for her as though she were a beloved grandmother.

Auntie Beers, when she was in her most cynical, grumpy and rude state, would make outrageous pronouncements as she was picked up for dinner or dropped off afterwards.

"Colleen, you pregnant with another wee bastard to feed? Sure listen, start thinking with your head."

"Damn hotel is full of fluthered old crocks. Otherwise it's a great place to live."

"Have these bloody weans ever had a face wash? Or do ye just let the sun do all the work?"

She was decidedly not the quintessential granny.

Bairbre insisted on living on her own. Independent if poor. After all, she was used to poverty. I'm certain that our parents provided her with a great deal of the beer she used as liquid food. Perhaps they figured since she'd survived this long without nutrition, a life of barley wouldn't hurt.

When I decided to write down my memories of her, there were some words I remembered as though they were my own. Others never fit my translated narrative.

I took the tales from my childhood and exaggerated them. Or applied Auntie Beers' notion of "if only/when" and "then." Add to that the crime writer's "what if?" and I was set for my fingers to fly over the keyboard.

As I have grown older, unearthed my memories of Auntie Beers, I've realized that life is never one way or another but a complicated mixture. In my fictional representations, I imagined happier endings for some of my relatives. Their difficult lives I couldn't completely ignore, however. Some of their ordeals, I wanted to share. As a kind of tribute to Auntie Beers' penchant for creating demons to teach a lesson.

Often, as the saying goes, Auntie Beers looked a little under the weather on a Sunday morning. She was most likely hung over. On those days her words were slurry and her movements slow.

Once she disappeared into herstory, though, she was electric. A vivid color of green surrounded by clouds of dark grey. To hear her tell it, Bairbre O'Sullivan had never lived an optimistic existence. She had inherited a dim, if ironic and witty, view. A self-fulfilling expectation of constant angst.

"I was born in Ireland on New Year's Day. At least that's the tale my mother told me. Although she said she was born New Year's Day too, and years later we discovered she was born in May. I suspect she just wanted to party very hard on New Year's. None of us girls had a registered birth. In those days, Catholic girls were as worthwhile as age spots."

My thoughts scattered a bit, as I pictured my mother. Strong, opinionated and feminist. I could not imagine anyone ever considering her worthless.

"The reason your grandparents came to Canada was because in the late 1920s Canadian farmers were in need of help on their farms. The government came up with a plan to get men from other countries to come to Canada. They were offered a job on a farm and a free house for their families to live in. Passage for everyone to get here. Feckin' governments. There's always a catch."

At this point Auntie Beers performed her dramatic pause. We held our breath, not only in reaction to the smoke that would be exhaled after a big drag on her cigarette but also because the excitement was palpable in that little room. We knew a lesson was coming. A moral to a story. Our great-aunt's "if only" scenario with its implied criticism of reality.

"If only that had been true! The catch was that the men had to work off the price of the trip across the ocean before they received any money. The cost was high if you had kids and a sister-in-law the way your grandda did. And the aforementioned free house turned out to be old shacks in the middle of a field."

She peered down her aristocratic nose at us.

"Remember, kids, there is always a catch. Nothing is ever free."

It was advice we never forgot. (Though difficult to apply in the late 60s when love and sex and sometimes drugs were all free.)

"There was no heat in those free shacks, so winters were very tough with that fierce weather we had in Canada. It never got that cold in the south of Ireland, you see. We had the Gulf Stream."

"What's the Gulf Stream?" Patrick asked.

He was always the one to clarify the details. To obtain facts from Auntie Beers.

"It's a big ocean current that comes from Mexico and circles around the world until it finds the greenest place on earth."

"Ireland." I supplied the prompts, which kept her narrative going even when facts were lacking.

"That first winter, we were nearly banjaxed. Wind whistled through the cracks in the walls. We had to wear our jumpers to bed. Usually we had a stove that stood in the middle of the front room but it was always going out. We burned wood in it to keep warm."

"Where did you get the wood?" I asked, child of a house where a gas-powered furnace roared.

In a subdivision devoid of big, old trees.

"We found the wood along railroad tracks or in stands of trees close to the shack. The fire of course always went out long before morning. You really had to hurry into your clothes. It was so cold."

Auntie Beers shivered, but I, sitting in that overly warm room, had to stretch my imagination to picture the frantic need to get dressed in frigid air.

One winter when my father took me to my uncle's cottage, the fire went out during the night. I remembered Auntie Beers' tale as I felt my cold nose and snuggled under big fluffy covers that I knew she never had. I imagined Auntie Beers, huddled on a bed with one or two of her nieces, facing the bitter cold of a shack where the wind had free reign. I could not imagine the strength of will it took to get up. To enter a day filled with hard work and so little joy.

"Why did you leave Ireland?" Grace asked.

My cousin's heart was both the strongest and the weakest. She couldn't bear others' grief, but she had the skills to help them heal. Her questions always zeroed in on the underlying emotions. Our great-aunt would often refuse to answer, but there were times when she opened her heart just a little. After all, my cousin was named after Bairbre's younger sister, who still lived in Ireland.

Auntie Beers took a drag of her cigarette. Her sensational green eyes held an echo of love, hope and selflessness.

"Sure, I didn't have anyone there to hold me back. And sometimes love of a person is stronger than love of a place," she said.

In those days, I always thought she meant Maggie.

After a beat, she took up the story as though Grace had not interrupted.

"Of course the 1930s were bad for everybody. Everywhere around the world, even Canada. We had to do a lot of moving. The first farmer we came to from Ireland couldn't afford to keep us and we had to leave not long after we got there. Your oul' wans were young and might not remember."

Our mothers and fathers rarely spoke of those years. Either Auntie Beers was right and they didn't remember or they didn't want to burden their children with bad memories.

"Michael and Kathleen were wee 'uns through those years and we didn't have the other two. I would sit in the wagon with your Grandda and hold them."

"A wagon?" I asked.

Visions of my sister's little Red Rocket wagon rumbling down the street danced in my head. I couldn't see Auntie Beers and my aunt sitting in one of those. Of course, picturing my uncle and mother as babies to be cuddled was even more difficult.

"Big. Pulled by a horse," our great-aunt clarified impatiently, using her hands to enlarge my imagination.

"John and Eddie had the job of picking up any small objects that fell off the wagon. Wee Peggy would insist on helping. Her chubby little legs would hold us up, but your Grandda had a special spot for his first little girl. Your Granny sat in the back and rearranged the stuff as we went. Not that we had many belongings, mind you. Not like we have nowadays."

Once again Auntie Beers waved her hand around the room as though to demonstrate a plethora of objects. She must have been thinking of my cousins' and my houses, though, because her little hotel space was bare in comparison. A single bed. A small refrigerator. A scratched dresser with a layer of dust on which two keepsakes sat.

A rusting rosary curled up in abandonment. A set of three black poodles, ceramic I suppose. One an adult chained to two smaller versions of itself.

Hate and Love

James/Benedict 1920s
Ireland, 1926
By Clare O'Sullivan Doyle

James loved the precision and beauty of the celebrations. There was control. Rigid ceremony followed the same routine each time. None of the chaos of his life could enter.

He donned the cassock, or soutane, a black robe that fell to his ankles. It had been sewn to measure for his height and broad shoulders.

"Ye take after the Viking ancestors," his mother told him. "We can't deny that those bastards were here and sent their progeny down the line."

James was grateful that his mother had been alive to witness his ordination. She was proud of him, a phenomenon that hadn't occurred in his life until that moment.

Next came the amice, a soft white cloth that he placed over those same thick shoulders, tying it into place with silky white ribbons. Over his cassock went the long white robe, or alb, which he tied up with a cincture. He liked this belt, for it resembled a rope and was comfortable around his waist. He enjoyed knotting it up correctly, as it held his stole in place.

As a symbol of his priesthood, the stole draped over his shoulders. A scarf that gave him status. A local woman had designed his for him, green with two Celtic crosses, two Pax symbols, both in white, and a delicate red flower embroidered near the bottom on each side.

For the outer garment, the chasuble, James had one in each appropriate color for the liturgical year.

Every piece of clothing had a deep, rich history and tradition. As he dressed, James said a prayer for each of the vestments. Mostly asking that he would have the strength to be the man he should be. He often found the daily process of living to be difficult. Never allowed to be his true self. To even acknowledge what that would mean.

When he stood on the altar, repeated the ritual prayers, gave sustenance to the congregation, sang the lovely hymns, he could disappear into another world.

Though he often still thought of himself as James, he was now Father Benedict. He had been Benedict for a long time now. He liked this name. It was strong, a Pope's legacy, something he could grow into. He hoped.

The day everything changed, Benedict walked from the church to his father's house right after morning Mass. As he passed the tall stone houses stacked side by side along the dirt road, his heart pounded with shame and pity. Little ones, their bones protruding from ripped shirts and slack dresses, played in the stubbly grass, using rocks instead of toys. Made up games that he couldn't follow. They looked up at him with desperate hope, smiled when they saw it was Father.

This morning he was able to distribute some small pieces of bread that had not been blessed and were left over. Whenever he could do this, he felt less guilty. If only their mothers would bring them to Mass, perhaps he could feed them a little more.

Go raibh maith agat, a Athair, the older children mumbled reverently. The little ones were mostly mute, but their eyes shone briefly with appreciation. As soon as he was gone, the bread eaten, the light went out and they returned to their silent games.

Benedict felt very little guilt in ensuring Joseph, his father, and sister Molly, as well as Paddy O'Brien, were fed and clothed. Paddy was a distant relative whom his father treated like a son. Especially since losing Joseph's younger brother Timothy, Paddy's presence in the household was extremely important for the older man's health.

The priest knew parishioners who had to scrape to give a shilling to the church, but he also knew those who could well afford to donate. Those were the people who invited him to dinner. To whom he paid a great deal of attention. They were the church councilors, deacons, and attendees at functions which included the Bishop. Theirs was the crowd who received invitations to the Castle, where they drank and ate to excess while the people starved along the oceanside.

Benedict was certain that God had a plan. There were those who would be rich and happy on earth, but perhaps whose afterlife would not be as comfortable. When they reached heaven, surely those ragged children would be raised up forever more.

As he traipsed over the bridge, Benedict picked up the scent. A thick fog snaked across the horizon. He knew what it was. There had been enough incidents in West Cork to make the smell familiar. A house was burning, its chemical and mechanical contents spewing bits of poisonous ash into the sky. Smoke that burned the eyes and scorched the throat. He pulled his stole up over his face, picked up the skirts of his cassock, and ran.

Benedict had, even as a young boy, learned to step on his emotions. Ever since he could remember, his mother had spent all her time in the church and his father had lived at the local pub. He and his sister had scrambled for food, watched their house deteriorate, and experienced the deadening of the little town around them. Violence and starvation had chased most of their neighbors away.

The arrival of Paddy and James's ordination into Father Benedict had made a difference in their financial state. None of this could save his mother from cancer, however. The Irish Fighters began to permeate their lives. Paddy brought talk of rebellion and hostility to their table. Benedict didn't question O'Brien about his whereabouts, nor where he got the food or money that he brought home after one of his wanderings.

Paddy had a golden crown of wavy hair, sky blue eyes and freckles that, even in his thirties, dusted his nose and cheeks like a child. He was extremely bright, having attended college. As a student he'd won a gold King's Medal for conduct, industry and attendance. Though Paddy sometimes laughed at himself, he still coveted that gold medallion.

James/Benedict loved Paddy O'Brien more than anyone else in the world.

When Benedict made it to the top of the hill and turned the corner toward the spiral of smoke, the sight brought him to his knees. The insides of their house had been sucked out, leaving lopsided, scorched stone, and bits of burnt thatch strewn around the outside. A thick column of smoke poured into the sky, forming a black cloud above their heads. The chimney stood embarrassed and useless inside the crumbling walls. The windows stared sightless at him, nothing behind them but ash.

There was no fire brigade. No hoses. Nor a source of water had there been. No nearby houses to worry about. Their house was being left to smolder and die.

A rustling from behind the house caught his attention. Benedict stood, bereft among the charred bushes and dead flowers. Suddenly he saw his sister, her face blackened and ten years older than this morning. Her arm tucked under their father's shoulder, nearly dragging him through the debris.

Benedict raced forward, his heart kicking into high gear, pounding in his ears.

"Molly," he breathed when he reached them. "Da." A prayer. A caress.

Molly fell gracefully to her knees, her long skirt resembling her brother's cassock, except covered in ash and burn holes.

"Are ye hurt?" Benedict asked, as he threw his arms over his father's shoulders and pulled him upright.

The old man said nothing, saving his energy for each tortured breath.

"We're all right, we are. But Paddy…"

"They riddled the place with bullets first," his father said hoarsely, "so we couldn't get out. Then the fire started, and they scattered. Only Paddy came and got us, so he did."

Benedict looked around, puzzled.

"Where is he then? Where's our Paddy?"

Those words would echo and repeat for months to come. Where's our Paddy?

Benedict lowered his father gently to the ground to sit beside Molly. Stole over his face once more, he stepped through the burned doorway, pushing aside the shards of wood that still clung to the entrance. Enduring the smell was like diving into fetid liquid.

His footsteps were slow and methodical. A slow-motion sweep, his boots scraping through the ash and the detritus of their lives. Odd items still recognizable, others a mash of dirt. Burned into nothingness. As he kicked his way through, he imagined coming upon Paddy's body, his feet making contact with something soft and dead. The horror of it almost made him stop, but not quite.

Halfway through, he connected with an object that still shone gold through the black ash. He bent over and pulled the King's Medal from the debris. The ribbon that had held the keepsake was gone except for a few charred threads, but the gold still shone. He slipped the medal into the pocket of his soutane.

"Paddy?" he called, but his muffled voice merely drifted on the air and disappeared. "Paddy…"

At that moment, the fire brigade arrived with their small engine, chugging up the hill, their clothing and faces still dark with ash from a previous fire. The chief walked through the doorway, suited up and determined.

"Father Benedict," he said, "You can leave this to us now."

Benedict wanted him to clarify what he meant by "this." This was gone, this was destroyed. This might just be the body of someone he loved more than life. He wanted to lie down, moan. Sink into the nothingness too.

Instead, he nodded regally, picked up the skirts of his cassock, despite knowing they were already covered in ash. Shoulders back and head high, he made a priestly exit. Pulled a mask over his face and feelings to perform as an ordained soul. Someone who cared for others and did not ever show his own emotions nor become bowed by them.

He led Molly and Joseph down the hillside, across the bridge and up the embankment to the church and rectory. They walked slowly to match Joseph's ragged breaths and his need to talk.

"Paddy was in with those Irish fighters," he said. "This was the work of those bastards the Black and Tans."

Molly said nothing, only emitting a kind of squeak as she breathed.

"The bloody British are determined to keep Ireland under their filthy thumbs. Starve us. Burn us out of our homes. Make us give up."

Joseph turned his furrowed, blackened face toward his son.

"They will not win. We will have our freedom."

Benedict simply nodded. He felt numb. Dead inside. When the blond freckled boy-man's face tried to surface, he pushed it aside. The price for freedom, it seemed to Benedict, was far too high.

Lacking an assistant or a housekeeper was now a plus. The priest's house was a decent size, with three small bedrooms, a dining room and kitchen, as well as a parlor. He gave his own ordinary clothing to his sister and father. Once dressed in a shirt and pants that she tied up with a rope, Molly began to move about the kitchen. Gathering food, cleaning the counters. In silence.

Joseph lay down on the bed and soon, his mouth wide open, he was snoring.

Benedict went back along the pathway to the road, across the bridge and up the hill. The fire brigade had spread over the burned house like ants. They dug quickly and efficiently, tossing anything useful into one pile.

The chief turned toward the priest as he hovered in the doorway.

"Any sign of Paddy O'Brien?" Benedict asked, his voice stiff and formal. "As ye know, he was living here temporarily."

"No sign at all, Father," Chief McCarthy answered. "No human remains have been discovered. We're not quite finished, as you can see, but it's not looking as though he's here."

"My Da is convinced this is the work of the Black and Tans."

McCarthy nodded his head, not looking at Benedict. "Aye, he's probably right. Two farmhouses and your cottage were hit today, so. Strafed by bullets then burned to the ground. I suppose there were groups of them so they could do it all at once. Made it impossible for us to save the properties. My team is wrecked."

"The bullets kept the people inside. They meant to murder them."

"It appears so. But they didn't succeed. Word got around and everyone was out."

"Word got around?"

McCarthy nodded. "Sure, someone ran from place to place. Somebody who knew where they were going to hit."

"Get up outta that. A double agent, like?"

McCarthy looked at Benedict carefully. "Look no further than your man, Father."

At the priest's look of shock and dismay, McCarthy put a hand on his shoulder and shook his head.

"You're all right, Father. Get on now. We're nearly finished here."

Outside, a crowd of neighbors had gathered on the blackened soil to give their sympathies to the priest. He walked among them, shook hands, gave hugs and blessings, and assured them that God would provide.

Most of them were angry. The destruction had served only to strengthen their will and the determination for freedom. Ireland would break away from the yokes of the English landlords, they said either in words or looks. Soon, Benedict was certain, they would say so in deeds. More burned homes, more destroyed lives. Would freedom feel good enough to erase the misery?

Over the next three weeks, Father Benedict tended to his congregation. Molly kept house, cooked and shopped for him and Joseph. Their father read books off the many shelves in the rectory.

A telegram arrived from the bishop on the fourth week. You're shite, Benedict thought. He searched for the word for coward and found it. A banóglach. Could not summon the nerve to use a telephone.

Improper to have family living in the rectory stop. Move them out immediately stop. Sending a curate to help in the parish stop.

"You're all right, Jamie," his sister said, using her childhood name for him. "Thomas O'Sullivan has asked us to come and live with him in Bantry. They've a large farm and things are tolerable. He's got three motherless children since Theresa died. Lots for me to do and room for Da as well."

Thomas, a distant cousin, had always been sweet on Molly. Benedict wondered how improper this arrangement would be.

"He's asked me to marry him, and I have said yes," she said after a pause. "He knows I'm past childbearing age but that I will be happy to take care of his own. Sure you don't have to worry, Father. Would you do the sacrament for us before we leave?"

A week later, exactly one month from the day his father's house burned to the ground, Benedict sat in his bedroom for some privacy. Gone were the quiet, efficient motions of his sister and the intelligent sighs of his father as he read a beautiful phrase.

Instead, the curate sent by the Bishop mumbled loudly to himself. Talked incessantly if Benedict appeared. Crashed into things. Left all his dishes and leftovers for the new housekeeper. A small, but mighty woman, he had to admit she tried her best to keep up, but the Bishop had only given them two days a week.

There was a hole inside Benedict's stomach. In his heart, he supposed, but the acid seeped up from the knots in his intestines and clouded his mind. Each passing day made it worse. He lay down on the bed and allowed sleep to take him. Where's our Paddy?

At first, he thought it was a dream, but gradually he realized that the knocking was real. He gathered his cassock around him and went to the front door. During the night, rain had begun and was slashing at the windows. The man on the doorstep looked diminished by the water flowing from his head and shoulders. He was small, thin, and breathless.

Benedict pulled him into the vestibule and half carried him into the kitchen, where he sat him at the table. Father found a blanket and tucked it around the other man. At the same time, he turned on the kettle and placed a teabag in a cup. Shivering, the visitor clung to the hot drink as though it were the source of life.

Benedict sat down across from him. "Who are you?" he finally asked. "What do you want?"

The stranger looked up and the priest realized this person was more boy than man. His eyes were a piercing blue. His hair was likely lighter than it appeared as it was soaked and plastered against his head and forehead.

"I've been sent to tell you about our Paddy," he said, his teeth chattering between words.

Despite his best effort, Benedict's eyes filled with tears in anticipation of bad news.

"What's happened?"

"They've sent him to Canada."

The padre sat back in his chair, both dismayed and thrilled. Canada. A country to which so many of their compatriots had flown that it felt both familiar and strange. This meant Paddy was alive. Yet so far away.

"They threatened to kill him if he didn't get on the ship. Gave him a third-class ticket, one way, they did."

"Where in Canada will he land?"

The little man sipped on his tea and shook his head. "Some place called Quebec. They told him if he wanted to stay alive and safe, he should go to a city named Urbston. Somewhere north of Toronto."

"What's your name?"

"Tim."

"You seem to know a lot about Canada, Tim. Even how to pronounce the city names."

"I've been there, Father. Sure and I spent a few months in the prison. I was not a nice man. I came back to the motherland to change my ways."

"And that has worked for you, Tim?"

The man nodded. He no longer shivered. His mouth was set in a straight line.

"To a degree, Father. I'm not here to do my confession, however. I will do what I must to gain freedom for Ireland. Some of those deeds are not anyone's idea of good, but..."

He shrugged his shoulders.

Benedict made Tim eat some leftover soup and bread, but the man would not stay the night. Despite the pounding rain, he slipped back into the darkness.

Over the next few weeks, Benedict told himself he should be happy that Paddy was alive. It should be enough. He ought to turn his face back to God, to whom he had dedicated his life. But he couldn't manage it. His grief was a deep wound that became more and more infected as the days rolled by. No longer did the ceremony of Mass hold his attention. He found little sympathy for his congregants. He was angry and sad. After a while, he realized he could not continue.

He made the trek to Dublin and spoke to the Bishop. His superior, too much of a coward to face the problem, was relieved that Benedict had come to him. He was able to erase a suspected freedom fighter from the ranks of his diocese.

On the return trip, Benedict stopped in Bantry to see his sister and father. They were healthy and happy.

"I'm going to Canada," he told them. "The Bishop has provided me with a first-class ticket. One way. He's happy to be rid of me. He thinks I'm a freedom fighter. I've been assigned to a city named Urbston."

He hugged his father and sister, knowing it would be unlikely that he would see them again.

Benedict carried only his stole, rosary, and his suit. In his suitcase, he packed the green chasuble. A symbol of charity and a color that was used most of the year. One cassock. One alb, ironically a symbol of purity in its judgmental white linen. Benedict felt most like James when he placed it over his head and body. Ashamed, guilty, out of place. Each time, he hoped the garment would hide James forever, but it hadn't yet worked.

An amice to cover his sinful neck and a cincture to hold it all together. Some socks that had been darned by Molly and a couple of long and short unmentionables. Paddy's gold medal.

The Bishop had sent yet another chatty curate by the name of Brother Francis to accompany the Father on to the ship. The slightly younger man immediately grabbed Benedict's suitcase and walked briskly along the dock, talking all the way.

Benedict knew the Bishop wanted to guarantee he used the first-class ticket. Did not trade it for a lesser one and keep the difference. Also, to ensure that he got on the ship and disappeared from the Bishop's circle. Benedict had not caused a great deal of difficulty in the diocese, but he had ruffled feathers a few times. He wondered what they did with the real troublemakers. Perhaps they got third-class tickets? Thrown overboard? Sent to Africa?

Benedict was slightly embarrassed to skirt around all the people waiting in line. Laden with bulky packages, food, clothing, babies. The queue went the length of the enormous ship, seemingly impossible to deal with. How would they all fit? By the shabbiness of their clothing, the thinness of their bodies, the priest could tell that these were the poor immigrants. Sent away because their land had been appropriated and they had nowhere to go. Perhaps, with any luck, they would not starve in Canada.

By now, in 1926, shipboard accommodations had improved, or so Benedict was told by the curate. The Brother was very young but appeared to be confident in the knowledge he had at his disposal.

"Do not carry on worrying about them," Brother Francis said, pointing his chin toward the human column. "Sure they are given free passage to a new life and nowadays they have more privacy. New berths, so they tell me, with families and married couples in their own areas."

"Free passage?" Benedict asked, his tone one of disbelief.

"Ex-servicemen of His Majesty's armed forces and their dependents sail free," the curate said, his tone one of certainty. "Others are sponsored under one of the receiving country's agricultural schemes. I believe there is a contract for a certain amount of work in exchange for passage and accommodation."

Benedict scanned the line, startled by the number of children and women travelling alone.

As though reading his mind, Brother Francis said, "Many of the men came across earlier to start working. Their dependents have been approved and will join them. As long as they are not idiots or immoral or alkies or anarchists."

The young man laughed.

"The bishop has sworn you are none of these, Father, so be sure to behave yourself on board."

Benedict was astonished by his room. One large bed encircled with flowered drapes. Two basins and, on the other side, a bed that had not yet been unfolded and formed a bench instead. A comfortable looking armchair covered in the same material as the curtains.

Brother Francis placed his suitcase on the bench.

"You will not have to trouble yourself with anyone else in this room, Father. The Bishop has ensured you have the stateroom to yourself."

Likely afraid he would speak about changes he wanted to make in the church and its structure, Benedict thought. Perhaps even in his sleep.

"This is lovely. Thank you, Brother Francis," he said aloud, using his kindly priest's voice. "Thank you for all your assistance. Much appreciated, so."

"Sure it's no trouble at all. You'll find a smoking room, dining hall, and even a library on board. And seven days to enjoy them."

The curate put out his hand and they shook.

"May fortune and happiness shine upon you," Brother Francis said.

Benedict could think of no graceful return, so he simply nodded, and the man was gone.

Despite the relative luxury—certainly relative to third class and even his room at the rectory—Benedict became bored after the first three days. He didn't smoke, so the smoking lounge was of no interest. After scanning the reading selections in the library, he simply sat in one of the snug chairs and stared ahead.

No one seemed interested in talking to a priest. He wondered if he should remove his cassock and wear his suit, but it was too warm for that to be comfortable. So he took to wandering the ship, up and down the stairs, landing on various decks. In the lower decks, he saw the crowded conditions of the people who could not afford a first-class ticket. Or did not have a Bishop who was highly motivated to send you away.

They were crammed into tight quarters. Despite having better lodging than the old steerage passage, the rooms were crowded with several open bunks. The dining area did not appear to have elbow room. Inside the smoking lounge a grey cloud clung to the walls and ceiling like sludge. Their outer deck had only enough room for some to sit and some to stand along the edges.

Benedict saw her on the first-class deck on his fourth day. He knew immediately that she did not belong. Her clothing had obviously been stitched and darned several times. Not only that, she was smoking.

Though he did not desire women, he admired them. This female was stunning. Tall, thin, red haired. Long legs. Her face was sculpted with all the elegance that defined beauty.

She sat comfortably on the deck chair, alone, the smoke from her cigarette drifting out to sea. Although clearly out of place, she appeared confident, poised. Even smug. Her expression said she belonged here and would stay until she wanted to leave.

"You're not fooling anyone," she said.

"What do you mean?"

"I can tell immediately that you are a homosexual. It's in your eyes when you look at me."

Benedict struggled to control the flush of anger that spread from his stomach to his face. Years later, he would admit that his hatred of her began right there. On that deck with the ocean rolling underneath.

"And you are obviously third-class, yet here you sit making outrageous pronouncements on first-class strangers."

He sat in a chair with one between them as though to cement the claim of who should sit where.

"Class is arbitrary and unfair. Depends solely on where you were born. If you are in the poverty class from birth, the church and the state work very hard to keep you there. If you are a person who does not belong, you are sent away. If you rebel, you are silenced by a gun or prison. Or Canada."

"The church is not complicit in…"

Her laugh was large, unfettered and delightful. In other circumstances, he would have been entranced. Instead, the sound made his skin crawl and his head throb.

"Sure, you are either in denial or think you must repeat the Catholic mantra. God may smite you should you detour from the mandated message, right enough."

She drew heavily on the butt of the cigarette, savoring perhaps the last of her tobacco. Her perfect lips furled in lines that would stay there if she wasn't careful.

"You are an ignorant woman," Benedict said as savagely as he could muster.

His anger and hatred had filled his mind, detracting him from words or coherent thought. He did not know when he had felt this way before.

At that moment, a rotund, grey-haired gentleman walked through a compartment door onto the deck. Benedict stood quickly, separating himself from the woman. He stood at the railing and watched the waves.

"Here you are," the man cooed to the woman. "A real chancer, are ye, Bairbre?"

"You tempted me with the tobacco, so you did," she answered as she watched the butt flare and go out on the deck floor.

The man glanced over at Benedict.

"A friend of yours?" he asked her.

"No. Most definitely not."

"You earwigging, mate?"

"This deck is for first-class passengers, of which I am one." Benedict pointed to the woman. "And she is clearly not."

"Feck off, eejit. Come, Bairbre, let us go and have some fun."

She stood up. Her weathered dress gathered around her body as though it were a ball gown. Her hair fell to her shoulders in perfect symmetry. She looked beautiful.

The man tucked his arm in hers and they headed for the doorway from which he had come. She whispered something to him. He laughed.

"Feck off yourself, fella," Benedict said, not loudly enough for them to hear.

The woman turned her head to look at him just before they disappeared. Her expression told him that she understood his sentiment exactly. She smiled mischievously and then she was gone.

Benedict seethed all day. Slept badly that night. Yet the next afternoon, he could not resist going back to the deck where he'd found her.

Bairbre was smoking again. Same deck chair. She wore the same dress, though today a ragged shawl sat on her shoulders. She managed somehow to look graceful and lovely.

Benedict could smell the mustiness from her. He wanted to gag but some odd emotion compelled him to sit in the deck chair he'd commandeered the day before.

"What's your name if I might ask, Father?"

Her voice and posture were languid. As though she belonged, and he did not.

"Father Benedict," he answered primly.

"The real one."

He paused, then said, "James."

"I like Benedict better, to be honest with ye. James is rather plain and very common. Benedict. That's different."

He nodded, agreeing with her on this point at least.

"How have you stayed with the Catholic church, Father Benedict? Ye must have a rebel in your circle and the Holy See does not like rebels. Otherwise you would not be on a ship to Canada."

Benedict looked out at the sea, a grey mass of water moving in a rhythm unknown to him. Slightly menacing, its weight and volume capable of taking his life in an instant. He envisioned Paddy's earnest face. His eyes lit with fervor.

"Freedom for Ireland," he would whisper, his head resting on Benedict's shoulder, still together but already apart. "It's the only thing that matters to me, Jamie. Even more than you."

Bairbre waited. Into her silence, he finally spoke. His voice had shed the superior tone, as though they were friends. As though he did not hate her kind of woman.

"Perhaps I know one or two," he said. "But the Church has supported the rebellion and freedom for Ireland. Sure listen. You are incorrect."

Bairbre drew heavily on her cigarette and gave a hoarse laugh. She huddled under her thin shawl as a breeze from the sea swept over the deck.

"Don't you believe it, Father. The Catholic Church has always sided with the British. They ex-communicated Fenians in 1867, so my granddad told me. The higher clergy were afraid they'd lose control."

Benedict said nothing, but the telegraphs he'd received moved across his eyes. The Bishop urging all priests to influence their rebel parishioners to surrender.

One of his parishioners, stuck in a small jail cell in Bantry, had refused to see a priest even as he took his last breath.

"He is at odds with the church, Father," his wife told Benedict sadly. "I'm terribly sorry but he believes the church to be on the side of the foreign oppressors, don't you see?"

Bairbre continued, as though she were giving a lecture. Which, perhaps, she was.

"The bishops wrote to the parishes and wrote to the newspapers condemning de Valera, Sinn Fein and the IRA so they did."

"They condemned the violence, woman," Benedict said, ferocious once again. "They were criminals who hurt and killed people."

Yet in the presence of her calm, learned speech, he felt whiney and ill-informed.

"There was violence only when they were attacked, priest," she returned. "They were fighting a war. The Church gave support to the enemy. It ran the Magdeline Laundry and threatened the children or siblings of the rebels with incarceration there. Many priests were informers for the British."

"I was not."

"That's likely why you're on this ship, Father. They wanted to be rid of you, they did."

A thick silence fell upon them. Benedict shivered. He stood, wondering why he felt compelled to listen to this ridiculous person. She herself would be a candidate for a Laundry. Obviously, a fallen woman and likely ex-communicated from the church as well.

He pulled his stole up around his neck and walked away. He heard movements and could tell she had thrown the nasty cigarette butt overboard. He couldn't help but turn to look at her.

She stood at the railing. Her hair tossed about in the wind, a red mass like a halo around her head. Back and shoulders straight, squared, Bairbre held herself like a lady.

Her entire long-legged, attractive personage was a lie, Benedict thought. A lovely spider.

He returned the next day, as though drawn by that piece of webbing. To his surprise, the fat uppity man who was clearly her lover sat in her chair instead.

When the man pointed his chins, Benedict sat where they directed.

"I'm Robert Foster," the fellow said, holding out a chubby hand to shake.

It was wet with perspiration. Benedict nearly shivered as they clasped.

"Father Benedict Collins," he said.

"Catholic?"

"Yes."

"Same as my mackerel snapper, who's gone off to check on her sister."

Benedict's hatred of Bairbre diminished somewhat in the realization of how he felt toward Foster. Though he was embarrassed for her that she would sink so low as to sleep with this man.

"I have made sure they have more room and more food for the journey," Foster continued, sounding magnanimous and superior.

Benedict suddenly understood Bairbre's motives.

"Her stupid sister has five children to feed. Does she not know what makes babies?"

"The church teaches that…"

Foster waved a hand to stop him.

"Your church is ridiculous. Maybe the sister should have a little talk with Bairbre. She knows how to do it right. Anyway, never mind. Where are you off to, Father?"

"A city called Urbston."

"Go way outta that! I'm heading there, too. Being placed in the Orange Order at a nice high level. Have you been assigned a parish?"

"No...I've been...retired. Kind of on my own from here on out."

"Well, if you need a hand, and you're ready to give up that terrible religion, come and see me. I'll set you up."

Benedict shivered. The slimy, snobbish horrible man.

"What about your paramour and her sister? Will you be setting them up?"

Robert Foster laughed.

"I will deny all knowledge of that clart. My wife would not approve."

He laughed harder, as though he'd told an enormously funny joke.

"Bairbre's off to join her brother-in-law on some farm. Scrabbling like a slave to pay off the cost of their passage. With any luck, I won't be seeing her again. However, Father, if you want a ride some time, maybe you can look her up."

Once more, he roared laughing. Benedict could still hear him as he walked-ran away.

For the remainder of the voyage, Benedict avoided that deck. He never saw Bairbre again until years later.

His hatred and disgust for her weakened once she was out of sight. Mainly because he knew, deep within himself, that she was right about the Catholic religion. On every count.

When he thought of how she had pimped herself out to Robert Foster, he wondered what he would do for Paddy. Would he be as selfless as Bairbre was? She spent that trip with a pig of a man to improve the circumstances for her sister and the children. He wasn't certain he could do that.

The ship passengers disembarked into a cold, grey cloud that sat on the dock and devoured each group as they walked away. Benedict had no one to pick him up. The Bishop had suggested that he get a lift to the rectory in Quebec City, where a basilica to St. Anne was being built.

His superior had patted him on the shoulder, while Benedict had wondered what was so wrong with his old life. Other than harboring a criminal, that is.

"Out of the ashes, Father Benedict, like St. Anne's parish. This can be you. Don't you think? They are erecting a beautiful church. You can start a new, beautiful life if they are generous enough to take you in."

The "if" was bigger than his Bishop let on. Benedict's connection to Paddy O'Brien followed him everywhere. Either in terms of being an Irish rebel or, worse still, a homosexual.

Benedict began to walk toward the harbor, hauling his old suitcase. He felt bent over, soaked through, by the clawing mist. Water dripped over the lid of his cap.

"Can I help you with your bag, Father?"

A soft voice. Irish lilt. Kindness seeped through the simple words. Benedict lifted his chin.

Freckles. Sky blue eyes. A golden crown of wavy hair.

Benedict sighed with joy. Never again, he thought. Never again will I let you disappear. 'Til death do us part.

They hugged long and hard, neither one caring who saw them.

"I've landed a good job and a place to stay in Urbston," Paddy finally said. "You can come with me. Ye might have to take off the cloth, though..."

Anything, Benedict thought. Anything for you. Perhaps he could even be as selfless as Bairbre.

"I've got us two bus tickets to Toronto and then on to Urbston. The new Grand Master, Colonel Robert Foster, has arranged everything for a group of us. We're to help him get established in the town. In exchange, we've got all the comforts we could want. You don't have to believe in the Orange Order, Jamie. They won't quiz you. I'm not letting go of you again."

Benedict thought of how often life provided joy along with sorrow. Paddy. Good with bad. The Grand Master Robert Foster.

He decided to be content with the love he had for this man. To focus only on the two of them. As for the rest, he tucked it away along with his cassock.

The Outhouse

Auntie Beers 1931
By Clare O'Sullivan

"Nobody could beat the view we had from our outhouse back in the old country," Auntie Beers once told us.

Immediately my mind conjured up a nice big hut with flowers and carved smiling moons and fancy wooden doors. My image was shattered as she continued.

"Da found some red tin sheets that had been thrown by the roadside."

Her long legs were crossed at the ankles. At the end of every sentence, she sipped gustily from her beer bottle.

"He got some discarded wood for the seats. Spent hours scraping and polishing with whatever he could get his hands on. Beeswax or even alcohol. They were the smoothest and shiniest seats in the county. Just like our bottoms."

We tried not to laugh, but we weren't entirely successful. I caught Auntie Beers' mouth lifting in a smile. Recognition that her joke had hit its mark.

"We'd sit staring out over the hills," she continued. "You could see the ocean from there. The greens in Ireland, my poor deprived nieces and nephews, are like nothing you've ever seen."

"Isn't that because they get so much rain?" Patrick asked.

Auntie Beers didn't acknowledge his question, though she mumbled loudly enough for us all to hear, "Ara, Patrick, may the great rains beat upon your spirit."

After which she began again.

"Sure look it, we only knew it was summer because the rain got warmer. Did you know in Ireland we call the place we do our business the jacks?"

We giggled and waited for Patrick's reaction. It was quick in coming.

"Why do you call it that?"

"I thought you'd never ask. There was a man called Jack who had thirty-eight children. You can just picture the mountain of shite that would produce, can you not? He had to invent something to take care of it all. So he built a line of huts where they could all go and do their jobs in one area. Every few years he'd move the shacks to a different part of his land. Nature has a way of using everything and those soils mixed with shite were extremely well fertilized, you see.

"The idea caught on and spread all over Ireland. Soon the poor fella's name was hooked up to shite. Even became a phrase: you know jack shite or you don't know jack shite, as the case may be. Eventually he had to move to the land of the enemy to get away from it all."

This was one of those occasions when we had gathered at Aunt Brigid and Uncle Alan's place for dinner. Even my father, Steven, was having a good time, encouraged by the free-flowing wine provided by Uncle Mario. All the adults besides Bairbre played euchre in the kitchen. We could hear the thumps of hands being slammed onto the rickety card table. Hoots of laughter and grunts of dismay.

Auntie Beers sat in an armchair, served beer by Alan, surrounded by most of her grandnieces-and-nephews. The boys were especially interested in the outhouse story.

"Boys do love their poop jokes," Bairbre chortled. "My brothers used to have farting contests. One of them had to fart before they counted to ten. Until Michael tried so hard to get one out that he shat himself. Ma banned those contests after that."

When our great-aunt was in this mood, which only happened at relaxed family parties where the booze was plentiful, she would treat us to her mirth. Blessed with a sound that arose from her belly, her laughter was a contagion that caught everyone in her path. We laughed along with her, delighted by her lack of adherence to the rules of politeness.

Loud and lusty and "completely unladylike," she would say. "I laugh like a woman."

"More like a horse," my father was heard to mutter, followed by a reprimand from my mother.

"Isn't shite a bad word?" Patrick asked.

We were already used to feck or feckin'. Shite was relatively new.

"Depends on how you use it, boy. Say shite with an Irish accent and you just mean the stuff that gets rejected by your body. Say it without an e and an accent, like you little shit, and you would be swearing.

"Outhouses were not created equal," Auntie Beers continued. "Here in Canada, there was a laudy daw farmer named English—he wasn't just from England, he had to have his name announce it—built a shanty that was good enough to have a picnic lunch inside. Windows with lacy curtains. TWO seats so youse could sit side by side farting and shite-ing."

The boys rolled around clutching their stomachs. The girls laughed so hard tears ran down our cheeks. Auntie Beers was right. There was nothing so funny as a fart and some poop.

"That outhouse was probably nicer than the shack we all lived in at the time. It was the victim of some good and some not so good-natured mischief. I remember a particular Hallowe'en as one of those times. In those days the kids mostly played pranks on Hallowe'en. There wasn't a lot of treating in the Depression. But this year, it involved his

Majesty's outhouse and was one of the funniest. Mostly for me, truth be told, because I got back at those wild boys like a right banshee from hell."

She tilted her head and roared.

"That year I walked the girls for miles to the upmarket side of town where they could get some genuine treats..."

Sometimes when Auntie Beers recounted a memory, I would move into the story. My imagination would piece together remembrances and experiences of my own, mix them with my great-aunt's, and create vivid word pictures. Later, I would blend her truth with my imagination.

One little person walks with a stick, dressed in a threadbare men's jacket, face smeared with lines from a piece of coal. She looks nothing like an old man, with that lift in her walk, her straight strong bones and her pinkish pale complexion. Peggy darts back and forth, in front of me, beside and behind, until I yell at her to settle down.

Kathleen takes queenly steps forward, acting the part, the tin foil crown somewhat crooked on her head. The cape, an ancient slice of drapery that someone tossed away, is a faded red. Color rusted into the fabric by time.

Brigid, the youngest, is the only one who has a store-bought costume. It's been handed down from the boys through the girls to the baby. Saved for with pennies stolen from the food budget.

At almost three, Brigid is tall for her age and stocky, gifts from her Irish ancestry. She wears the skeleton jumper, stitched and restitched as it is, with enormous pride. Over the years, the mask has been glued and taped, but it's still creepy.

Lured out by the unusually warm weather and the promise of sweets, kids line up at various doors and along the sidewalk. Somewhere out there, hoboes John, Eddie and

Michael cruise the streets on their own. Old enough to do so at eleven, ten and nine, as judged by their mother. Daniel remains at home, glued to his Ma's side. He has none of the courage of his younger sisters, but he pretends he's staying home to protect her from mischief makers.

Maggie would be here except for a persistent cough. She doesn't have the strength to walk too far. Brigid would likely want a piggyback home.

Reluctant and therefore crabby, I pull the girls along with the sole purpose of getting the begging over with. Maggie has rehearsed a phrase with the girls, even with the little one. I must admit they can make the rhyme sound sweet.

"Hello, it's Hallowe'en. Give us some candy and don't be mean."

"We have to say please and thank you, too," Kathleen says, ever conscious of being polite and kind.

Yes, please give us some of those sweets you give your own kids every day of the year while these wee 'uns eat cabbage and thank you for thinking this old smock is a costume instead of my everyday dress while you sit in your grand house like the Queen of bloody England, I think, but keep all of that to myself.

I only shrug and say, "Of course" as though it were a given.

As my nieces traipse from house to house, I wait on the sidewalk or roadside with my arms crossed. I can't help tapping my foot. I also can't prevent myself from responses to snide remarks from other minders. Even though I mumble too low for them to hear, I get satisfaction from my witty returns.

"What are they doing on this side of town?"

Help us, we're lost in a land of heathens.

"Bloody Catholics are multiplying like fleas on the back of a dog."

I'd say bite me but I believe it's t'other way around.

Not everyone is rude. Some smile. Try a word or two about how cute the kids are. I remain true to my creed that I dislike people no matter their color, accent, religion or station in life. I don't return any greetings at all.

A witch strides by, her crepe costume sounding like the crushing of crackers into soup. Two kids, dressed as clowns with bathing caps on their heads, triangles drawn for eyebrows, sad mouths edged in dark red, make Brigid cry. Peggy chases after them, waving her stick as a weapon. The clowns laugh but run away. In my opinion they're dead creepy.

A real enough looking devil child waltzes past, a grotesque head disconcerting as she twirls in her frilly white dress. By the haughty, dismissive manner with which she treats her parents, I predict a hell of a time raising this one.

When someone walks by with what appears to be a real pig's head, I nod my head and say without thinking, "That's a real porker."

Pig Person does not reply.

The girls' sacks bulge with cookies, fruit, nuts. A bit of real chocolate. Some used toys. I scoop up the coins that were nonchalantly tossed inside. The residents are pretty much paying the kids not to play pranks.

I decide we've had enough fun.

"All right, girls, let's head back to home and show your Ma all the goodies."

"Do we have to share?" Peggy asks.

"Don't give a shite if you do or not," I reply.

"That's a bad word," Kathleen says.

"Not if you say it with a long I for Ireland."

"We better ask Ma." Pious Kathleen again.

I'm not sure if she's talking about the sharing or the swearing, but at this point I'm too tired to care. My feet ache and my back sends twinges down my leg.

When we cross the road to head off toward our shack, we hear them. At first the words are indistinguishable, but as I veer off in their direction, the girls grumbling and whining behind me, I can make them out clearly. I have to chuckle with a mixture of pride and chagrin. Those boys had actually listened to the rhymes and ballads I'd recited. Even memorized them and changed them to suit their own purpose. I could just imagine what Maggie would say.

> *Rise up, oh dead of Ireland!*
> *And rouse her living men.*
> *The chance has come to us at last*
> *To win our own again.*
> *To sweep the English shite away*
> *From hill and glen and bay.*
> *And in your name, oh Holy Dead,*
> *Our sacred debt to pay!*

The boys add their own line in tribute to Farmer English's pigs. The animals snort and grumble from their pens, which aren't far away. They're probably frightened, but they sound as though they're joining in.

Piggy, piggy, sweep the English shite away!

Maybe the poet, Brian O'Higgins, has arisen from his grave to spur on the antics of boys who don't know a thing about Ireland except from the mouths of their parents and me. My nephews tend to be easily roused to mischief and mayhem. I know I must intervene.

"This isn't the way," Kathleen pronounces. "We have to go that way, Auntie."

As though I am stupid enough to have wandered off course.

"I can hear the boys!" Peggy says.

She begins to rush forward, but I drag her back by the collar of the old man's shirt.

Ahead of us is a row of maples. Boulders in a ring in front of the grove make a perfect sitting area. Beyond the tree line, I know, is the English property. Specifically, their jacks.

"Wait right here," I command them all. "I'm going to see what's happening."

Peggy and Kathleen complain for different reasons, but they obediently sit together on a large, flat rock. Brigid immediately curls up with her head on Kathleen's lap.

"Ye can have a couple of treats," I say to mollify them.

When I leave, they are happily munching, though the little one appears to be sound asleep. I make my way through the underbrush and halt behind a big fat tree.

The boys' chanting is very loud now.

Piggy, piggy, sweep the English shite away!

They've formed a line that resembles a string of monkeys bent on destruction. The outhouse is already leaning. Six or seven pre-adolescent boys stand or crouch on all fours along one wall of the jacks, rocking it back and forth.

In the moonlight, I can see the gaping hole underneath as the shed lifts from its moorings. I can already smell its contents.

John is at the top of the structure, legs braced wide, moving side to side. Chanting maniacally and waving his shirt like a victory flag.

Cautiously I take one step forward when I feel a squishing sensation underfoot. I almost gasp out loud as I jump back. When I look down, I see the pig mask. Naturally, that gives me an idea.

It's a disgusting thing, rubbery and smelly and hot. I struggle to put it on, but manage nevertheless, chortling to myself.

When I jump out of the bush, the moonlight strikes me perfectly, as though nature has conspired to give those boys a comeuppance. I screech at the top of my lungs. Manage to be loud and fearsome despite the leather covering. I wave my arms and scream.

Just as I do so, the outhouse gives way and lands on its side. John flies off but lands upright. Takes off with a squeal of fright. With a loud cry, Michael scurries away toward the tree line. Five other boys, including Eddie, disappear into the darkness. All of them grunt and sob. Race as though chased by demons. I throw the pig mask on the ground. Double over laughing.

At first, I think it's an echo. When I turn around, I realize the laughter isn't all my own. Peggy, Kathleen and Brigid are howling with mirth. Peggy still in the process of waving her old man's stick. Kathleen's "wand" at her side as she bends over to hold stomach muscles contorted in giggles. Brigid the skeleton is a frightening blast of shocking white bones. All three of them are awash in moonlight, looking at least as scary and foreboding as the tall skinny woman with the pig's mask.

When I catch sight of them, we throw our arms around each other. Fall on the ground. Tears of laughter and howls of glee consume us. Right up until the moment we hear Farmer English shout.

"What the hell has happened here?"

We crawl away into the brush, scoop up the spoils of the night, and race home.

None of us mentions the incident to one another. Especially since Maggie might overhear. But now and then, I lean close to John, Eddie or Michael and whisper, "Piggy, piggy, sweep the English shite away."

Depression 1931

Auntie Beers 1960-1965

"Most Irish came to Canada because of the famines over in the old country," Auntie Beers told us. "Our family of course thought this country was giving away land by the cartload. Never considered that we were decades too late. The free land in this area had already been distributed. If only..."

This was the point at which our great-aunt inserted a dramatic pause. Harkened to her practice of living between 'if only' or 'when.' Mostly she'd fill the space with a sip of beer and a deep draw on her cigarette. The smoke wafted over our heads in the small, over-heated room.

Sometimes my cousin Grace coughed and her eyes watered, but she kept her attention focused on our great-aunt. We knew what rewards lay inside the small refrigerator and were not about to jeopardize that for a little reaction to secondhand smoke.

"If only your Grandda had not made the big mistake when he came over here."

I was usually the one to fulfill the role of prompter once the drama had been staged. Grace, Mario and Patrick rarely contributed to the conversation unless Auntie Beers gave them one of her sneers or asked a loaded question. Or left out some fact that Pat needed to process.

"What was the big mistake?" I asked.

"Your Grandda landed in the middle of Orange country," she answered. "Urbston. Right in the center of the Proddies who had no time for Catholics."

"Why did they have no time for Catholics, Auntie Beers?"

Me again, prompting only. The facts had been repeated many times.

"In my well-read yet humble opinion, I submit that everything, the migration, the starvation, the hatred, is to be found in the dusty past and the Irish penal laws. Those fiendish acts were passed far back in the sixteen and seventeen hundreds."

Perhaps Bairbre—if she hadn't been the family caregiver and alcoholic—could have been a history lecturer. She knew historical details, local stories and the geography of the land. She was opinionated and fierce about her beliefs.

"The feckin' Protestants decided the way to reward Catholics for their Papist ways was to subtract the only thing that had any value in that godforsaken country: land. Catholics couldn't own it. They couldn't lease it for too long, lest memory fade about whose was whose. They sure as shite weren't fit to vote let alone run for political office."

She took a deep breath and another drag on the cigarette.

"We might have had some clout if we held an elected office. An Irish Catholic couldn't be a feckin' lawyer. Couldn't own a horse. Some Protestant might get kicked in the head or run over. Couldn't die for the country neither. At least not as a soldier. Not until the world war came along and they needed some human fodder. Until then, you were quite welcome to die of hunger so. "

In hindsight, perhaps the history Auntie Beers related was more fiction than fact. Not to mention that she would've had to choose more socially acceptable words had she pursued a career as a history professor.

When she sat and lectured, she looked like one of those stars in an old-fashioned movie. A beauty who kept her distance. Long, free hair. Slim and cool. Auntie Beers' face was built for sneers and curled lips rather than smiles.

Clouds of bitterness had long ago hidden any lightness in her. Her humor was accidental.

"Things did change by the time your oul wans were born, but only because of the fierceness of the Irish spirit. Speaking of being kicked in the head, that reminds me of a story about your Grandda."

We shifted on our bottoms, excited. Especially me. Her stories about our grandparents were always vivid. Auntie Beers had been an observer. A kind of troubadour who sang about the past as she experienced it. An adult during the Depression, contemporary of our grandparents, she could open a window that no one else had available.

Cossetted child that I was, I thought poverty, farmhand toil, desperation and humiliation were somehow exotic. Perhaps in the way some people thought war was glorious until they actually experienced it.

I drank in the stories about my mother. For me she was the heroine of every tale. Mom told us only a little about her childhood, which made our great-aunt's stories all the more intriguing.

In Auntie Beers' tales, our family was chock full of brave, feisty, hardworking, resolute characters. It was difficult not to glorify. At least for a child who'd never had to beg for food at the side of a road while her family starved.

"I was home for the noon meal when your Grandda came in from the barn. He'd started a new job, one of so many. In those days, you see, when they discovered we were Papists, they'd kick us out."

"What are Papists again?"

This time Patrick asked the question, interested in the details and getting them right. A thinker.

I cringed because I knew Auntie Beers had explained all this before. Papists were people who followed the Pope, the deity in Rome who was never wrong. Try as he might, he only spoke the word of God and therefore could not possibly be incorrect.

If our great-aunt heard Patrick's question, her only reaction was a slight curl of the lip. In every other way she ignored him.

"When your Grandda Séamus came home early mid-morning, your granny was frantic. We stopped cleaning and cooking and together we watched him through the screen door. Walking in the dusty road. A dirty handkerchief pressed to his forehead. We were both frozen. In real shock. He was always gone from dawn to dusk. He never came home at the half day.

"I could feel Maggie's fear in the way she stiffened. The way her breath quickened. Her eyes were big and dark blue and that day they were wider than I'd ever seen. Maggie had been a beautiful woman, but this life had diminished her already.

"She rushed outside without a word and went to him. It was one of the rare occasions when I saw an open exchange of affection between them.

"She put her arms around him and looked at his head. When they got into the kitchen, she broke off some cubes from the icebox and wrapped them in a towel. That's when I saw the dent."

"A dent in his head?"

Already a crime writer, I couldn't stop the exclamation. Excited and appalled at the same time.

Auntie Beers looked amazed too, as if she were looking at her brother-in-law right this moment.

"Yes. An actual dent in his forehead. As though the bone had bent inward. He'd been kicked by a horse."

All four of us gasped. A horse. Like the one that pulled the milk wagon until it was replaced with a truck. We were younger then and the animal had looked like a monster. We couldn't imagine being kicked by one.

"A few minutes later, the ice seemed to make the dent swell outward. Séamus had a huge red and purple lump on his head. When the ice was nearly melted, he squared his shoulders and went back to work. I saw him later at dusk, the lump still big and messy. Your grandpa was also a good-looking man but that day his poor face looked more lined than ever. His eyes had lost some shine. He didn't get that back until years later."

"Did he get it back when the bad years were over?"

"Yes," Auntie Beers said simply. She looked down at me and scowled. "You remember what those bad years were called? I've told you a hundred times."

"The Depression," I answered, careful to pronounce it correctly. "Just like the depression in Grandda's head."

I have few memories of Auntie Beers truly laughing but this was one of them. A hoop of delight from her belly. A laugh from before she became disenchanted. There were even tears in her eyes.

"Yes, Clare, the depression was in his head in more ways than one. All right. I'm tired now. Get your treats and go."

We scrambled to our feet. Grace got to the little refrigerator first. She dutifully passed out the chocolate bars, one each, and two Cokes to share. We filed out of Auntie Beers' room, along the shabby hallway, down the staircase and into the sunshine on the street. As we had so many times before.

Most days, in good weather, we walked-ran to the city park and gathered on a bench under an enormous tree. A slight breeze often lifted our hair as we gobbled the bars and took turns sipping the cola. Chocolate and pop. A perfect combination of rare delight and forbidden fruit.

We never thought about the cost of the treats. The trouble Auntie Beers went to in order to buy us those gifts. How much that would put a hole in her meager budget. We never thought about why she would do this.

My cousins considered the treats rewards for listening to her ramble on about the "old days."

I never did tell her that I would have listened for hours without any chocolate or pop at all. The stories alone were sweet enough for me.

Famine 1800s

Auntie Beers 1962

In her later years, our great-aunt Bairbre talked more and more about the past. Even the past past. Events that happened before her birth. She retold the stories her grandfather had related. Passed on our heritage.

"My grandfather's face turned into a rotting apple when he talked about the Great Famine," Auntie Beers said.

As she aged, Bairbre retreated from her traditional seat on the bed, where she had swung her legs, to an old rocker in the corner of her room. No longer quite as tall and straight, her thin shoulders were somewhat rounded. Her hair was still lined with red among the silver strands. Years of smoking had created pinched lines around her mouth. Years of frowning had made a roadmap on her forehead. Yet she was still beautiful. Certainly no rotting apple.

Grace and I glanced at each other, confused by the analogy.

"How could he look like a rotting apple?" I asked.

It was one of the increasingly frequent times that Patrick and Mario chose a fishing trip over Auntie Beers' tales and their weekly Coke and chocolate rewards.

Auntie Beers grunted in response.

"No imagination, have ya? Picture this now. His face lit by the fire, reddened by the flames and drink. Sunken brown spots in his cheeks, put there by the terrible things he'd seen. By the awful life he was forced to live. Can't you see that's just like a rotting apple?"

Emboldened by the lack of testosterone in the room, Grace and I huddled closer. I even ventured to stroke Auntie Beers' hand. Tiny worms of blue veins pulsed upward through her soft as silk skin. She peered down at my fingers, then up at me. Her eyes reflected suspicion and disapproval, but she didn't move her hand.

"That's so sad, Auntie," Grace said.

"Tis. Also a crime." Bairbre's voice took on a hard edge. "I told ye about the penal laws. Well there were other laws too. Plenty of them designed to get rid of the Irish so the English could take it all."

"And the loving English feet they went all over us," I intoned in my head.

"Grandda, Great Grandda to you weans, was called Eamon Sullivan. He had a substantial farm for those days, about six acres, which was a grand size, for if ye had more than eight, you could be swallowed up by the landlords. In 1845, Grandda said, they had a splendid harvest of potatoes. Most of it got sent off to the English. Even when the blight first appeared, they said oh, don't you worry about that at all. It's all grand. And later they feigned surprise when half the population turned up starving to death.

"At first Great Grandda Eamon and the like were all right. They had a few cows and some grain. They had oats and milk to sustain them."

"That's all they ate, Auntie? Just milk and oats?"

"That's what I said. Look it up in the history books, lass."

Grace and I shook our heads at each other. I imagined mushy oatmeal and watery milk in a bowl at every meal. Felt sick and hollow inside at the idea.

"If only the Irish had paid attention to their own intuition," Auntie Beers went on. "Relied on more than potatoes. Demanded a place in the governing of their own land.

"They kept on saying, when the English leave, we'll be right as rain, but they did very little to rid the place of them. Work with them, they said. Take their money. After thousands of Irish had perished, we finally got our nerve back.

"Grandda told of the poor farmers thrown off their land, out their doors, by bailiffs and their henchmen. The landlords couldn't wait to see the back of their Irish arses. Can you imagine all those little ones, hands outstretched, no food for days, trudging behind their devastated parents?

"The charity food was stored or sold at outrageous prices. Barely a smidge went into the mouths of the starving. Bodies began to pile up at the side of the road."

Grace lowered her head and cried. Empathic and sensitive, she let the tears fall. Allowed the emotion to bubble over.

In contrast, although I was horrified, I retreated into my head. Tried to think of words to describe such a tragedy. Such cruelty. It was a technique I would use many times throughout my life.

> *Skeletal. Dirty. Asleep, barely breathing, in the cold mud of a ditch. The smell is a physical barrier to getting close. Big vacant eyes in the decimated face of a little boy.*
>
> *Lined up in the streets of a small town, starving people search for mercy. For sustenance. For signs of humanity that do not come. A tiny girl, her body seeping away like a sponge that has lost its moisture, finally curls up in fetal death. Flies hover for their own preservation. The stench in the air hangs like poison gas.*

I tried to consider phrases that might explain the cruelty of those who stole food and ignored the dying. What would it take for a human being to bypass the reek of genocide?

If my father was right, they were people whose livelihoods had been taken away. People who were frightened, whose fear turned into anger and hatred. But in Auntie Beers' story, the loss of land and livelihood was only true of the victims. What then caused the offenders to climb over that edge into an evil abyss of denial or brutality?

"Of course, no surprise said my Grandda, disease followed. Fever, typhus, dysentery, cholera. More efficient killing machines than starvation.

"Grandda hung onto his land like a bloodsucker to your toe," Auntie Beers told us. "He set up his own soup kitchen, too."

"Soup kitchen?" I asked. "Did they just serve soup?"

"Naw, ya daft thing ya. Well, aye, maybe mostly soup, but anything that could feed the masses."

"Oatmeal and milk?" Grace asked.

"And the like. The government set food distribution up in the counties to stop the riffraff from coming to the towns. Spreading their filth around, you see. Might get up the skirts of the gentry. Of course there weren't enough soup kitchens to feed everyone so Grandda and Granny would stand by the roadside and give out what they could. When they could.

"Some of the Proddies gave food, too, but only if the starving people agreed to give up their Catholic religion. Lots of rich folk made the poor ones work for food. As though they were being charitable by breaking the backs of the already broken. There had to be a payment for receiving enough to simply stay alive. Even the churches thought the famine was a way to change the cursed population. A gang of religious eejits went around preaching to just let God's will be done and go on and meet him in the afterlife. Get out while the getting is good. And the good was, good riddance to the Irish."

Auntie Beers leaned back and began to quote.

> *"Before us die our brothers of starvation;*
> *Around are cries of famine and despair;*
> *Where is hope for us, or comfort, or salvation,*
> *Where—oh where?*
> *If the angels ever hearken, downward bending,*
> *They are weeping, we are sure,*
> *At the litanies of human groans ascending,*
> *From the crush'd hearts of the poor."*

The poet Speranza, who was in reality Lady Jane Wilde, used her words well. She spoke of toiling through life with the thought that only death would set them free. Grace and I were unable to fathom that such a situation could be called living.

"Some of the landlords decided the best option was to send all the Catholic buggers over the sea. Pay for their passage to America in exchange for their land. The sleeveen bastards knew they could make a grand living without having to feed any tenants. So ya could go to a workhouse, which was worse than the worst prison, or ya could get on a coffin ship and probably die on the way over. Sure that was not much of a choice, my pets. By the time the governments were finished, they'd dumped a million Irish bodies in their own soil and dumped a million more in the ocean."

"What happened to your Grandda?" I asked. "Did he do the workhouse or the coffin ship?"

"He did neither one, did he? He stayed right there on his land. Kept his head down and used his brain and his brawn. Worked all hours planting different crops. Kept his few cows and chickens. Only god above knows how. His brother Patrick, now, he went on to America in Black 1847.

"Lived to tell the tale, too. Managed to get through the filth and disease and all other manner of devastation to be dropped off in New York City. He was lucky he didn't die on the shores of that uncaring country who also didn't want the Irish. Three years later, he was back, worse off than ever. Lucky for him his brother never gave up."

She stood up, almost as straight as ever.

"Now off you go. I'm knackered. Grab your chocolates and Coke and bugger off."

On those days, when our great-aunt planted terrible pictures in our heads, Grace and I would guiltily eat our chocolate bars. Gulped a shared can of coke like medicine that would cure the world's grief. We'd practically run home, as though we could escape the words and force them to be unsaid.

The day of the Lady Wilde poem, Grace was coming home with me while her parents went on some long-forgotten mission. When we reached the safety of my little room, my cousin flung herself onto the bed. Burst into uncontrollable sobs. I squatted on the floor.

"How can people do that to other people?" she cried. "How can they be so cruel? What if we're related to one of those awful English?"

"We're not," I assured her, speaking from the authority of a twelve-year-old who had done a modicum of historical reading by then. Of course, I did mix my disasters.

"We weren't English. We were Irish. Our family was IRA and all that. They became rebels to fight the English. Some of them even got killed or burnt out of their houses because they were on the side for independence."

Grace wailed louder. Where I considered the fact that our ancestors had been murdered and made homeless as badges of honor, she saw only cruelty.

My mother entered quietly and sat down on my bed next to Grace. Her hand was gentle on her distraught niece's back. Moved in calming circles.

I think my mom was always composed in the face of drama because so much of the gene ran through her family that she'd become inured. Or perhaps I am more like my mother than I know.

"Do you want to tell me about it, Grace?" she asked when my cousin turned over to face both of us.

Grace shook her head.

"Clare? Is there anything I can do to help?"

I never could withhold much from my mother.

"We're really sad about the stories Auntie Beers told us today," I answered. "We can't believe people are so mean."

"Evil," Grace said. "Cruel and evil. Human beings are horrible."

My mother gave a rueful laugh.

"You're right, honey, sometimes our species is very cruel."

"But why? How can they do things like that to other people?"

Grace began to cry again.

Just then my father opened the door.

"Kath…hey. Hi there. What's happening?"

My mother suggested we all decamp to the kitchen for chocolate milk and cookies. She knew my father would add an element to the conversation that needed to be managed with sweetness. Steven Doyle was far more definite in his opinions than most. For him there was rarely any grey. Especially when it came to Auntie Beers.

With motives I could not explain, I had an urge to fan the flames. Maybe I wanted the debate so I could tell my mother and father how much the words my great-aunt imparted meant to me.

"Auntie Beers told us some awful stories and they upset Grace. But the stories are true, so…it's life. Right, Dad?"

My father didn't answer me. He turned to his wife instead.

"I keep telling you, Kathleen," he said in a low, exasperated tone. "Your aunt doesn't know anything about kids. She's rude and inappropriate. Those girls are too young to be listening to that terrible history."

I sipped at my chocolate milk and nibbled on a cookie, watching the exchange of looks between my parents. In my experience, they almost never argued in front of us, though I was very aware of the difference in opinion over my visits to Auntie Beers. I wanted to say, in vocabulary that would have been far simpler at my age and in a naïve belief in the truth of what is written: if it's history, doesn't that mean it's true? Aren't the tales simply about life? Aren't human beings at the core a cruel species?

My mother took some time organizing her thoughts. Luckily my mouth was full, so I said nothing. Probably what my mother intended.

To this day I still remember in vivid detail the philosophy that Kathleen O'Sullivan Doyle shared with us. The vocabulary has morphed. Grown. Been seeded with experience. With research of my own. But in paraphrasing and repeating her words throughout my life, as Doris Kearns Goodwin has said, "The past is not simply the past, but a prism through which the subject filters [her] own changing self-image."

My mother folded her hands on the table. Sunlight danced through her auburn hair and backlit her fervent, intelligent eyes. I thought she was beautiful.

"Stories are always important," my mother said. "In some ways, the difficult and upsetting stories are the most important. They tell us where we've been. Teach us where we must go from here.

"The Irish descend from a group called the Celts. People who never wrote anything down. No pictures on cave walls or scrolls left behind. They told all their stories orally. Each generation handed down the history to the next one by telling tales. I think, as a result, the desire to tell stories is sort of built into us."

She smiled up at me. It was not a surprise that my mother knew of my penchant for writing. That day, her smile showed a pride I hadn't glimpsed before. A frisson of pleasure ran along my skin.

"And Steven, I think story is integral to human development. The fact that you are so upset, Grace, is inspiring to me."

She stroked my cousin's cheek tenderly.

"I think it means you are a human who is empathetic and kind. I believe Bairbre's stories will lead you on a path of healing, not only for yourself, but for others."

My mother couldn't have known how accurately she was predicting the future, or at least part of it.

"We learn from the sad, terrible revelations of what occurred in the past, and if those events make us determined to be better people, they are worth more than anything factual that you might find in a book, or nowadays, see on the television. You'll discover that change is smaller and more incremental than we want it to be, but the world is getting better. In tiny, slow steps, but evolving. I think if we don't listen to the stories because we're afraid they'll upset us…"

At this point, she patted her husband's hand in emphasis.

"…Then we'll fall backward. We'll slide away from the essence of what it means to be human. All the messy, awful, horrible things we can do to each other will be repeated instead of rejected. I'm glad we have Bairbe to lead us. I'm sorry that she allowed her past to make her often bitter and uncompromising when it comes to other people she labels the culprits or the enemy. But maybe that's her role in our lives. To model not what we should aspire to, but what we should avoid.

"We—at least, in this family—don't look at other human beings as lesser than we are. Deserving of contempt or having terrible things befall them. We don't believe what some of the English thought back then—that Irish Catholics starved to death because they were evil. We don't enslave people because we think they're not as smart as we are. There are so many lessons that we have learned, girls, and all those lessons came from the stories told by maltreated, courageous people. You do your namesake proud, Grace. She is a woman who has stood her ground, literally. She has helped to make Ireland a much better place. Along with her children. And I want you to remember that not all English or Protestant Irish were awful, the way Bairbre would have us believe. There were plenty of good people."

Later, when I read about my Irish ancestors and what occurred during the Great Famine, I found the infamous quote by Charles Trevelyan, who was in charge of relief for the famine. "The real evil with which we have to contend is not the physical evil of the Famine but the moral evil of the selfish, perverse and turbulent character of the [Irish] people."

My mother's eloquent denunciation of racism and hatred has echoed in my ears as I traced the shameful past. As I navigated my own turbulent present. My own herstory.

Unfortunately, Auntie Beers would never appreciate the extent to which she influenced her nieces and nephews and grands. Her stories of the past taught us acceptance.

Respect. To be activists, not only in words but also in action. Bairbre's own intolerance and prejudices had a reverse effect on most of her descendants. None of us turned out perfect, but we did have a fierce family love and loyalty to one another. We tried never to be judgmental, either.

Auntie Beers suffered from a kind of famine too, I realize now. In her teens, she was surrounded by stories of misery. From people she never knew. From family decimated by hatred. She was surrounded by the terrible results of greed. War.

Rather than leave the grief and anger behind, she brought them with her. Inside. Bairbre was not starved to death, but she lacked joy. Pleasure. Food was simply utilitarian. Love and respect were scarce. The little fun she did manage was found in the numbing effects of alcohol.

My great-aunt allowed the undernourishment of her childhood to seep into her bones. To weaken her ability for happiness and satisfaction. She became too ill to eat from the glorious table of love, friendship and family.

Fortunately for her descendants, that illness was not contagious. Nor did we think of Auntie Beers as a spiteful old woman. We loved her wit. The laughter that would sometimes bubble up from deep inside. The way she could dance.

Her ability to tell a great story.

Pulling the Wool

Auntie Beers 1934
By Clare O'Sullivan Doyle

When Auntie Beers moved into town, before any of us were born or even considered, she got a job at the Urbston Woolen Mill.

"I went to work in the woolen mill for eight dollars a week," she told us. "Ten hours a day, six days a week."

We looked at each other, aghast. Even at our pre-teen ages, we knew that eight dollars did not go far in the early 1960s. We also knew that working that number of hours was far more than our own fathers did (none of our mothers worked once we were born). Our parents lamented the forty-hour, five days a week regimen that most men had to follow.

Mario quickly did the math.

"That's thirteen cents an hour," he said. Referring to his older brother, he continued with a shake of his head. "Robbie makes a dollar and a quarter an hour."

Auntie Beers ignored us. She shifted her long legs to stretch them out in front of her. Took a long drag on her cigarette.

"Money went a lot farther in those days, mind," she said. "Right downtown Urbston, I saw a sign that said 'Now Hiring Full Time,' so I marched on into the factory. They took one look at me and hired me on the spot. I started the next day. Even though I had five miles to walk, I was thrilled to have a job."

Five miles to walk. Any kind of weather. Fiona and I had a mile to walk. Before Auntie Beers' story, I had been proud of that fact.

"Out of my first pay cheque, I bought Liam a cap gun. Eddie had a fit when he heard that I had paid 39 cents for it. He claimed that you could buy a real gun for 60 cents."

Two things pulled me out of the tale. First, the rare mention of Uncle Liam. He was the mysterious relative who had spent a lot of time in jail. A very bad man, we were told. Don't ever speak to him if he approaches you. A warning from my father.

"The gun came with a package of caps. Round stamps each with a circular arrangement of real gun powder. Tiny, but sure it made a sharp sound when you pulled the trigger. Liam used up all the caps in one day and had to wait for my next payday to get more. I very soon became tired of this practice. In short order that gun stood on a shelf like a decoration."

Second, the gun. We had very little experience with guns. None of our toys made a sound unless we made one with our mouths.

"What did you do in the woolen mill?" I asked.

The answer my great aunt gave was factual and distant. Though there had been a lot of years in between, I think she purposely would not go into detail.

The terrible explosions from her sister's trauma that caused Bairbre to quit the only real job she ever had, were not to be shared. Instead, she spoke of how strong she was to walk that far. How many hours she worked. What she bought with her wages.

"I kept fifty cents for myself, twenty cents to save, and put the rest toward the mortgage," she said.

Though it wasn't really a mortgage. When Séamus and Maggie died, Bairbre was homeless.

Years later, when I began to write about my great aunt, I had the luxury of the internet. I could research the past in order to fill in those gaps.

The building was enormous. Once inside the factory, a cacophony from rows upon rows of wool streaming from tightly wound bundles filled my ears. Spindles. Wheels turning slowly with high-pitched squeals. Workers, mostly women, pulling threads together. Some on their haunches twisting the bottom of the blanket of wool.

I quickly figured out why the women wore handkerchiefs or tight turbans on their heads. Scarves around their faces. Wool dust floated through the air. Salted uncovered hair with ash. Landed on eyelashes and stuck inside nostrils. No one thought about how the dust must look inside the hairs of their lungs.

The huge jaws of the wool processing machinery moved in and out, just at shoulder height. Any long strands of hair could be caught and yanked from the worker's skull.

Despite the overwhelming noise, I was happy to have a paying job. I imagined what I could do with all that money. Tried to ignore the bits of fluff as it flew through the air, scratching at my face. Tomorrow, I would be prepared with scarf and handkerchief.

Just as the thought crossed my mind, a small dark woman approached me with a long sheath of cloth and a wool scarf. She pointed until I understood that I was to lean down so she could reach my head and face. When I obediently crouched, I noticed that she had only one hand. The other arm was severed at the elbow. Tied up like a bow at the end.

She murmured in another language but quickly had me covered. When I straightened up, she pointed again, this time at her own chest.

"Bhairavi," she said, in an accent so thick I couldn't understand anything but B.

I pointed to my chest. Likely in an Irish accent that was unintelligible to her ears, I said, "Bairbre."

After a moment's silence, we laughed.

"Bee," I suggested. "Bee One." One finger to her. "Bee Two." Two fingers to me.

We laughed again and nodded in complete understanding.

"You bring back," she said, indicating the scarf and head covering.

To help other new workers, I was sure. I squeezed her hand in friendship and acknowledgement. She squeezed back.

The next day, Maggie gave me a headscarf that she'd kept from somewhere or someone. It was covered in roses, though would soon be smeared with ash. The scarf she found for me was, ironically, made from soft, fine-woven Irish wool. I was able to return the lent cloth and scarf, neatly washed and folded, to Bee One.

I soon learned why I'd been hired on the spot. Other than the high demand for soldiers' wool uniforms as the war dragged on, I was tall and lanky. Though thin all my life, I was strong from shifting bodies on their sick beds or lifting little ones in the air. The machine they put me on was at my shoulder in height. Later, I discovered the process was called carding. It was one of the first procedures to be mechanized in the industry.

The carding machine was a monster with giant teeth that moved up and down, untangling the sheets of scoured wool. The strands were pulled apart by the machine, sometimes blending different varieties together. From there, the threads wound around giant spindles that workers would pick up when the bars were full. Another worker would replace the spindle immediately with an empty one.

My job was to flatten the roll of wool at the top of the machine and feed it into the teeth. I had to do this very quickly. Elbow just above the rolls of needles. Other hand holding up the arm that would clamp down on the sheets once the feed began. Everything at frenetic speed.

Urbston had lower, cheaper machines because their factory was fairly small. Still, this job was normally done by men, who were generally taller than women. But our little city had sent most of our able-bodied men off to war. Taller women like myself took their places.

Except for Lenny, who was no longer able-bodied. He trained me on the carding machine. His absent limb was tied up under his shirt. Both he and Bee One had lost their arms in one machine or other. Luckily the Urbston employer kept many of these disabled workers as trainers.

Gradually, I heard tales of those in the bigger cities who had been thrown out onto the street if they could no longer work. The presumption being that the accident was their own fault. We thought our employer was kind.

I was terrified by the job but resolved to keep it. I suppose it was determination that carried me through the weeks that followed. I got very good very quickly, according to Lenny, and soon he left me on my own to supervise or train other workers.

Each day the factory whistle blew four times. Once in the morning, at seven, to start the shift. The one I stayed on throughout my employment. Next at noon for lunch. Twenty minutes later to get back to work. Five o'clock for the shift change. The whistle had to be very loud to overcome the noise of the machinery. I wondered how the neighbors stood it.

Bee One and I ate lunch together every day. All the other workers appeared to shun her. And me for that matter.

They were either shrunken into themselves or banded together in small, quiet groups of two or three.

Sometimes Bee One brought me bowls of rice and meat, which I greedily consumed. A few times, I would use some of my pennies to buy flour and sugar and make her a rhubarb cake. I squeezed out some of the rhubarb stalks for moisture. It wasn't as good as it could have been with eggs and butter, but she was very appreciative of my effort.

There were a few picnic style tables outside and some grass and trees. Bee One and I reserved a small spot of grass under a willow. I discovered why the area was left for us when the ants began to invade my hair. I looked up and saw the trail going back and forth from the tree to the ground and back up. When I brought an old blanket Maggie had shipped from Ireland and stashed away, that helped.

From our spot we gazed onto the factory wall. Red bricked. Wide windows that were often open but provided little relief in the summers. This factory was fairly well built, with high ceilings and a sturdy roof.

In my later years I would read about woolen mills that were structurally unsound. Roof collapses that killed employees. Bricks fell onto workers and permanently injured them. The machines were not serviced properly, which resulted in lost limbs. I felt lucky that the Urbston employer was kinder and more careful of the safety of his workers. Though there were, witness Bhairavi and Lenny, still accidents.

The only problem I really had with my job was the raw wool. Every day I would come home from the mill with little fluffs on my clothing. As did every employee except for the office staff.

I would inspect my clothing rigorously before entering McManis. I knew what would happen if even one tiny bit floated into the air or landed on the floor or a piece of furniture.

If she saw or felt a fluff of raw wool, my sister's entire body would become a quivering, shaking mass of fear. Her mouth would open in screams that wrenched every heart within hearing. She would back into a corner, collapse onto the floor with bent knees, hands over her head.

Whenever any of the children and later, the grandchildren, witnessed Maggie's terrible breakdown, they would ask Séamus why this was happening. Why did Mom or Granny have such an irrational fear of wool in its raw form? Woolen sweaters or scarves didn't bother her. A tiny bit of raw wool, however, sent her into a dark past from which she had difficulty emerging.

Séamus, beyond an occasional discussion of politics or religion, shared very little. So it wasn't unusual for the children and grandchildren to have their personal questions unanswered.

Fortunately, no one asked me. I pretended to be just as aghast and puzzled if a tiny fluff escaped inspection and tortured my sister. But I knew. I also knew that Séamus kept silent because he knew how hurt I would be. For everyone to know that I hadn't protected Maggie.

Eventually, when too many bits of raw wool came home with me, sending Maggie into a nightmare world of abject fear, I quit the factory job. I got another one clipping roses at the Urbston Flower Estates. Inside the row upon row of greenish glass, air humid and warm any time of the year. Thorns that pierced my cheap gloves. Pay that didn't leave me enough for presents. But worth the absence of fear in my sister's eyes.

The Well

Near Bantry, Ireland, 1902
By Clare O'Sullivan Doyle

Maggie's little legs carry her across the stubby grass as though she has trained for a marathon. She is small and slight, but she is strong.

What she loves best is the physical burst that freedom gives her. Being out in the air, the wind. Beyond the confines of coughing. Shouts and murmurs. The musty smell. The dark of the tiny cottage.

Since the last escape, Bairbre is supposed to watch her. They sleep together on a stuffed mattress on the floor, but her sister is a sound sleeper. Exhausted from all she does every day. Maggie learns how to wiggle out from under Bairbre's protective arm that she invariably tosses over Maggie's middle.

Sometimes she simply sits in the doorway, staring out at the dawn. But often when the sun's rays tip across the horizon, Maggie can't resist as the golden fingers beckon to her to run.

Her bare feet are used to the scrubby grass and rocks that cover the ground. She could fly over the prickly ones. Tiptoe around the big flat stones. The ocean roars as background noise. A soothing sound of rhythm and repetition.

This time she decides to climb the stone fence to the abandoned farm next door. It's further from the sea, but there is a withered crop of trees still standing along one edge of the property. It looks like fun to explore.

There is a spot in the wall where the mud has crumbled and freed the rocks from the fence. It's easy for a two-year-old to climb. Maggie goes over it in a flash.

She feels an even greater rush of freedom. She isn't at home anymore. She is somewhere strange. Somewhere different.

Not far along, Maggie discovers a huge pile of stones. She is unaware that these are the remnants of the old farmhouse. Abandoned by the former tenants because they could no longer afford the rent. Yet lying unwanted by a foreign landlord.

Her feet are unable to withstand the jagged rocks and rotting thatch, so Maggie walks away. Heads toward the clump of trees. One of the cedar limbs has grown out sideways from the original trunk. Seeking a space where it could touch the sky. Drink from the sun. In its climb, it has formed what looks like a swing to Maggie.

She remembers the one that Da made for her from rope and a flat piece of wood. Recently it fell from the broken branch, useless. This one is part of the tree. A permanent perch. Unfortunately she cannot find a way to scrabble up the trunk. The swing is too high for her to reach on her own. Maybe if she begs Bairbre she'll lift her up onto it. Sit beside her and swing their legs.

Maggie notices that the sun has climbed above the grass and rocks. Ma and her sisters will be up any moment. They'll see that she is gone. She doesn't pay attention to the ground as she races back toward the cottage. She doesn't see the gaping hole quite near the pile of abandoned farmhouse. She flies into the air for a moment. For a long time she doesn't feel anything when she thuds to the bottom of the dried up well.

When she stirs, her body sends out lightning strikes of pain along her back and neck. Her head pounds. At first, she doesn't know why she can't breathe. Maggie turns over without consciously realizing that she has been face down in a bed of scratchy material. She doesn't recognize the fluff, but she feels its choking presence in her mouth and lungs.

Above her, the sun lazily lights up the surface. Through the large round opening above, she can see the grey sky begin to tinge with daytime blue. Without a warning sound, a face fills the hole. Dark eyes surrounded by black fur. Enormous horns twist from the top of its head to its ears. Point downward at her. A sound rumbles from deep in its throat. It's covered in long scraggly fur that jiggles loosely as it moves its head back and forth above her.

Maggie screams. The monster, startled, shakes its head. As it does so, bits of fluff cascade down the hole. The air fills with scaly fibers that cover Maggie's nose and cram into her horrified, open mouth. She can't breathe. She takes in terrified clogs of oxygen as she sinks into a semi-conscious state. Her little body writhes with fear. The head withdraws, but Maggie is beyond seeing.

Bairbre and Ma finally find her, after searching through their property and eventually climbing the wall to the abandoned farm. At the bottom of the well, Maggie is twisted in a trembling ball. Barely breathing.

Ma discovers an old ladder on the ground, several rungs missing, but still sturdy. The way a farmer would construct it, using bits of wood and rope, ensuring it will hold.

Bairbre climbs down into the abandoned well and grasps her sister by the waist with one arm. Bairbre is only eight, but she is strong. Strong enough to carry the thin frame of the two-year-old, ragged as a doll, up the rickety ladder. It takes a while, but they slowly inch upward. A long breath-holding time later, Ma cradles Maggie her arms. She croons to her. Removes the bits of fluff from her face, neck, mouth and eyes.

Bairbre sees the small flock of Blackface sheep huddled in the trees. Away from the frightening humans. The ram, its horns wrapped around its head like a root seeking the sunlight, stares at her in horror. The animals are undernourished and stressed. Their fur drips off them like skin cells. Abandoned by the shepherd, betrayed by a summer drought, the animals stare at the three humans in desperation.

Ma struggles to her feet with Maggie's limp frame glued to her shoulder. She reaches out and slaps Bairbre hard across the top of her head.

"I told you to watch her," she snarls.

Hunger. Disease. Drought. Unable to care for or protect her family, Ma has become angry and violent. She lashes out again and again. Bairbre lets her. Takes the abuse in silence.

Years later, Bairbre leaves her other sister, Grace, and her country, to accompany Maggie and her children to Canada. Bairbre has lost her lover, so she becomes caretaker of her sister's kids instead. She will eventually be closer to her grandnieces and grandnephews than any other of the offspring.

She spins tales. Teaches them to dance and sing and chant in traditional ways. She is a moral compass of sorts, despite her many addictions.

Historian of herstory. An influence that helps produce a writer, a psychologist, a doctor, a teacher.

A woman of contradictions and intelligence. Someone whose violent altercation in the Queen's Hotel teaches a generation that hatred must not take up space in their lives.

Troubled Times

From the Irish News 1935

We regret to announce the death, at a ripe old age, of Mr. Joseph Collins. His passing recalls the Black and Tan reign of terror in this region. He was a respected resident of Dublin and the father of Francis Collins, who currently resides in Australia, and James Collins of Canada, also known as Father Benedict. Joseph Collins had a daughter Molly, Mrs. Thomas O'Sullivan of Bantry.

The deceased gentleman was a lifelong supporter of Irish nationalism. He endured a great deal of violence at the hands of the Black and Tans, including the death of his brother Timothy in the rebellions of 1919 and the disappearance of Paddy O'Brien, a beloved cousin currently of unknown status. He suffered the burning of two houses by the Black and Tans, by way of reprisal.

"I fought for the injustice," Mr. Collins was heard to say. "To rid us of the slums and tenements that plagued our streets and kept our native Irish in poverty and misery. We couldn't fashion a revolution in words, so we did it in action."

The late Joseph Collins was prominently identified with Sinn Fein in West Cork and as an elder was on the run from the Crown forces. His relative and boarder, Paddy O'Brien, was in the brunt of the National fight in those days too. Joseph Collins had some trying experiences at that time—he and his daughter once were forced to escape from their burning home amid a hail of bullets. Mr. Collins was poorly in his later years. No doubt the mistreatment he endured in his life undermined an otherwise robust constitution.

The funeral was large and representative, a fitting tribute to the esteem in which the old Gael was held. A statement by his daughter Molly was especially moving.

"I am quoting here," she said, "but it's true that when politics fail, culture fills in. The Irish culture demanded self-determination and my father helped see to it that the revolution of freedom took place. Not only in words but in action and sacrifice."

Auntie Beers 1920s-1960s

Until I grew up, it didn't occur to me that Auntie Beers' deep sorrow, her bleak outlook, must have begun in childhood. As the eldest girl, she became head of a sickly family. While Grace took care of the land, Bairbre became the caregiver. Maggie dove into her family with Séamus and, eventually, a new country that held the promise of happiness.

Bairbre was never allowed to be herself. To become a more contented version. She spent her life sewing, cleaning, cooking, and looking after siblings. Her brothers were physically weak and died, one after the other. She wouldn't have been very old when their parents also became ill. Became dependent on Bairbre too.

When her younger sister emigrated from Ireland to Canada, I imagine that Auntie Beers thought this was her chance at a new, unchained life. Off she went with Maggie and her children, expecting land. A house. A chance.

Instead, she got the Depression. Once again, she cared for children who were not hers. Lived the "if only" and "when/then" for years. Until circumstances, boredom and bitterness removed the possibility of when or then. Later in life she consoled herself with alcohol, witty repartée, and flirting with men.

Despite being flawed and cynical, Auntie Beers served as our moral compass. She told us stories to warn us. To prepare us for life. Albeit one that was more often unforgiving and cruel.

Unfortunately, Auntie Beers would never know the extent to which she influenced her nieces and nephews and grands. Her stories of the past taught us acceptance. Respect. To be activists. Not to simply talk about the wrongs, but to do something that makes a difference.

Bairbre's own intolerance and prejudices had a reverse effect on most of her descendants. None of us turned out perfect, but we do have a fierce family love and loyalty to one another.

The altercation in the Queen's Hotel taught us that violence was not distant, or pretty, or unharmful like the images we watched on TV.

Somehow, between the pessimistic lines and the accidental humor, the cousins learned to be strong, feisty, outspoken, determined—and optimistic.

My sisters, cousins and I heard tales from my mother, Kathleen, too. Auntie Kate to everyone but me and Fiona. Kathleen was forced to leave school very young, though she loved learning. She pursued education after she'd given birth to her last child and took up a highly successful career. Kathleen gave her first born—me—her surname as a middle name in a society where that was rare.

My mother and aunts struggled against a system that favored males and was rampant with prejudice, poverty and sexual harassment.

As they aged, they became outspoken feminists. They were strong, confident women who'd fought through the worst of times and won many battles.

They couldn't erase the past, but they sure could try to change the present and therefore the future.

The Farm

Kathleen 1935
Near Urbston, Ontario, Canada
by Clare O'Sullivan Doyle

Once I am up there, the fear is gone. Now I stand sovereign over it all. Feel the wind as it whips my hair around my face. The scent of freshly cut hay fills my nostrils. The field lies at my feet, swaying and bowing in the wind. I am filled with fear and power at the same moment. Even the disinterested cows seem to lift their sad eyes to gaze at me. I salute my subjects.

Tenuous, lurching slightly on the doorframe, I grasp the stiff twine of the rope and take a deep breath. From here I can see the laneway and the Bradshaw's beautiful white house, the horses in the distance, the river beyond. Even our little house at the edge of the west field looks fine from this height.

I turn back to the hayloft, not daring to look at the floor. Closing my eyes, I breathe out and let go. In that moment of surrender, my heart seems to explode in me. The fear is like a cascade. My whole body responds. It seems an interminable minute before I thud to the hay pile below. My knees tremble as I dust myself off. Again the feeling of fear and power all at once makes my face flush. It is the first time I have ever hugged the rope in all the months that we have lived here.

"Kathleen! Kathleen! Where are you?"

At the sound of the magnified voice, I remember my mother and my promise to hurry straight home. I sprint across the dusty yard. Leap over the fence. Head for the house. My legs are long and lean, used to running.

By the time I stand in front of my mother, my long red hair is tangled. I feel beads of sweat on my nose.

I lower my head and scuff my foot in the dirt. The porch of the little shack is sagging a bit, but my mother still towers over me.

The affectation of guilt does not faze my mother.

"And where have you been my girl?"

Mother is angry. Her body is stiff. She glares.

The truth is impossible. Hugging the rope is absolutely forbidden.

"Well, Mama, you see...I found a little doggie on the way home from school, and it was lost, and I couldn't leave it there. I mean, it was so little and cute. So I picked it up and went to every door and I asked and I finally found who owned it and well, they were so happy that they asked me in for tea, and..."

The words tumble out, pushing each other in their rush to escape. Almost believable.

"Never mind the stories, girl, go in and wash up. I have a dozen chores for you. Henhouse now."

But my mother's tone is gentle. Her eyes are not angry as I scoot between her large frame and the door.

While I gather the eggs from under the chickens' soft bellies, I talk to them.

"Well, Hilda you are a fine one. This morning, I found nothing under your lazy little bottom. Smarten up, will you? Gladiola, girl, what a surprise! You're just so good! A nice big egg for me today. And Francine..."

The hens mutter and blink at me, lulled by my soft voice, my hands passing warm and smooth in and out of the nests. In the yard, they follow me, clucking and talking, telling me the barnyard news.

Whenever I am given the job of collecting the eggs at evening, I have to pretend to mind. My mother must not see the tiny fire of joy that leaps into my eyes, for I am convinced she will guess the reason.

When I bring the eggs to Mrs. Bradshaw's door, I know that the farmer's wife will be there: white starched apron, smooth dress, unwrinkled nylons, fingernails shiny. Her red lips will curl into a smile for me.

The screen door will open and always, always, the scent of floor wax and baking. I step gingerly on the mirroring tiles, hand over the eggs, and wait for the invitation to take a cookie or a piece of pie or a tart or some other delicious treat. I especially love the chocolate chip cookies, which are warm and moist and stay on my tongue for hours.

I always stuff the treasure into my mouth as I race back to our house, making sure no sign of it is left on my clothing or face.

In contrast to the sprawling Bradshaw farmhouse, we have no furnace. No indoor toilet, no running water and no electricity. We use coal oil lamps, an outdoor well, a two-seater outhouse (where you can read the Eaton's catalogue) and rely on the kitchen stove as the only source of heat. The house is about 700 square feet in size with two bedrooms, a kitchen and a living room slightly larger than a closet. Aunt Bairbre sleeps on a mattress in the living room. In the morning, she hides all her bedding behind the old sofa.

Auntie Beers is the only adult who will explain things to me.

"Our country's in what they're calling a depression," she says, when I ask why a man has come to our house to do an inspection. "Sure look, it's all over the world. The whole financial system has fallen apart. The Canadian government has come up with a method of providing assistance, you see, but you have to prove you're poor enough to take part in the scheme."

Da is nowhere to be seen. The two sisters, my mother and my aunt, stand during the inspection, as though their height will give them some control.

When the inspector arrives, his scrutiny makes me feel strange. Invaded. The man, who is tall and bulky and looks as though he gets his three meals a day, holds a clipboard and a pen to make notes. He looks in every corner of our small abode. He's brusque and aggressive, as though he owns our place. Owns us, in fact.

My mother makes us stand in a line. Her face is a mask. Tight and closed.

The man checks the soles of our shoes one by one.

"Only a couple of holes," he says. "Shoes can wait until next time."

He writes out and signs a rectangular piece of paper that he hands to my mother. He turns his back and leaves at a pace that suggests he's afraid fleas will stick to his clothes.

Later, I understand that the piece of paper is called a money voucher, which my mother can use to shop for food.

My mother is proud and strong. She is used to being able to speak out. Although raised in poverty, as an adult she had command over her own home.

I understand perfectly why my mother hates Mrs. Bradshaw. Not only does the other woman live in a beautiful home while assuming the hired hand and his family can make do with a house that has never been updated, but she had the nerve to offer charity.

Combined with the visit by the inspector, the gesture fills my mother with rage.

I can still see Mrs. Bradshaw's starched straight figure standing inside our little shack, thin lip-sticked mouth curled up in distaste. Her eyes alight with something I cannot fathom.

When she offers the basket of food and clothing, I suddenly notice my mother's face. Flushed with anger and embarrassment, my mother straightens her tall broad back and blocks Mrs. Bradshaw from our view.

"We do not need charity, Mrs. Bradshaw, though I thank you very much, I'm sure."

My mother's voice is shaky. Words clipped. Her breath heavy.

The door opens to sunshine then closes again, leaving the shack thick with tension. My mother turns and faces my brothers and me.

"Never...never..."

Her voice is slow, measured, holding back an explosion.

"...take anything from that woman."

We nod. Speechless, frightened, we watch as our mother turns her back and prepares our meal in silence.

But I have never been able to resist those treasures. Soft, chocolate cookies, crumbly cakes, sweet juicy pies. Each visit, when I return home from that clean, waxed kitchen, my heart beats heavily with fear and with joy.

I can see that same look of pity in Mrs. Bradshaw's eyes after I reach out for the delicacies. My greed overcomes my pride every time. I don't care that she feels sorry for me. Someday I will have a kitchen better than this one and ladies like Mrs. Bradshaw will have to beg to come and call.

Today I gobble the chocolate cookie and fly back home. My mother is tense and grouchy. I am afraid she will smell the wax and the baking sticking to my clothes.

I make it to the house just in time for dinner.

There is something different about the table. John has set it as usual. My mother is finishing off boiling the potatoes. Peggy fills our glasses with watery milk. Michael, Daniel and Eddie have planted themselves on their chairs long before everything is ready. As usual, Aunt Bairbre sits in the corner, rocking her old chair, a glass of something dark in her hand. Still, there is a silence that none of us seems able to break.

I don't let the screen door slam as usual, but come in, wash my hands in the basin. I place the two eggs that we're allotted into the pantry.

I sit beside Brigid, who wiggles with anticipation. She smiles at me, quiet only by strength of will.

My mother spoons some potatoes, mashed up with water, and a small piece of chicken for each of us, onto our plates. Neither she nor Auntie Beers take any good, though I know they will gobble up any leftovers. If there are any.

"John, you go ahead with the prayer. Da won't be coming down tonight."

Her tone is brisk, hard. Her eyes do not see us. John, trembling with the responsibility, stumbles through the prayer. Peggy sits down finally. We begin to eat slowly and quietly. Bairbre rocks without saying a word. My brothers look bewildered and frightened by the silence. Brigid focuses on her food.

I cannot bear it any longer, this pinched silent meal.

"What's wrong, Mama?"

She stares into the eyes of her willful daughter as I stare back. I see pain. The complete and utter frustration that lives behind her proud face. She blinks and turns to all of us.

"Mr. Bradshaw is letting your father go," my mother says finally, keeping her eyes carefully on the table. "Da will have to find another job and we will have to find another place to live. Times are hard and farmers can't afford as many helpers nowadays. Of course we had to be the first to..."

Perhaps she feels our shock, for she suddenly stops, lifts her eyes and shakes her head.

"There will be no questions. You are to say nothing to your Da for a few days. He feels very sad. You are not to worry. He will find something else. Finish your dinner quietly."

After dinner, the boys and Auntie play jacks in the living room. Mother is in the jacks with Brigid. The little girl still hasn't learned to sit and do her business independently.

I slip out the back door. The sun begins to set just as I climb the slight hill in the east meadow. Its yellow and orange fingers grasp for a stronghold somewhere in the field. Slowly give up the struggle to remain on this side of the world.

I curl up under the maple tree, hugging my knees. I carefully stare across at the farmhouse. All the little buildings huddled around the barn. The small shack that is our home. The rows and rows of wheat and corn.

I was too young to remember the trip over to Canada from Ireland, but I have often heard my father speak wistfully of the "old country" and of the dreams he had about Canada. None of them have come true, he said.

But I have never thought much about this. Not until now. I never believed that we would be anywhere but here. This is my farm, more than it is the Bradshaws'. I know they don't love it the way I do. For the first time, I feel some of the resentment that my mother has always felt toward Mrs. Bradshaw. Why hadn't she told me? Why had she simply offered me the cookie, as always, without telling me that it would be the last? The shame that I feel for "taking charity" makes my face hot.

But I won't cry. Maybe the next farmer and his family will be nicer. Maybe they'll have a girl my age. And Mother might even like them. I could play with the farmer's little girl every day and share things and have make-believe parties with our dolls. Even though we are poor and the girl...her name will be Rebecca...is rich, it will make no difference in how we feel about each other. We'll vow to be friends to the death.

And then one day Da will get a letter from Ireland, telling us that a rich relative has died and left us all their money...then Rebecca and I will become rich society girls and throw parties. And we will never invite the Bradshaws. They'll feel ashamed that they were so mean to my father.

I bury my head on my knees, feel the little hairs rub softly against my forehead. I cannot picture another farm. The white Bradshaw house, the hens, the cows, the fields, keep coming to my mind. It seems that there can be no other farm for me, just this one. With all its ups and downs, all its good points and bad, this collection of buildings are always what I will see when I picture a farm. I wait until the last orange fingers of the sun slip beyond the fields and then I go back to our little house.

Miss Burton

Kathleen 1935
by Clare O'Sullivan Doyle

I love school. Most of all, I love Miss Burton. Her skirts folded neatly around her legs, her hair always tied strictly away from her long face, Miss Burton can make a story come alive. Her voice is low and soft when she reads but the pictures that the words form are loud and colorful.

I always rest my head on my hand and gaze at our teacher. Watch her lips trace over the words. Pretend that I am the girl or boy or animal in the story. I especially love Alice in Wonderland, with all the funny poems and fantasies.

Miss Burton often asks us to write a little story or poem of our own after she has read to us. This is the part that I like best. Carefully I try to paint the pictures with sentences. Fit the lines and words together like a puzzle. Miss Burton sometimes reads my poems to the class. She tells me they are "very good for a little girl."

In fact, Miss Burton tells me that I am a wonderful student. "Always interested and enthusiastic," my report card said. I get As in everything except arithmetic. Numbers are so different from words.

Today John will tell Miss Burton that we are moving. I watch my tall skinny brother move uncertainly to the front of the room, quickly rush through his little speech, and race back to his seat again. John's face and eyes twitch with nervousness. His freckles stand out under his deep red blush. I know that John is only relaxed when he is making something from wood or stone.

Miss Burton's face shows genuine sadness as the teacher says that she will miss us. She looks directly into my eyes.

"Make sure you stay in school, Kathleen," she says. "You are very smart. It would be a shame to waste that mind of yours."

I am surprised and pleased and feel myself blush. My brothers and sisters politely chorus good-bye. Miss Burton takes back our books and our pencils. We open the schoolhouse doors and it is over.

I glance back at the little building as we head for the laneway. Feel an ache of longing and a fear that seems to have lodged itself permanently in my chest. Never again will I hear that low, sweet voice painting those word pictures. Never again will I sit in that seat near the front. Lean on my elbow and stare at two birds making a nest outside that window.

My eyes fill with tears. I feel them clog my throat. Angrily I jerk at Brigid's arm to pull her down the lane, suddenly feeling that it is all my siblings' faults.

We trudge back slowly, the hot sun on our heads and backs. The air is thick and heavy. Bees hum around our ears. Flies tickle the sweat on our arms. John and Peggy race ahead and soon disappear in the distance.

Michael drags a stick through the dust while Eddie kicks at stones. Daniel marches beside us, stiff and silent.

I still fight the tears in my head. Blink and blink until I am dizzy. Afraid I will explode. Finally, Michael speaks.

"We'd better hurry. Mother told us the wagon is coming to pick up all our stuff after we get home. And they need strong people to help load."

"That counts you out," I snarl, speaking hurtfully from my pain.

Michael turns and sticks his tongue out. Suddenly we are running. We scream and breathe heavily. Release the pressure, the fear and loneliness, in noise. Twice Brigid falls with a thud in the road, until finally Eddie piggybacks her, squealing with delight, toward home.

When we reach our little yard, our squeals and screams cease. Shocked, we stare in silence. Every possession that the little shack had once housed lies stacked unsteadily in the yard. A testimony of daily life, our treasures and our necessities, lie uncovered and grotesque. A parade of pride and of shame.

Boxes filled with faded and stained shirts and pants. Chipped china with worn red flowers. A silky black porcelain poodle, her family trailing on a chain behind, our aunt's only ornament. Greyish sheets and rough and grey blankets. Lumpy mattresses. A couch with the stuffing peeping from behind. All stand stark and unfamiliar in the indifferent sunlight.

Our mother appears in the doorway, red-faced, annoyed.

"Everything gets piled out here," she says without preamble. "Now."

John and Peggy already carry boxes from the house. The other boys get to work without a sound. Michael tries his best to drag furniture onto the lawn. Aunt Bairbre barks directions at them.

Ma tells me to look after Brigid. I feed her some bread and a bit of cheese. Her nature is a seesaw. One minute happy and cheerful. Unaware. She's satisfied with a meager lunch. The next minute she might erupt in a tantrum that doesn't appear to have a source.

I curl my fingers in her soft hair. My eyes fill with tears again. I feel ashamed.

A rattling empty hay wagon rumbles into sight. Backing into the yard, it settles like a giant camel kneeling for its burden. My father, his powerful shoulders bent with the strain, begins to load our possessions into the back.

"Eddie! Help your Da out here."

The horse stamps and snorts impatiently. Kicks up dust in tiny swirls. Eddie soothes the animal in minutes. I listen to the clutter and clang but cannot bear to watch. My father, my aunt and siblings are unable to load everything into the wagon.

"Maggie," he calls. "Pick what ye can live without."

By the time she is finished, there is a small pile in the yard. We plunk ourselves on top of the rest of our things as my father whips the horse. We jerk up the road. Brigid falls asleep on a sack of clothing, held fast by Aunt Bairbre.

We don't get very far when several items fall off the wagon. Da signals to John, Eddie, Michael, Peggy and me to jump down. Tells us to pick up anything that falls and throw it back into the wagon.

"If ye can't throw it in, toss it aside," Da says.

We trudge up the road once more. As items fall off, we throw them on again or into a ditch. I look back at the little house as it recedes in the dust behind us. The tears are so thick inside me I am unable to breathe. We are almost to the top of the laneway when I see it.

Discarded on the pile of things we can live without. Once embraced and loved, it lies on the pile, head broken and leaning over its chest. One eye open.

Dust and tears cloud in front of me. They block the view of my doll. Become the curtain on childhood.

Farmer Knudson

Kathleen 1936
by Clare O'Sullivan Doyle

Back I go, out through the open barn doors, clinging tightly to the thick rope. The wind is strong as it pushes and pulls at the long strands of my hair. Directly to my left is the west field. Green corn stalks wave at me. A cat races through the dirt. Dances through the stalks after a mouse. I can see the maple clumps and, beyond those, the river as it bends through the fields.

On my next swing through the door I twist toward my right, to the east field, with its rows and rows of straight brown wheat. The wind ripples through the lacy hair of the endless ocean of plants. The scent of musty grain fills my nostrils.

Beyond the field I can see the white of the Knudson's house splashed against the blue of a summer sky. I can't see the details but I can picture them. The wide front porch. The beautiful red of the front door with its cut glass window. The brass knocker. The ruffles on the rockers lift slightly as the wind skirts under their bottoms.

One more swing. Slower than the others. I focus straight ahead on the henhouse and the dust of the yard as chickens flutter and scratch in the sun. Back inside, the horse stamps behind me as I swing into his territory, clearly disapproving of this activity.

At the Knudson farm I am allowed to swing. Each morning before school I collect and deliver the eggs for the wife. Once a week, I am allowed to keep a few for us.

Farmer Knudson decreed that the rope hanging from the wide double-door opening is mine to enjoy. Most of the time, he spreads hay into the pens and watches me. Chuckles and tells me I look so pretty and brave.

I never think of myself as pretty. Thick reddish-blond hair and a face full of freckles, I am tall and thin with wide shoulders. My mother says my best features are my big blue eyes. I think that's because they're the same as hers.

When Farmer Knudson says I'm pretty I feel a flush that starts in my stomach and turns my face pink.

"Would you like to milk the cow, girly?" he asks one morning.

Knudson has a long thin face that's always red and blotchy. He says you as 'oo', which sometimes confuses me. He's thick and short, not much taller than I, but his arms seem long and are covered in black hair. There is something about his eyes that make me shiver. Piercing light blue that look hungry.

I stop with my hands on the thick rope, itching to swing, but too polite to ignore him. I have been taught to listen to my elders.

He seems to think I need more incentive.

"I'll teach you how and you can even take some milk home to your moeder."

Immediately the saliva runs into my mouth unbidden. I imagine the taste of the milk. The look on Ma's face when she pours her tea. The frantic begging from my siblings to have some too.

I let go of the rope and nod.

He takes me to the cow stalls and invites me in. The creatures look around, chewing. Thoughtful. Farmer Knudson takes me to the side of one huge animal.

The cow turns to look at me. Her neck movement is so restricted that I can only see one big brown eye. Our images reflect back to each other, mirrors of fear and want.

I feel guilty. She is tethered while I am free to swing out the door on a rope.

The farmer puts his hands on my shoulders and eases me down, firmly, on to a stool. He reaches over me, his arms around me, as he puppets my hands forward to the cow's teats. I feel heat simultaneously from the man's body and from the cow.

Knudson guides my fingers to pull on the teat. It's a surprisingly strong appendage, soft with stiff little hairs on the outside. The strength and sinew of a well-honed muscle; a conduit of life. Connection of body-to-body. Designed to feed her baby or dump her precious fluid into the bucket for me.

The farmer pushes my fingers, cupped by his sweaty hands, up, then down. Close to the cow, then away, we push and pull until the white watery liquid splashes into the bottom of the pail. He releases my hands to repeat the motions on my own.

Suddenly I feel Mr. Knudson's hips rub against my shoulders and my head in rhythm. A hard sinewy part of him that is both foreign and familiar to me, a girl who has five brothers. I don't move as his hands trail back up my arms to my breasts. He squeezes in the same fashion as I squeeze the cow, hard, soft, up, down.

I hear his sharp moan and intake of breath. A shudder runs from him to me to the cow. She seems to breathe a huge sigh at the same moment. Huffs and turns her one free eye to blink at me. Again I drink in her fear. Shame floods me. We are both prisoners, but in my case, I have made a choice born of greed and want.

Farmer Knudson turns away for a moment. My fingers stay automatically in place. Keep the rhythm. In the silence the milk continues to splatter into the pail, a quieter sound as the level rises. The precious liquid becomes a slow drip then stops.

"All right there, girly, you did a great job. Look at all that milk!"

His voice is high and giddy, falsely jovial. Perhaps some of the shame has infected him.

"I'll get you a bottle and off you go home."

He jerks the pail out from under the cow. I still don't get up or turn around. I am afraid to look at his face. I am appalled at the heat that still lingers from my shoulders down to my waist.

When I finally turn to face him, I keep my eyes lowered. He hands me a bottle, capped with a small round cardboard lid, filled to the brim with white gold. He also hands over a small basket of eggs.

"I put in a couple o' extra eggs for you. I know your family can use it."

When I see the look of delight on my mother's face as she takes the milk and transforms it into mouthwatering treats for the family, I almost forget how I earned it.

The next day is Sunday, and I am reminded. The Knudsons are a rarity. Catholics who own a farm.

"Mind you," my mother has told us disdainfully, "they aren't Irish. They come from the Netherlands."

We haven't studied that country in school. Thus I have no idea about the location of the Netherlands. It sounds far away. Unreachable. Perhaps it is a difficult place to live, poverty-stricken like Ireland. Maybe that explains why he did those things to me in the barn. My mother has said that poverty can force people to make bad choices.

Farmer Knudson and his family march down the middle aisle of the church. The females wear fancy hats while the patriarch twists his own in his hands. Mrs. Knudson has short dark hair nearly covered by a bonnet of red and white flowers. Her forehead is hidden beneath a veil that drags from the brim. I can still tell, by the set of her mouth, that she is frowning. Her forehead is probably lined with disapproval.

I think to myself that hiding her condescension from the Almighty with a flimsy piece of tulle won't work. The priest told us that He sees all, even our innermost thoughts.

I touch the piece of used cloth pinned to my hair. Peggy, Brigid, Ma and I have no fancy hats.

Shame courses through me once more. Whether at the memory of the incident in the barn or the sudden recognition of our different stations, I can't tell.

The Knudsons sail straight toward the pew at the front. The one they have purchased from the church. Meanwhile we have difficulty finding enough empty seats for our whole clan.

We hunt for nine seats together. Brigid has to be dragged down the aisle by the arm. She wails loudly until Ma cuffs her across the back of the head. Everyone seems to be looking at us.

"Why can't we just go sit in one of those pews?"

My eldest brother waves toward the empty benches at the front. John is playing head of the family, something he does only when our father is nowhere close.

"Woe betide to anyone who tries to sit in a pew they didn't pay for," my mother says in a hard, sarcastic tone. Albeit whispered. "Not so they can be closer to God, mind. Strictly so they can be seen. Arrogance is a sin and they don't seem to know it. Don't ever be arrogant."

My brothers appear not to hear her because they have spotted some empty seats and leap to capture them. We are squished, but together. Brigid sits on Auntie Bairbre's lap. I memorize the word arrogant, determined to discover its meaning.

I keep my head down as the Knudsons complete their swan up the aisle, even though I am far along in the pew we have finally snagged at the back of the church. I don't need to fear, however. Mr. Knudson shakes hands with several of his fellow farm owners. He never even looks at us.

My mother sits ramrod straight. Her wide shoulders back. Her pale face impassive. Colored fingers of light through the stained-glass window rake her red and gold hair. She looks beautiful.

She gazes neither left nor right but zeroes in on the altar at the front. All through Mass, she stares at the priest's back as though he has answers.

Ma is a puzzle to me. She is often sad and angry and frustrated. I can't remember a gentle touch. Occasionally I will catch a glimpse, a softening in her eyes when she looks at us around a table. Or when she speaks of the old country.

In church I drift off. Think about the meaning of woe betide. Trip my tongue over such phrases as "Agnus Dei, qui tollis peccátamundi: miserére nobis." I have no idea why we follow these rituals. What I do know is that "miserére" sounds very much like the feeling I have at that moment.

Later that week, in the giant dictionary at school, I read, "arrogant: an exaggerated sense of one's own importance or abilities." Given the fact that the Knudsons own a successful farm and a pew, I'm not sure my mother's use of the adjective is correct.

My father isn't allowed to leave the farm when Farmer Knudson is absent, so my mother brings Da a host to go. After we traipse up for Communion, we slip out the side door. We must get to the chores before the Knudsons return.

My brothers and I practically dance all the long way home. Peggy, as usual, races ahead and leaves us all behind. Aunt Bairbre and Ma chatter all the way home. About what I can't imagine.

Once again, I almost forget. Until we are back at home in the shack. Until we have had our meager breakfast.

"Kathleen, Mrs. Knudson will be wanting her eggs for their Sunday brunch. Go on now."

I shiver from something deep inside.

"I don't feel well. In my tummy."

Which is true.

"You were all right a second ago when you filled that belly with oatmeal," my mother responds. "Now get on with you."

"Can't Michael do it this time?"

Her eyes search mine. I try hard to maintain a look as impassive as her church face. I fear her wrath if I tell her why I'm reluctant to go. I am afraid she will be mad at me. Ashamed of me.

At that moment Michael passes by and gives me a shoulder punch.

"See if you can get some o' that milk again, Freckle Face."

"Oh, that reminds me."

Ma disappears and reappears with the empty milk bottle. For some reason the sight of the perfectly preserved cardboard cap makes me feel genuinely sick. It's also the extra brightness in my mother's eyes. A hint of something I rarely see in them. Anticipation.

I slip on my boots and grasp the milk bottle as though it's a chalice.

The barn is empty. I breathe a sigh of relief. Look around for a place to put the empty bottle. I decide the railing in front of my donor cow is a good spot. She doesn't turn to look at me but sighs heavily.

The rope swings slightly in the wind. Sails placidly. Innocent. Everything is silent. The farmer and his family always spend time with the other parishioners and the priest after Mass. I have these moments to myself as though nothing has ever happened.

I can't resist. I grasp the rope. Climb the haystack. My ankles cross carefully over the knot. My hands clasp tightly. Out the door into the light I swing. Back into the darkness of the fusty barn.

When I sail into the sunshine, I feel some of that former delight. It's not quite the same exhilaration as before, but it's still there. A moment of freedom. Air. Sunshine. The soothing scent of the fields.

Suddenly a column of dust from the road smears my sightline. The Knudsons drive that expensive car toward their house. They're early. Hastily I let go of the rope, pick up the egg basket and scuttle into the henhouse.

I haven't named any of these birds. I don't talk to them the way I used to at the other farm we lived in when I was younger. Today I am swift and not even very gentle, fueled by a shimmer of fear through my limbs.

When I'm finished, I think about the empty bottle in the barn. Would Ma expect me to deliver it to the house along with the eggs? Should I leave it to be found on that railing? I decide not to take the chance.

I shiver and walk back through the yawning barn doors. Only darkness beckons.

I set the egg basket down at the entrance. When I reach the cow pen, I look up at the railing and take a step back in fright. The bottle is filled with milk once more.

He encircles me from behind. Slides his hands up and down the raised hairs of my arms. Gradually migrates over to my very small breasts. Squeezes. Pinches.

I make a sound in the back of my throat as though I am about to vomit. He doesn't hear it. His moans are too loud in the quiet heavy air.

He rubs against my back, up and down and side-to-side. Slowly at first. Faster. One arm wraps around my chest, his hands opening and closing over my breast. The other grasps my hips, holding me against him as he moves. In the next moment he makes a strangled noise and abruptly stops.

He lets me go and turns into the dark of the barn. I stand still. Not motionless, because tremors spread throughout my body.

His voice is gruff and throaty.

"You can go now. Take the milk. Take some eggs. You're a good girly. I'll bring the rest of the eggs to Mrs. Knudson myself."

For a moment I can't move. This time his voice is harder.

"Go now, girly."

I force my legs into motion. Reach up for the bottle. Reach down for the eggs. Tuck a half a dozen of them into my shirt pockets, two more than usual. I deserve them, I think to myself.

All the way to our little shack I am suffused with shame and fear. I keep the eggs still and safe in my shirt, cuddle them like delicate treasures. The milk bottle is sweaty in my hand.

I am jittery with shock. I don't know what to do.

Even from outside I can hear the screeches. Her distress fills the tiny shack.

"Brigid's on a tear," Michael says cheerfully as he skates by and grabs the milk bottle.

He places it delicately in the icebox. One by one I put the eggs carefully into the carton on the shelf. Fragile wonders. Repugnant payments.

John has disappeared somewhere to help Da. Peggy is nowhere to be seen. Eddie and Daniel wrestle on the floor. Elicit squeals and grunts from each other.

Ma's voice rises in frustration as she unsuccessfully tries to soothe Brigid. The shack is a cacophony of irritation.

I sleepwalk to the outhouse. Lock myself in and cry. Hear the words, "you're a good girly" over and over in that stilted accent. My mother would be so ashamed of me.

All that week, I duck into the henhouse with lightning speed. Eschew the rope. Place the eggs on the porch without knocking. I am afraid Mrs. Knudson will complain, but she never does. I don't see the farmer. I begin to relax. To shut it all out.

On Saturday morning, I'm surprised by the sight of some baby chicks. Once in a while the hens are allowed to roost until hatching time. There are twelve of them. Tiny yellow balls of soft feathers. Rows of sunlight filter through the boards and turn them into bright wisps of fluff.

I fill the basket with eggs and squat down by the plaintively peeping chicks. Pick one up. Immediately it settles in the palm of my hand. I gently drag a finger over its silky body. Its tiny heart beats fast against my skin. Vibrates with what strikes me as pleasure in the warmth of my touch.

Behind me the sun is blocked by a sudden shadow. In fear I stand straight up. I don't turn. I know it's him. I can smell him. Feel his heat. I keep my eyes lowered on the chick.

"Haven't seen you for a while, my good girly. You likes them baby chicks, ja?"

He moves and plasters himself against me. Transfers his sweat to my back. This time he lifts my shirt, his hands playing all over my bare chest. Squeezes. Pinches. He runs his tongue around the back of my neck.

I stiffen. Freeze. My heart matches the racing pulse of the tiny chick in my palm. Tears run down my face.

Farmer Knudson forces my legs apart. I feel the thick mound of him through my clothes, the long hard roughness of him, rubbing hard. He gyrates and pushes. Bends me slightly forward. Strokes. Kneads. Faster. Against me and through my legs as he mauls my breasts in rhythm with every move.

The moan tells me he is finished. He drops his arms. Steps back. Pants and groans. Once again, his voice is gravelly.

"Ah, good girly, see what you make your old farmer do. You're such a lovely girly. So pretty and sweet. So tender."

He picks up the egg basket. Counts out six eggs and places them on a cloth. Sets a bottle of milk beside them.

"You have a feast today, my good, good girly."

The farmer is long gone when I finally move and realize that my hands are fists. I open my palm and feel the stillness. The baby chick is as lifeless as I feel. Its feathers matted and limp.

"I am so sorry," I cry into its soft stillness. "I am so sorry."

I feel a tide of regret so deep that I am certain it will swamp me. Why did I pick up this baby bird? How could I let myself be distracted when I knew he might be lurking? Was I so bad, so dirty, that I could so carelessly lead this wee creature to its death? Why didn't I run?

Hail Mary, I try to mumble through my sobs, pray for us sinners now and at the hour...

Weeping, I bury the tiny body in the dirt just outside the henhouse.

As I carry the milk and eggs home, I can't control the tears. The shame and fear are thick knots in my chest that force saliva and choking sounds to hiccup through my mouth. By the time I get to the tiny porch of the shack, I have to sit on one of the crooked steps to breathe.

Through the long brown stalks of wheat, I can see my brothers' heads now and then as they comb the field. They bend down frequently to check the irrigation tubes that run through the rows.

Bairbe walks through the bushes, picking some berry or other.

There is silence from the shack. Clothes dance on the line in slow motion in the very slight breeze. I can hear the brush of Ma's sweeping motion across the floor. Back and forth.

I gulp deeply of the sunlit air. To dissipate the well of shame. I imagine Ma's face if she knew. If she smelled his sweat and filth soaked into my shirt. I wish I could yank my top off and throw it away. I shiver as I feel his fluids on my skin. Nothing works to self soothe.

The door opens abruptly and my mother stops. I don't turn but I know I have interrupted her sweeping of the dirt temporarily to the outside. I make an attempt to halt the hiccups. Force the tears to stop streaming down my cheeks, but I simply cannot do it.

Ma places the broom along the steps and sits down beside me. I can't remember the last time I have felt her arms around me, but she reaches out across my shoulders, and I fall into her side. She is hard and soft at the same time. Warm and comforting. This feeling of safety makes me cry harder. I don't deserve it.

She puts her head against mine, strokes my hair.

"What is it, Kathleen? What's wrong, a stór mo chroí?"

Inside I am broken by her use of the old Irish as my parents call it. I know 'chroí' is heart and my own opens up in grief. My mother's usual aloof guard has been set aside by my anguish. She holds me tightly, rocks me. Whispers, there, there, tell your Ma what ails you.

I don't want to drag her into my shame, but I can't think of any other way to do this. I can't imagine ever returning to that hen house.

"Farmer Knudson," I stutter finally. "He...he touches me."

"He what?"

She puts her hand gently under my chin and lifts my face until my eyes meet hers. Our identical sky-blue eyes. Mine cloud with tears. Hers darken.

"He touches my...my titties." I point as though she might misunderstand. "He rubs against me...here..."

Once again, I point to between my legs. I have no words for there. I have been taught nothing about my treacherous body that heats up when he rubs it.

"And then he makes these noises. And...and...then he gives me the milk and the eggs. And calls me a good girly."

When she lets me go, I expect a slap so I instinctively duck my head. But Ma has flown down the steps, the broom in her hand. Like the witch in the Wizard of Oz, a movie I've only heard about, but imagined. I am terrified.

"Watch your sister," she flings behind her.

She is gone from my sight in the time it takes me to let out a shuddering breath. After a moment I take the eggs and milk into the shack. In my parents' room, I sit by the wooden box in which Brigid sleeps. Her little face is covered by soft downy hairs. Just like that tiny, helpless chick. I weep silently. I am confused, terrified. Stiff with shock. I cannot think.

A few minutes later the commotion in the yard brings me to my feet. I am too frightened to go outside. I peek through the filmy window but I can see only blurs.

The screech of Mrs. Knudson's voice is ear-piercing. I hear nothing from my mother but I know she is there. My brothers take turns calling her name and whining. Michael keeps asking what's going on?

"Your daughter is a lying slut. Think you can hit my husband with a broom and get away with it, you bitch? Think you're all high and mighty? Get the hell off our property.

Pack up all your dirty Irish shite and get out. I don't want you here another minute."

I can't hear my mother's reply but suddenly the deep tones of my father interject. His words boom clearly.

"I have spoken to your husband, Mrs. Knudson. You will give us until tomorrow to gather our belongings. In the meantime your husband will do his own farm work. Our daughter is neither a liar nor a slut. Mr. Knudson, on the contrary, must be taken to the priest."

There is a brief silence.

When my parents come up the porch steps, the boys trip behind them, uncharacteristically quiet. They have witnessed something extraordinary.

"Kathleen?"

I automatically follow my father's command and stand, head bowed, in the doorway. He walks over and, like my mother before him, gently tilts my head to look into his eyes.

"In this family we don't let people take advantage of us. We may be poor but we are not to be made a trifle of. We don't roll in the shite with bastard dogs."

He turns to Aunt Bairbre, my brothers and my older sister.

"We will hold our heads high while we pack. Mr. Knudson has wisely found us another position at a farm in a little place called Riverside."

Michael's voice is more adult than I expect. I look at him and see hardness in his eyes, but not toward me.

"Why should we move? Let's go and beat the shite out of that old bastard."

"Language, Michael," my mother says.

"Da just said it," he complains.

Brigid stirs behind me. I go and get her, steady her as she blinks sleepily at all of us.

"Bad language seems appropriate just now, Maggie. However, son, your mother has already taken care of beating that old bastard. We don't have the luxury to stick around. I have used our current leverage to secure a new place for us. We need to take care of our own. We'll leave that filthy man to the Lord Almighty. Now let's get packing."

We begin to move but he stops us once more with his words.

"We will never speak his name again. But do not forget him. He is our lesson in what the devil can tempt a weakling like him to do. He is also our lesson that we will never tolerate a devilish act upon our family. No matter how poor, we are rich in pride and love. Let us say no more."

I watch in astonishment as my reserved father and my detached mother look at one another with devotion. Their smiles are bittersweet and determined. He leans over and kisses her lightly on the mouth.

"You are a fierce one, Maggie," he says proudly.

They both straighten those broad shoulders. We all begin to pack up. To once again leave an innocence behind.

Taking the Piss

Kathleen 1936
by Clare O'Sullivan Doyle

Stiff and achy, I open my eyes to a grey and pink dusk. Tucked as I am between a dresser and a mattress, all I can see is sky. The wagon feels tilted and I realize we are slowly making our way down a steep hill. The road sounds gravelly and loose under the wheels. I am suddenly afraid that the horse will slip and careen us forward.

Aunt Bairbre isn't coming with us to the new farm. She's got a job at another farm, so she's boarding with some other women. She looked forlorn as she strode away from the Knudson property.

Brigid is deeply asleep on my chest. I wriggle out from under her weight, settle her back down on the blanket underneath us. She crams her fist into her mouth and sucks fiercely. She's nearly five, but she's still a baby in many ways.

I sit up and look around. On either side of the hill, mature maples and tall evergreens stand as silent honor guards. Even with the burden of the loaded wagon behind him the horse is steady and strong. I notice my father and brothers on either side of the animal as though they could prevent a slip. My mother sits in front holding the reins. Everyone is silent.

When we get to the valley, I am relieved and excited. Though it's not completely visible in the darkening sky, I can hear a creek rumble over rocks and splash off to the distance. I'm thrilled by the presence of water close to where we will live. Rather than the flat unrelenting fields, here I will savor my favorite combination of rock, tree and sky. Temporarily I forget the disgust of the Knudson experience.

The wagon jerks to a stop. Everything rattles. In the silence Brigid's sudden wail sounds even more strident. I make her stand up and hand her over to sit beside our mother. Then I jump onto the soft green embankment.

Ahead of us is a slight hill with a muddy dirt path that leads to a small house. The shack stands inside a semi-circle of trees. Stretching out beyond the hillock, fields undulate along the creek. Stuffed with corn and grass and unknown shoots. The land starts a slow descent into darkness as the sun sinks.

To my left is a creek. I race over to play my fingers across the surface. The water is clear and cool, shallow but teaming with minnows and water bugs. A frog grunts in disapproval. Several birds flit from branch to branch, disturbed from their slumber. I am overjoyed by the evening life.

We begin the tedious trek up the path with our belongings. Although the hill is not steep, the path is too muddy for the wagon. Da is his stern, distant self. In charge.

"Put everything on the lawn by the stoop. Kathleen, go with Ma into the house and start hauling everything to the inside."

"Da has to return the wagon," Ma says to explain his urgency. "Let's get this done before it's very dark."

"How's Da getting home again?" I ask.

"He's riding the horse. We get to keep Old Joe."

"We do?"

I am astonished. Owning a horse is a luxury beyond description. Even an old one like Joe. He was obviously strong enough to get us here. I wonder if Da will use him around the new farm.

In a few seconds it hits me that Farmer Knudson must have been in more trouble than I thought. I push the flush of guilt away, the one that reminds me that initially I sort of liked the way he petted me.

"Jacks is out back," Michael yells and the boys race to see who can pee in the outhouse first.

John, older than his years, shakes his head and continues to haul items to the porch. Peggy works with him.

Ma grabs Brigid, who had been close to stamping in the mud, and heads through the door. I am right behind her. We begin to look around.

This shack is deceivingly smaller than the Knudson cottage. The front room is small but looks swept clean. Next to the kitchen there's a space that could be a bedroom.

My mother is agitated. She mumbles and complains, not quite a whisper.

"Where are we all supposed to sleep? One bloody bedroom?"

There's a ladder propped in the corner. I try to be helpful but I'm not sure she hears me.

"Ma, look. I bet that ladder goes to an upstairs."

Running along the back of the house is the kitchen. It's tiny and not very clean. Our old table and a couple of chairs might fit but that's all.

"Jesus wept when he saw Jerusalem," my mother quotes to avoid swearing.

Ma opens the icebox door and glances at the stove. She looks around and pokes at a hob in the front room. While Brigid follows in her footsteps, my mother continues a litany of muttered complaints.

A musty, unpleasant smell drifts from the bedroom. I am drawn to it like a fly to shit. Sure enough, there's a pile of excrement on the floor. Above it, in all serenity and perfection, a picture of the Blessed Mother hangs on the wall in an old glass frame.

I squat in front of the crap to study it. Verify that it is, indeed, shit. Long funnels of poop curl around on top of one another, giving it the look of a child's toy. Annoyed at my disturbance, blue black flies buzz at me. In less than a minute the smell drives me back.

"Kathleen! What are you doing? Let's get our things into this shite of a..."

"Ma, look, someone pooped on the floor."

My young girl self is excited by the exotic discovery, so I am not prepared for my mother's reaction. She steps closer to me and the excrement. Her face flushes deep red. Tears sprout from her eyes even as she fights them. She glances up to see the picture. Shakes her fist at Holy Mary.

"Goddamn you to hell!"

She picks it up and throws it against the other wall. Glass shatters across the wooden floor. The frame breaks into several pieces. The Blessed Mother lands upside down in the pile of debris.

"Why don't you just strike us all dead right now and get it over with?"

My mother wails for several seconds before she takes a long shuddering breath. Her voice is thick and forced. Brigid stares up at her, silenced by the outburst.

"Start getting the bloody stuff into the house, Kathleen. I'll be there in a minute."

I scoot out of the bedroom, terrified. Brigid runs around the sloping floor of the front area, entertaining herself, so I leave her there. From the grass, I grab baskets and boxes and bags and other loose detritus of our life as quickly as I can. I am filled with energy fueled by dread. John and Peggy keep up with me.

The priest taught us that God hears everything. The Mother of Jesus is a sacred person, which means she is perfect and never sins. Never says bad words or does bad things with her body. I am uncertain what those body things are, but I have an inkling it is like the things Farmer Knudson did. I do know for sure that you are never to curse at the Blessed Lady. Especially condemn her to hell.

I am a whirlwind of effort to get our belongings put away before God strikes us dead just as my mother asked. For all our transgressions. For my own. My greed, that allowed Farmer Knudson to commit his sins. For that poor wee chick.

When my brothers and sister tramp all through the house with our meager possessions, I notice that the floor in the bedroom is pristine. No glass, no bits of frame, no picture. Perhaps my mother has apologized to the Blessed Lady. Will that be enough?

I study Ma's face when I can. She still looks angry and exhausted. I see no sign of remorse. What if God takes out his disgust on me instead? After all, I have done much more than break a picture. I have killed a living thing. I am terrified.

The weedy lawn has sagged under the weight of our possessions, trampled over by our feet, when I go out for the last of the stuff. In the distance the sun has left fingers of orange in the sky and darkness beneath. I can barely see my father as he forces Old Joe to pull the wagon out of the laneway toward the road. My throat is thick with tears. I want Da to turn around and make everything all right.

Inside the house Michael, Eddie and Daniel are nowhere to be seen but I can hear their whoops of joy and the thunder of their footsteps overhead. From the hooting it seems they are thrilled with the loft. John continues to unpack, silent and distant in his efforts.

Peggy and Ma drag the old mattress that Ma and Da use into the bedroom. Brigid jumps on the lumpy padding and laughs. She is so different from any of us. Her natural state is joy and simple fun. When she wails, though, she is as fierce in her unhappiness as she is in her exuberance.

Unlike Daniel, who cries over every nick and tumble, Brigid rolls through life with a determined and mostly happy spirit.

Peggy helps Ma to put the slats together for Brigid's bed. One at the top, one at the bottom, straightening the planks. From found wood Da cleverly fashioned a tongue and groove frame that holds the mattress made of horsehair and feathers. I kneel down and wordlessly help my mother.

"I'm afraid you and Peggy have to bunk in with the boys upstairs, Kathleen," Ma says quietly. "As you know, Bairbre is boarding with another woman in the town. She'll come out when she can."

Ma continues to be upset by how little room there is. I think she misses her sister's help. I don't really mind, though. I can handle the boys, even my older brothers. I am the middle child boss. Peggy, her head always in the clouds, is comfortable as a bed mate.

"It's fine, Ma," my sister says. "We're used to it."

That doesn't seem to mollify our mother.

"I'll have Da string up a curtain as soon as he can," she adds.

"That's okay, Ma. It's fine," I echo Peggy. "Honestly."

I don't ever want her to be as angry and despairing as she was a while ago. As she still is. I vow to do everything for her.

"It should be warm up there in winter," she says. "We'll hook up the stove pipe then. There's a window too, for breezes when it's hot. I'm glad it's the middle of the summer, but I hope it won't be too warm up there. "

Peggy and I repeat our phrases of reassurance.

"It'll be fine, Ma. Really."

She sits back on her haunches. Tries to straighten her shoulders.

"You're good lasses, Peggy. Kathleen. Thank you."

My mother has never complimented me before. Although I have to share this one with my sister, I am speechless. Normally I am the mouthy one. The one with all the questions. The one who often causes trouble with the boys. The one who is the cause of this latest move to a literally shitty house.

We finish the bed in silence. Brigid has fallen asleep on Ma's mattress so I move her onto her own.

Afterward I follow Ma into the kitchen and help her put things in the small cupboards. Peggy goes upstairs to see to our sleeping arrangements.

Ma and I scrub the old stove and clean out the icebox. We have no ice or food tonight but Ma says we'll fill it up tomorrow. There is nothing but bread for dinner so we eat a whole loaf. Ma warns us too late to leave some for our father.

Michael and I go outside in the dark because he says there's a peach tree out back. Scrabbling in the pitch black with our feet and our hands, we return with a dozen sweet fruits.

"Dinner for Da," Michael says and I laugh at the phrase.

Up in the loft, the boys have dragged all our mattresses, blankets and clothing across the floor. Peggy has put ours by the window, which pleases me immensely. Eddie has to stoop a bit under the rafters in places, but the attic is fairly large. The wooden boards across the joists rattle a bit as we walk. Ma shouts up to us not to jump.

On one side we discover a hole into the front room. This is where the stovepipe will go in winter. Right now it serves as a window into our lives. I imagine looking down at soft, fine furniture and a table laden with chocolate cake and chicken and beef and potatoes and corn. Someday soon I will buy Ma a beautiful table and chairs with a fancy cloth to put over it. Fancy plates and bowls too. She won't have to shake her fist at the Blessed Lady ever again.

"Where's John?" I ask. "He's been gone for a long time. Where's he going to sleep?"

"He built himself a shed," Michael answers.

"What? How?"

"Well, there was a broken-down shed at the side of the house, so I should say he fixed it up. Found some wood and some mud, didn't he? Just like the old country or the people who live on the land. Smart. Our brother. Eddie helped him."

"He's going to sleep there? That's okay for now. It's summer. But won't he freeze in the winter?"

"He says he'll worry about that in the winter. Fall should be okay."

Peggy curls up on the window side of our mattress. She hardly takes up any room. My sister is often apart from the rest of us. Not wishing to take up any space. Her thoughts somewhere else. She clasps a worn book.

The boys take a long time to get to sleep. They use the chamber pot so often I have to scold them. Shortly after they quiet down, I hear Old Joe trot into the yard with Da.

Soon I can hear the murmur of my parents' voices somewhere below. The sound is soft and loving. I wonder if Ma will confess to my father about the curse she may have brought upon all of us.

I lie awake long after their voices turn into silence. Shining through the window, a sliver of bright moon traces the dirt along the pane. A couple of flies buzz in fruitless circles.

All I can imagine is the angry face of Mother Mary. Her eyes are black and bore straight into my head. She shakes her finger at me. Tells me my whole family will die in the flames of hell.

"It's all your fault," she hisses in my ear. "You wanted that bloody milk so badly, didn't you, dirty girl? You killed that baby bird. It's all your fault they are here in this terrible house and now they have been cursed."

I get off the mattress and kneel. Mumble prayers. Promise everything. I will do anything to make up for my sin.

I wake up half on and half off the bed. Peggy is already gone. The boys sit up and throw pillows at each other. Michael looks over at me. He walks to my bed and squats on the floor.

"What's the matter with you, Kath?"

I'm not sure how he has figured out that I'm upset until I put my hand on my curls and realize my hair must resemble a bird's nest. I probably look exhausted because I didn't get much sleep.

I tell him about Ma's curse. Michael is good at listening to me. His freckled face wrinkles in concentration and his green eyes show concern.

He hesitates for a few moments. Raises his head toward the window and thinks. I love that he doesn't give me some quick answer that will make me feel stupid.

"I read a book that Miss Burton gave me," he finally says. "I have an idea from one of the stories. We have to wait until Friday night, but we can fix this."

"Why do we have to wait?"

"The moon will be full on Friday. If God wants us gone in the meanwhile, there's nothing we can do about it. He can strike us dead by lightning if He wants. But I think He'll give us a chance."

He pats me on the shoulder. I feel better, though I am sluggish and tired from a night of worry.

Downstairs, daylight fingers the dirt and dust of the kitchen and the sags in our old chairs. But Da has brought home eggs and milk and bread. We have a feast. He's off to meet with the new farmer and begin his duties, but we are free for the day.

Ma even gives Peggy and me the time off too, though we have to take Brigid with us wherever we go. We put her in a makeshift wagon and pull her along the rough paths. She laughs and points and gabs about everything she sees.

If daylight makes the inside of the shack look worse, the outside is a delightful surprise. The land is very different from the Bradshaw and Knudson farms. Instead of a flat dull horizon we are greeted with pockets of tiny valleys. In each one there is a different crop. Apple and plum trees blossom everywhere. A field of strawberries has begun to redden slightly. There are many other trees that we can't identify, but when we charge through the branches, we are amazed by the various kinds of fruit that have ripened or are on their way. We help ourselves to all the sweet treats. Apricots, peaches, cherries. Brigid's cheeks and fingers turn various colors as she smears the juices all over herself.

Off in the distance we see corn stalks that have sprouted. Fields of grass and clover. The peak of a barn displays a bright red weathervane. Although we spy only a few cows, we discover a big herd of sheep nosing through the grass. We race up and down the trampled pathways through and around the crops and trees.

We're exhausted and thirsty when we reach home. Brigid's curled up in the wagon sound asleep. At the back of the house we discover the pump. Clear cool water flows out of it. We drink until our bellies are full. There are big clumps of rhubarb and the straggly sprouts of potatoes too. Old Joe stamps his feet and huffs.

Ma steps out of the back door and watches us. There's a slight smile on her face. She doesn't look quite as tired.

"Da's come home for lunch," she announces.

We squeal with delight at this hard to believe news. As the boys and Peggy tumble through the door, I lift my little sister from her uncomfortable position and settle her on her feet. She stumbles toward our mother, snuggles against Ma's hip and sighs.

"Go on with ya," Ma tells me, nodding toward the door.

The boys, my sister and my father sit around our old kitchen table on spindly chairs. Everything feels slanted. I shove Daniel over and we put a butt cheek each on one chair.

Da eats a large tomato and a slice of bread. He speaks mainly to John, Eddie, Michael and Peggy, who are old enough to help out even more this summer.

"This is a different kind of farming," he explains. "Mr. Reid calls it diversified."

I can barely imagine such a word or how it's spelled. When school starts again, I will look it up.

"It's very modern and brilliant in my view. It means there are lots of different ways to run the farm and you don't count on just the one way to make money. Through the summer he has the strawberries, fruit trees, grains and corn to tend. Farmer Reid seems open to having you lads—and Peg—help out in exchange for milk and such. There are sheep and some cows. As well, the Reids run a lumber mill through the winter months, so we'll have work all year long."

Just as my hope for a new life begins to surge, our mother appears in the kitchen doorway.

"Have you mentioned to Farmer Reid that we're Catholic?"

Da doesn't raise his eyes.

"We'll deal with it, Maggie. Reid has some connection to Knudson, so I can't foresee a problem. That terrible man was supposedly a Catholic as you well know. In the meanwhile we'll just lay low on the subject."

"You explain to the Almighty why we're not at Mass then," she says and stomps into the kitchen.

She grabs a pail off the counter and hands it to me.

"Get some water from the well, Kathleen."

I hurry out to the yard and pump as fast as I can. Da has no idea how much he has added to God's anger. If we can't praise Him at church, after Ma's curse on top of my sins, we are probably doomed to the fires of hell. I hope that God will wait until after Friday to get around to us.

Unfortunately, the next morning brings an incident that will surely get the Almighty's attention. Two ladies in hats and gloves appear at the door even before we are down from the loft and sorted. With the exception of Peggy, who has likely been walking through the fields since dawn. Ma helps Brigid up the ladder to me and tells us all to be quiet.

We huddle around the hole in the floor and peer down as much as we can. Ma tries to smooth out her old smock. She gives one last despairing look around the front room before she opens the door.

Even before the women step stiffly into the room, their perfume drifts upward, assaulting our noses with fabricated scent. Unaware that we are judging them from above in the same way they judge us right below the pipe hole.

Ma is polite but clearly nervous. Her hands move up and down her dress as though she could change it into a fancy gown. The two visitors are dressed in lovely shades of green or blue and both sport extravagant hats and gloves. Perhaps they think gloves will keep away any fleas or ants or spiders that surely inhabit this shack.

"Do ya want some tea?" Ma asks bravely, knowing we'd have very little of it to offer.

"No thank you very much," the taller lady says in a cultured British accent. "I am Mrs. Reid, the farmer's wife, and this is my friend and head of the Church Women's League, Mrs. Moore."

"What church would that be, if I may ask?"

My heart pounds at Ma's boldness. I don't know if she or I can handle moving again. The head of the Women's League answers obliquely.

"St. Andrew's Presbyterian Church is just up Ambleton Road at the bottom of the hill," Mrs. Moore explains.

Her accent is flat and nasal, not a British or Canadian sound that I have heard before.

"We trust you found everything to your satisfaction," Mrs. Reid says.

For a moment I hold my breath as my mother pauses. Will Ma tell her about the shit in the corner?

"Everything is grand, thank-you, I'm sure."

When Ma is sure, she means the opposite, but the church lady and Mrs. Reid seem to take the phrase at face value.

"The church puts together a basket for..."

The farmer's wife hesitates long enough to reconsider what she was about to say. Likely she notices the stiffening of my mother's shoulders and the compress of her lips.

"For all newcomers," Mrs. Moore says. "How many weans do you have?"

She looks around as though we are hidden in a corner somewhere. Little does she know that our malevolence radiates right above her head.

As Ma answers and Mrs. Reid issues a polite response, I turn my head. I remember Ma's cold refusal of a basket from Mrs. Bradshaw. Her admonition to never take charity. Her anger toward the Blessed Mother. I make finger puppets for Brigid to distract myself from the tension below me.

When I glance toward my brothers, I notice Michael. His face is red with embarrassment for our mother. Perhaps mixed with a learned hatred of that British accent. He fools with the buttons at the front of his pants and at first, I am puzzled.

When Michael gets up in a urination stance, his legs slightly apart, his penis grasped in his hand, I realize what he's about to do.

My last look through the hole displays the church lady's hat directly below it, the feathers and ribbons ostentatious and ridiculous in our little shack.

Eddie tackles Michael just as he lets the urine go. A small spray dribbles down the hole but the rest soaks my smock. My eyes follow the squirt down the hole. A light mist of urine spreads over the feathers of the preposterous hat on Mrs. Moore's head. She doesn't move, so I assume she hasn't noticed. However, my mother's broad face appears. She turns her eyes up to look directly into mine.

My brothers meanwhile have tumbled onto the mattress in a heap of hard breathing, face to face. Michael's eyes fill with tears as he sits up, tossing Eddie to the side.

"She's a right bitch to our mother," he whispers. "They all think they're so high and mighty."

"I know," Eddie whispers back, but he has no words of comfort.

Brigid tiptoes over to the boys and heaves herself on top of Eddie, giggling. Her assumption that they're playing makes us all smile. Daniel joins in the mock wrestling.

The sounds of hurried leave-taking float from downstairs. Lots of false "thank-you-I'm-sures" from our mother. A few moments after top of the ladder. Her look is neutral as she gazes around the attic.

"Whatever is going on here? You kids taking the piss in more ways than one?" she asks.

"I spilled a bit of pee down the hole when I was moving the chamber pot," I respond.

My mother is not stupid. The chamber pot is in its usual spot. My smock is visibly wet. But she doesn't argue or blame. Her eyes glow with a cross between pride and annoyance.

"Well I suppose when feathers are still on the bird they get covered in piss now and again."

We all grin at her, sheepish yet unrepentant.

"Maybe the church lady will think the pee was left there by the bird she stole them from," I offer.

Ma laughs then. A sound we rarely hear from our mother. We are so astonished we don't even join in. Simply sit there with those lopsided smiles on our faces.

"Come down once you're dressed," she says when her laughter stops. "There's a grand basket with all kinds of lovely things in it for you."

I'm uncertain as to whether my mother took the charity in exchange for discovering that someone shit in her room or whether she was so anxious to remove the women from the house that she simply forgot about the basket. Either way, we make those treasures last for days, savoring every bite of the donations. We kids never mind taking some charity now and then. We don't yet possess the kind of pride that overcomes desire.

A few days later, on Friday, Michael and I camp out in the yard. We bring a blanket each and some water. We tell our parents that we want to stay up to watch the sunset and wait for the sunrise. They shrug and don't ask why.

Once the sun goes down the air is chilly. We curl up in our blankets like sausages. Lie on our backs and track the stars. The moon, as predicted, is a big white ball that lights up the tips of the trees around us. Old Joe teeters nearby, purring in sleep.

"In the story that I read," Michael explains, "ancient priests and priestesses would dance around fires all night and sing songs under a full moon. They would ask the gods to make this night a new beginning. All sins forgiven."

"And we can do that tonight?"

"Sure we can. As long as we stay awake and see the sunrise. We just have to tell the gods our sins. When the sun comes up all the bad will be gone."

I talk to the night air and the dome of starlight above me. How Ma cursed the Blessed Mother. My guilt about Farmer Knudson. How I squeezed that poor baby chick to death. About not having a lot of faith in what the priest tells us at church.

Michael speaks of hatred toward the high and mighty English. He admits he shouldn't have taken the piss on the church lady but confesses he's struggling to feel bad. He asks that his sins now be forgiven, so I add that too.

We spend the night at a level of reflection that only young minds, open to possibilities, can experience. We are penitent, hopeful and forgiving. It's not the first time that I am amazed by Michael's intelligence. It would not be the last.

CATHERINE ASTOLFO

Auntie from Red Hills

Kathleen 1937
By Clare O'Sullivan Doyle

Michael and I are allowed to go to school by default, even though I am in the seventh grade and he is in eighth. All having grown tall and strong over the winter, John, Eddie, and Peggy are exempt from school to work on the farm at least until winter comes. None of them seem to mind. Michael, however, has begged to continue with his education. Since there are already three hands in addition to Da, our parents allow it.

As required by law, Brigid has to attend Grade One in September, and she's eager to do so. I am thrilled that I get to go, too. Unfortunately for walkers, but lucky for me, the school in Riverside is up a steep hill along the main road. Trucks and tractors and even cars move rapidly through the corridor from one town to the next. Along Mississauga Road, Riverside is the little bridge for commerce and trade. Most people live elsewhere, except for the farmers, their farmhands and their families. Brigid cannot walk that route by herself.

Children of all ages and economic levels attend Public School Number 87. Mr. Winter is the principal, the teacher, and the caretaker. Tall and very thin, he wears small glasses and has a long nose. He's always clean shaven and dressed in pressed, white shirt and trousers. Unexpectedly, his voice is deep and loud, booming from somewhere inside that skinny frame. You'd be forgiven if you imaged a ventriloquist was hidden in the closet.

Mr. Winter is nothing like Miss Burton. He runs the classroom the way I imagine an army sergeant runs a base. Depending on our age, we are given various assignments and tasks in addition to the schoolwork. As the two eldest, I am paired with a girl named Raeni. She is the first girl I've ever met whose skin is brown. When she speaks, I fall in love with her lilting accent.

Mr. Winter makes both Raeni and me go to the front of the room. We are to print our names on the chalkboard and say them aloud for him. If they are still unpronounceable—he says this as though we've wilfully chosen our names in order to baffle him—he will simply call us something else.

Caitlín, I write, using the Gaelic form of my name, the one that my mother says is on my birth certificate. None of us has ever used our Irish names outside of school. Ma, however, needs to use them when she registers us.

Raeni, the other girl writes.

"Like it's rainy outside," she tells Mr. Winter, looking straight up at him. "Except it means Queen."

The teacher pulls his glasses off and stares at her.

"Fine. As long as you remember you are not the queen of this classroom."

He turns to me. Points at my neat printing.

"And pray how do you pronounce this?"

This dangles from his mouth like a distasteful bit of food he's trying to remove.

"Kathleen," I reply slowly, enunciating both syllables as clearly as I can. The Canadian English way.

There is a silence during which I can hear only impatience.

"We'll call you Suzy," he says.

Raeni catches my eye. Face reddening, I can't decide whether to cry or stomp my feet and walk out. She gives me a slight nod in acknowledgement of my feelings, which makes me feel better when I do nothing. We return to our desks.

Raeni and I are assigned to help the Grade One's with their work. Besides my sister, there are two other little girls and a boy. Brigid is tall, stocky and blond, while the other children are tiny and dark-haired. All four of them are fidgety but quiet. We help them print cat and sat. Drag our attention back to the history of Britain.

Lean over to whisper questions to one another, where do you live, what does your father do, how old are you, when is your birthday. By the time Mr. Winter rings the dismissal bell, we are fast friends.

When Michael, Brigid and I head home in the early September heat, our little sister drags her toes in the dirt and whines with exhaustion. I cuff her across the back of her head the way Ma always does, but she doesn't stop. The string of complaints aren't even words but one-note half cries.

Finally, Michael puts the little girl on his back, but she still sniffles and whines. When we get home, he deposits the child on the lawn and disappears into the house. Brigid keeps up the complaints non-stop.

Ma's voice startles us from our yard. She sits on the front lawn.

"Brigid, sure that's enough now."

Brigid raises her sky-blue eyes and claps her hands. She races toward her mother and throws herself at our mother's feet. Ma scowls but threads her fingers through her wispy blond hair. Brigid settles comfortably and falls asleep. When I gaze over at my mother, I realize that she looks exhausted and swollen.

"You all right, Ma?" I ask.

"Oh, Kathleen."

Her voice is a half-whisper of grief. I am shocked by the tears that well in her eyes. Now that I look at her directly,

I see dark smudges and lines across her face. My voice is silenced by the fear that my stoic, fierce mother is vulnerable.

"I'm going to have a baby," she says.

There's a beat of silence as she stares off into the day. Her eyes don't really see us.

"I thought that after all this time…"

She pauses for a moment.

"How can I stand another one?"

She sounds angry and resentful.

How can I stand another one? Not feed or clothe or handle another one, but stand another one. Abide, put up with, bear, stomach. I interpret it from my own selfish point of view. Drink in her unhappiness as a rejection of us. As a statement of dislike for her children.

Peggy opens the door and I watch Brigid walk tiredly over to her big sister. Peg hugs her and disappears with her into the shack.

I feel the grass prickle my skin. Feel the sweat yanked out by the relentless sun.

Suddenly I am embarrassed by my mother. Shiver in indignation that she and my father would still perform the act which creates babies. At their ages. With our lack of money and space.

I spit something back at her, a phrase she often levels at us when we misbehave.

"I guess you made your bed so you'll have to lie in it."

By the narrowing of her eyes and the scrunch of her nose, I can see I have wounded her. I flounce into the house and scurry up the ladder to my small corner of the loft. My face to the window, I let the tears fall. It is my first taste of what it's like to head toward adulthood surrounded by miserable circumstance.

From this new more informed and more cynical perspective the vast fields stretched out before me are scrubby and dirty. Still laden with green and red and purple fruit, the trees are no longer lush and beautiful. Now they represent long hours of work for little pay. The shack looks grey and shoddy.

Suddenly ashamed of the clothes I wore to school, I tear them from my body and slide under the thin, over-washed sheets. Later I ignore the call to dinner. I even rebuff Michael's entreaties to eat something.

The next day at school, I am tired and irritable. The only lifelines are the exchanges I share with Raeni. At one point, she squeezes my hand as though to demonstrate an understanding beyond words.

It is Raeni to whom I go when I emerge from the outhouse. We're supervising our first graders in the yard at lunch. We all take turns using the jacks. I don't use it because I have to pee but because I have strange cramps below my stomach. Fists clench inside. Flood me with a pain that drains all the animation from my face.

I look down at my underwear and it's streaked with blood. Some of it has run down my leg. My heart skips with fear. I am pale and shaky when I throw myself at Raeni.

She turns, startled, but opens her arms immediately.

"Wah gwaan?"

Her lilting voice is a comfort in itself.

"I...I think I'm dying," I gasp. "I...there's blood on my smallclothes and I have this pain and...Raeni, I want my mother."

I burst into tears.

"Blouse and skirt!" she swears.

I am no longer confused by the cuss she uses. I tug at my dress, but I am too absorbed in my terror to care if the thin cloth is torn or twisted.

"You got the Auntie from Red Hills," Raeni continues. "We gotta tell the Mister."

I shake my head vigorously. Consider the auntie from Red Hills to be some shameful disease that only Irish Catholic farm families get.

"I can't. I can't."

"Yes you can. You gwan tell him you gotta go home. I'll stay with the littles here. You come collect Brigid on your way back."

Reluctantly I consider that if I am going to bleed to death from Red Hills, I want to do so at home. Which necessitates going to Mr. Winter with some kind of excuse.

I take a deep, shuddering breath. Choke back the tears.

"You're not gwan die," Raeni clarifies. "This happens to all girls. My mama says it's the sign that we are strong. We hold life inside our bodies but when there's no life yet, we don't need the nesting stuff. So we're smart and get rid of it. All girls become women when the auntie from Red Hills arrives."

Some of what Raeni says penetrates. I think of Ma. Of her pregnancy. Of those times when she demands any small amount of privacy that she can get out in the jacks.

My urge to see her face, feel her arms around me, to apologize and receive her comfort is stronger than my fear of the teacher.

When I enter the schoolhouse, Mr. Winter is alone. Behind his desk, eating. He looks up from his sandwich and scowls at me.

"Yes, Miss Suzy. Approach."

I walk up to the desk, feeling the blood seeping slowly along my thighs.

"I have to go home. I...my sister did a dirty in her pants and I have to go home with her."

He looks into my pale face and wide eyes and sees something there that I don't mean to show. Perhaps he even notices the red snakes appearing below the hem of my ragged dress.

I feel naked, exposed. Ashamed until he suddenly smiles at me. A kind, understanding, comforting sort of smile.

"That's just fine, Suzy. I'll mark ye absent for this afternoon only."

As though he is giving me a gift for only a half day's mark against my attendance record. A flash of anger flushes my white cheeks. I know my freckles must stand out like bits of dirt. For that moment I don't care.

"One more thing, sir."

He looks up from the attendance register. Doesn't answer but raises one eyebrow in a question.

"My name is Caitlín," I say, picturing the Gaelic spelling but speaking the anglicized version. "In Canada, you pronounce it Kath. Leen. It's not very hard."

We stare at one another for the seconds it takes to hold my breath to near bursting.

Mr. Winters smiles again. The same one that makes his stern face look human, humane. When it disappears, all the kindly crinkles and the light vanish with it.

"Take good care of Brigid. I'll let Michael know you have left."

He nods a dismissal. I turn my back to leave.

"And take care of yourself."

He pauses, then says, "Kathleen."

I walk out the door with my shoulders back. Ignore the progress of Auntie of Red Hills as she sneaks down my legs.

Later, when I think of that day, I swear several things. Should I ever have a child, I shall inform them about the mechanics of the human body. I will celebrate my daughter's menstruation and teach her how to manage it. I won't allow someone, even someone in authority, to be lazy and therefore diminish me. Such as not bothering to learn my name.

When we arrive home, Brigid almost delirious with the freedom of a whole afternoon off, Ma is once again sitting on the front lawn. Brigid squeals and races around in circles. Her laughter is the background as I try to explain why we're home.

"Auntie from Red Hills has arrived," I tell her.

"Quit acting the maggot. What are you on about?"

"It's like...ketchup. Ketchup between my legs."

It takes my mother a few moments to understand. For confirmation, she glances at my legs. The thin lines of red now stretch all the way to the edge of my socks. When she looks back up at me, her eyes flicker with various emotions. Amusement. Anger. Shock. Embarrassment.

I stand quivering under her scrutiny. Try not to allow my body to respond to the furious cramp that seizes my belly.

My mother gets to her feet.

"Go to the jacks," she says. "Take everything off."

I stumble to the outhouse. Once seated I pull off my stained clothing. Sit there in just my undershirt. I shiver as blood drips down the hole. Hunched over like this, pushing down, seems to relieve the cramps.

Ma reappears with another sundress, this one sewn and washed less often. She hands me underpants and a folded cloth.

"You put this cloth in your panties to draw up the blood," she says. "When it's full, just wash it out with cold water. I'll give you another when you need a dry one."

I nod. I haven't noticed, but tears flow down my cheeks. Ma sighs. She's not unkind but I feel guilty. As though I have done something wrong.

"You're younger than I was when I got my flowers," she says.

"I'm almost twelve," I say.

"I was over fourteen."

As though it is a contest over who can hold out the longest and I have lost.

She turns her back as I begin to adjust the cloth into the crook of my panties.

"Ma, what is the flowers? Why does Raeni call it the Auntie from Red Hills?"

Again, she sighs. As though this burden is hers to bear and not the one who sits dripping into the outhouse pit.

"It's the monthlies," Ma replies.

I shake my head, no less muddled.

"We have lots of different names for it. Women get it every month. It means you're no longer a child."

"Why do we have different names for it?"

"Men don't like to hear or think about it," she explains. "It's kind of a womanly code. Let's call it ketchup between you and me. Our secret. And Peggy's. She started her monthlies too."

"Okay."

Once again, shame passes through me like an illness.

"Do you still get ketchup, Ma?"

Her sigh is longer this time.

"Not now that a baby is coming," she answers, her tone bitter.

I recall Raeni's words then. The nesting material isn't needed when there is no life yet. I have some idea of how the life begins, from the lack of privacy in our shack. Knowing it has some connection to the men who do not want to talk about women's nests makes me vow I will never do whatever men and women do to create a baby.

I keep that vow until I am twenty-six.

Months later, my brother Liam arrives in darkness. The midwife stays for several long hours. My mother writhes and screams.

Da paces the little shack, a jabbering Brigid following him everywhere. She responds to the tension and fear in her own way while Michael, Daniel and Eddie hide upstairs. Peggy disappears into the night. John stands sentry at the door, as though he is Da's partner in a crisis.

Left as the midwife's helper, I have no choice but to taste, feel and witness my mother's pain. I run back and forth, to and from the pump, wash and rewash rags thick with blood and mucous.

When the infant's scrawny bum squeezes from between Ma's legs, he's covered in the same gelatinous fluids. He's determinedly bent over, foetal position. As though he knows at birth that once he is forced to put his face to the world, he will bring it heartbreak and harm.

The midwife pulls him into shape. He gives one sharp cry as he stretches. The woman expertly wipes and wraps him in a blanket that has held all of Maggie's babies.

I am bewildered when the midwife hands him over to me. As I grasp the infant in my arms, I notice my mother. She has turned her face into the pillow where she sobs as though she will never stop. The midwife waves me away.

The tiny boy grunts as I walk slowly out into the other room. Da looks down at the baby and gives a short smile.

"A boy?"

"Yes."

"What name do you want, lass? You got him first, so why don't you choose?"

I look up at my Da. I haven't thought much about my new brother until now. Too wrapped up in the sea of new navigation points in my own changed world.

"How about Liam?" I ask.

"Good Irish name," my Da says.

When the midwife signals for my father to enter the bedroom, I sit in the old rocker. Brigid stops crying to stare at the thing on my lap. She touches his face tenderly.

"Our new baby brother," I say. "His name is Liam."

"Liam," she repeats. "He's so tiny."

Her little face looks much bigger now. She's approaching five years old but she's a bit slow with her words and her understanding. She's naturally sweet with her brother, although it's clear he's a mystery to her.

I feel such love for Liam. A lack of hair and eyebrows means he will be blond like Brigid. His tiny fingers are wound so tight. His forehead creased. Forewarnings of an inner torment that we cannot see. As my mother mourns his birth, I fall completely under his spell.

It turns out that my mother is right to be suffused in grief. Little do we know that Liam will grow up diseased. His mind a twisted tangle of anger and irrational thoughts. Handsome on the outside but ugly and mean on the inside. Incapable of empathy or real love. He will manipulate and destroy.

Yet in that moment, he reaches out and wraps his tiny hand around my finger. He clings with all his strength. I promise to protect him always.

A promise that, in the end, I am unable to keep.

Corky

Kathleen 1938
by Clare O'Sullivan Doyle

When I open the door of the schoolhouse to step onto the porch and begin the trek home, I am almost pushed back by the wind. The weight of the kids in line behind me forces us all at once into the weather. Darts of icy snow bullseye our faces as we stagger to the ground. We scamper out like deer, all in different directions. Heads go down. Eyes protectively squint. Those of us who don't have mittens hide our hands in the sleeves of our coats.

The only boots I have once belonged to one of my older brothers. Too big and loosened around my legs, the snow wedges itself inside and freezes my toes. I trudge along, unable to walk very fast. My Geography book, tucked into my waistband, creates a space for the wind to grab at my skin. I hate Geography anyway. Resent my teacher for assigning a project to do over the Christmas break. I am unsure where I will get the paper on which to write. Luckily, fuming fuels each step.

Now I am surrounded by a cloud of snow that swirls in frozen currents around me. It's dark with winter storm clouds. I stumble forward. Travel with instinct in place of sight. Feel the cold deep inside like an illness. Every bone and muscle aches.

I'm so glad Brigid was sick today. I couldn't imagine hauling her along with me in this whirlwind. Michael stayed home too, and I resent him for it.

At one point I begin to cry but realize quickly that the tears on my face make things worse. I crunch my shoulders back. Fling myself forward. Determination fills me only because I am afraid to die. Each foot forward is full of pain.

Each foot forward takes an interminable minute to accomplish. I feel as though I have walked forever.

By the time I reach the long laneway that leads to our shack, I am shivering uncontrollably. My cheeks, fingers and toes are numb. The sudden warmth of light that spills over the snow makes me stop despite the scream of cold that wracks my body.

Our house is lit up. From every window a flickering finger beckons. Little streams dance along the snow, turning the ground into crystals of light. Diamonds of green and white flash past my eyes. It's stunningly beautiful.

I stumble up the short veranda and fall into the house. Shut the door behind me. There is a hush inside. Not an absence of people. More a collective holding of breath.

The wood stove blazes. Every kerosene lamp, every homemade waxed candle, has been lit. The result is a hot, smoky, smelly room that feels like I have been rescued. The flickering light is seductive. I want to fall asleep in its circle. My eyelids begin to flutter.

Michael reaches for me from inside the haze. I sit abruptly on the floor at his feet. He yanks off my coat, hat, and boots, dripping with rapidly melting snow.

"Good thing Brigid wasn't feeling well this morning," he says. "I don't think you would have made it dragging her along too."

I feel like saying that he should have been with us. Even without Brigid, I could have used his help. But I'm too tired to speak.

Loose limbed and half faint, I flop like a raggedy doll under his ministrations. He rubs my feet and hands. As they return to life, my blood vessels twinge with pain.

I curl up in front of the stove and whimper.

My mother's face hovers above me.

"The light looks so pretty, Ma," I whisper.

She leans down and spoons some sweet tea through my chattering teeth.

"It's not pretty," she says. "They cut off the hydro because we couldn't pay on time."

"It still looks pretty," I insist.

Ma sighs and straightens up once I have drunk the tea. "Well."

She says the word as though I have made a ridiculous statement. Obviously, her tone implies, I have very little commonsense. But I don't care. It'll soon be Christmas. I fall asleep as the pain subsides and the warmth tucks me in.

Later, Michael helps me up the ladder to the loft, where he leads me like a sloppy drunk to my bed.

"Are you all right, Kathleen?" he asks.

I look up at his pinched face. Eyes full of worry.

"I'll be okay, Michael," I say. "I guess we won't be getting much from Santa this year if we can't even pay the hydro."

My brother looks around the loft, as though to calculate how many siblings we have to buy presents for. Eddie snores slightly in the corner. Daniel and Brigid snuggle together on the large mattress that Da stuffed for them. Peggy sits cross-legged on our bed, reading a tattered book. I want to ask where John is sleeping on a night like this, but I'm afraid I won't like the answer.

"Ma always seems to get just the right thing," he says in a tone that is both tender and respectful.

"That's true, she does. I don't care, really. It's for the littles. I love to see their faces."

"Good thing we have Liam now," Peggy says. "We were running out of littles."

As soon as the baby was born, Michael hammered out thin planks from leftover barn wood to prevent Brigid from stepping into the hole. Now Liam sleeps in the box next to our parents. Brigid shares a mattress with her adored brother.

As soon as winter hit, the stove pipe filled the hole and pumped warmth into the attic.

As I fall asleep, I dream back to a few years ago. Michael sat in the outhouse and I stood outside the door. Stamped my feet on the cold hard ground. Shivered inside my coat as I waited.

"Michael, do you think Santa Claus is real? Some of the kids at school don't believe in him."

There was a short silence.

"Santa Claus is the spirit of Christmas, Kathleen," he said. "He's invisible and can float everywhere even though you can't see him. At Christmas he touches everyone with happiness. It might be a present. Or it might be the love of family."

After that, for a few years, I was a little confused about the difference between God and Santa. Not to mention the Virgin Mary, who got a lot of attention at church. God, I decided, must be a woman. She was always busy taking care of everyone, even providing presents for children at Christmas. Just like any mother.

When we climb downstairs that Christmas morning, there is a beautiful evergreen branch lying across the floor in front of the pot stove. It's sprinkled with popcorn on strings and small pinecones. Our presents are placed along it, colorful and shiny, wrapped in pages torn from a magazine.

I glance at my mother. She sits back on the sofa and nurses Liam. Her face is impassive, stern, as though she waits for us to misbehave or complain. When she flicks a brief smile at me, it doesn't reach her whole mouth but resembles a muscle spasm. The outward language of my mother gives no sign of the person who carefully assembled this beautiful display for us. The woman who must have put so much thought and love into this act of making Christmas special.

Da steps into the house bringing a blast of cold air and droplets of snow with him. It's only when he turns to stand and face us, one arm out as though he is about to make a speech, that we notice the wriggling under his coat. We hear a high-pitched mew. Two little ears poke out from our father's collar. Next a sweet little tabby face with huge blinking eyes.

We are all astonished when he puts the kitten on the floor.

"What shall we call him?" my father demands, as though this were not the greatest surprise in our lives but a duty to be fulfilled.

"Oh, Séamus," Ma sighs. "How are we supposed to feed that one too?"

Da brings something else out from under his great coat. A huge turkey, wrapped in newspaper, cold and pale with no sign of its potential to be delicious.

We gasp, even Ma.

"Turkey?" she says in disbelief.

Just then, the light in the kitchen snaps on. Da grins as he slaps the huge bird on the old stove.

"There you are. The cat has brought us luck already. He'll eat mice and scraps from the barn, don't you worry, Maggie. Farmer Reid gave the turkey and the cat to us. Now what shall we name our little mouser?"

Michael is the first one to gather the kitten in his arms. Peggy, Daniel, Eddie and I follow. We hold the wriggling body out to Brigid and she laughs as she pets his soft fur. John reaches out and scratches the kitten's ears, but doesn't take a turn holding him.

"Corky!" Michael says. "After the county where you were born."

A rare sound fills the shack. Da emits a huge laugh and begins to sing.

> *"We had one million bags of the best Sligo rags*
> *We had two million barrels of stones*
> *We had three million sides of old blind horses hides*
> *We had four million barrels of bones*
> *We had five million hogs, six million cats*
> *Seven million barrels of porter*
> *We had eight million bales of oul' nanny goats tails*
> *In the hold of the Irish Rover."*

We all burst into laughter.

"Have you been drinking?" Ma asks.

"Just a wee nip with Farmer Reid," he answers as he snuggles in beside her.

"At breakfast on Christmas! Jesus wept!"

"He's a good man. We'll have heat and lights from this day on, my love. The boys and I can work the whole year round at Reid's mill."

"And me," Peggy says. "I want to work too."

"You're as strong as a boy," Da says. "You can work too."

Peggy briefly throws her arms around Da's neck, as though he has given her a wonderful gift. I wonder that a girl who loves to read, who is dreamy and fierce and creative, would want to work in an arena dominated by men. Instead of going to school. My sister is a mystery to me.

Little Corky nips at our toes and chases us around the room until Ma tells us to sit. The kitten collapses in Eddie's lap and immediately falls asleep.

"Go on, open your presents," she says.

I unwrap a pair of beautiful mittens, knit from soft wool and lined with something that feels like fur. I am filled with wonder. Ma has somehow fashioned magic out of nothing.

I look up at her, eyes shining, careful not to thank her out loud for Brigid's sake. She still believes in Santa.

Ma smiles back at me, a real smile this time. A tentative step toward belief in redemption and perhaps even joy.

Da takes Liam onto his shoulder and grabs our mother's hand while he pats the baby's back with his other hand. He croons more softly. With a small chuckle, changes Maggie to Magleen.

> *"I'll take you home again, Magleen,*
> *Across the ocean wild and wide*
> *To where your heart has ever been*
> *Since first you were my bonny bride.*
> *The roses all have left your cheeks*
> *I've watched them fade away and die*
> *Your voice is sad when'er you speak*
> *And tears bedim your loving eyes.*
> *Oh I will take you back, Magleen,*
> *To where your heart will feel no pain*
> *And when the fields are fresh and green*
> *I will take you to your home, Magleen."*

It's only years later that I realize the deep grief and sadness of those lyrics. Words written for another immigrant, not an Irish one, but perfectly suited to my father's lilt. Fitting for the message that taking his Maggie 'home again' means he will work to bring her renewed happiness and security.

At that moment, it sounds like a love song to me. At that moment, it's a song of hope. My mother's eyes fill with tears and her cheeks go pink. They gaze at each other with such adoration that I am forced to look away. To give them a private exchange.

CATHERINE ASTOLFO

One day, I vow, someone will look at me that way.

As luck would have it, the schoolhouse burned down during the holidays. That meant several weeks of boring, cold days in the house in exchange for freezing walks.

However, Ma was determined to make us study whatever was to hand. The only book I'd brought home was that damn Geography text.

My Uncle Michael Searches for a Model of the One True Faith

Urbston, Ontario 1930s
by Clare O'Sullivan Doyle

From pictures and statues in our church, saints appear to be a weepy bunch. Tears and pained expressions. Not a smile in the lot.

None of them look directly at you. They gaze upward as though pleading for help. Or cast their eyes downward as if they carry a heavy burden.

Father MacGee encourages us to model ourselves after the saints of the church and the outstanding Catholic citizens in our community.

I'm not sure I want to be a saint, though my name is famous among the blessed. Or so Father says.

"Michael is the Archangel," he tells me as he throws his cassock over his head.

At the sink in the sacristy, I wash the chalices in holy water and prepare them for wine or hosts.

"He's the true guardian of the Faith. You must emulate him, Michael, as his namesake. Fight for the cause!"

He says the last sentence as an exclamation. A rallying cry. I imagine punching the noses of some of those pagans just like the school bully, Samuel Beasley, used to before he disappeared. Through the fence that separates our school from the publics, blood would spurt whenever a difference of religious opinion occurred.

When I ask why all the saint pictures are ancient, Father MacGee tells me, "You could do no better than to look to the prominent people in our parish for living examples of true Catholicism."

If prominent means well known, the adult Catholics in Urbston don't project a much happier image than the old saints. Father isn't ever specific about what examples of true Catholicism are, so I watch the elder models carefully.

I imagine Mrs. O'Leary is one of the paragons. After all, she teaches Sunday school, which surely demonstrates a deep knowledge of catechism. She always wears black. Her facial expression truly reflects those of the saints in the pictures. She attends Mass every day; three times on Sunday. Once in a while she even acts as an altar boy if none of the kids show up.

Which, in my mother's opinion, proves that church rules are more amenable than the priest would like to admit. The underlying premise that females would desecrate the altar is suddenly tossed away.

"For expediency!" my mother declares indignantly. "You'd think the gravity of the rule against having women on the altar would warrant a delay in the Mass and not a complete disregard of something that's supposed to be an instruction directly from God Himself. But if a man—such as a priest—needs something, then sure it is grand to ignore any rule."

Mrs. O'Leary, however, stands well away from the priest when she serves at Mass. I suppose she wants to assure people like my mother that her femininity, such as it is, won't profane the altar. Her hair is invariably in a bun curled into a flat circle that looks like a spare tire stuck on the back of her head. I can't remember ever seeing her without the square black hat that comes halfway down her forehead. Her lips are pulled tight together, which makes her always look like she is about to whistle.

My friend Lorenzo Malpensa once said that Mrs. O'Leary's lips "are pulled in like a cat's ass." From then on, I think of her whenever our cat walks away. Which doesn't help with my investigation of her as an example of the One True Faith.

Mrs. O'Leary's idea of teaching is to have us memorize questions and answers in the green book called The Baltimore Catechism. Not bowing our heads when we hear the name of the Lord or not genuflecting as we pass in front of the Tabernacle are both considered serious offences. For which we receive several prayers to recite silently, on our knees. When my mind veers off the text, I have to remember that God can see and hear everything. Even inside our heads. I have to consider this phenomenon every few seconds.

There are other well-known Catholics in town, but I doubt if Father MacGee has them in mind as models. When Lorenzo discovered that I attend Mass—the Malpensas being the only Italian family in town who never admitted to Catholicism—he asked me to let him know if I ever saw Frank McCarthy or Herman van der Berg there. Then he laughed as though he'd told a great joke.

Both Herman and Frank are known as Catholics within the community although I think they stretch the definition to the limit. Surely, they are not examples of the One True Faith. But since Father MacGee was so vague, I study them anyway.

To the local puritan Protestant element the two men are proof that God considers Catholics the Lord's lost sheep. Souls who've been bent by the "jiggery-pokery" of papist teaching. People to be both pitied and avoided.

The only occasion on which Frank McCarthy overtly declares his faith is during the Orange Parade. Held each summer, it's one of two large processions that annually march through Urbston. The other event is the Santa Claus Parade, which Frank ignores. But on July twelfth, he stands on the main corners downtown, shouting obscenities and admonitions. He rebukes the marchers for their bigotry.

Shouts that the battle of the Boyne was a lie, the Catholics having been the victorious party. He is always ignored, but not unnoticed. It's the only instance when Frank shows a measure of aggression, so I suppose that's one mark in his favor. He's clearly fighting for the faith.

On ordinary days, Frank spends a lot of time on the main street. I watch people cross the road to avoid encountering him. He does not beg but he does like to talk. Frank is, apart from on July 12, essentially harmless, though decidedly not pleasant company. For one thing he smells. Wine breath mixed with urine and strong body odor is not a scent that people admire.

Frank has a habit of approaching passers-by. Leaning his face close to that of the target, he asks questions.

"Do you know the difference between a dangling participle and a split infinitive?"

Most people pull a scarf or sleeve over their noses and rush by, but the odd one—mostly newcomers, I've observed—answers in the negative. Frank never tries to educate.

He shrugs his shoulders and says in a rueful tone, "Most people don't know the difference."

As though this is one of the great ominous signs of the decline of western civilization. Senior townspeople claim that Frank had hardworking immigrant parents who provided him with a reasonable education. On the death of the father, the legend says, Frank received a small legacy.

"Which he is determined to spend entirely on cheap wine," my mother declares.

Frank clearly does not see the point of squandering money on such unnecessary commodities as accommodation and clothes. Undoubtedly there are occasions when Frank is both awake and sober, but no townsperson can ever recall seeing him in both these states at any one time.

Two mysteries surround Frank's life.

No one knows exactly where he lives or where he gets his booze (presumably the cheap wine to which my mother referred). Rumor has it that Frank owns a shack out by the Wadopika River, about a half hour's walk from downtown. There is no record to indicate that anyone has ever actually seen the hut, but it's believed by most townspeople that it's out there somewhere. A minority of them believe that this cabin doesn't exist. They find it hard to believe that Frank could stay upright for half an hour at a time, never mind spend it walking from the shack to downtown.

If the place exists, Frank doesn't spend much time in it. He often sleeps overnight on the steps of the Bank of Commerce at the corner of Delby and Wellington Streets. My mother opines that he chooses this spot because it's sufficiently off-center from the heart of downtown to allow the police to ignore him. Colder nights he passes in any empty railroad boxcar that happens to be in Urbston and available.

Frank wears a fedora and a long tweed great coat in the winter, which he sheds in summer to reveal a woolen knit sweater and black pants with a piece of rope as a belt. No matter how hot the summer day, Frank never abandons the woolen sweater. This does little to enhance his odor.

Perhaps poverty is the Catholic model that Frank sets. St. Francis of Assisi, his namesake, is the patron saint of poor people and animals too. According to legend, the venerable man took Lady Poverty as his bride and gave up all his wealth. Since St. Francis lived in a hut and got an entire following of people to also become poor, Frank emulates the saint in two ways. If he actually owns a shack. Our Frank does have some street dogs that he shares scraps with.

However, he only gets one other person to follow him. Sort of.

Herman van der Berg cannot be more different from Frank. Herman comes from one of the town's prominent families. His father was born in The Netherlands and came to Canada as a teenager. Horst van der Berg quit school early, got a job as a carpenter's apprentice and over the years he established a local reputation as a quality builder.

Herman has been on his father's payroll since leaving school at sixteen although he is absent from work more often than he is present. Herman does not have a knack for the carpentry and construction that are the very fibers of his father's being. Horst can't understand this lack in his own son. His disappointment is painfully obvious to everyone, including Herman.

According to my mom, Herman's mother runs a perfect household but believes that outward expressions of endearments are inadequate and improper.

"She is such a stiff old thing," my mother says. "She demonstrated very little affection for that poor child. When they came to Mass and Herman was a little fella, she'd cuff him across the head more often than she prayed. No wonder her son mostly stays away from church nowadays."

I don't dare point out that this description fits my mother herself as much as it does Mrs. van der Berg.

Herman keeps himself reasonably neat and, as far as anyone can discern, bathes regularly.

While Frank is harmless and even friendly, Herman can become volatile and vicious. (Traits that will cost him his life before his thirty-fourth birthday.) If Frank is the ideal of poverty perhaps Herman represents the fight for proselytization.

Herman's father provides him with a home and the necessities of life but limits his access to cash because he knows that his son will spend it on alcohol. Drink is what attracts Herman to Frank. Love of cheap booze unites them. Frank always has some. Both always want some.

Although Herman tries to avoid being seen in public with Frank, they are occasionally overheard arguing vehemently over some real or imagined slight. Everyone assumes that somehow alcohol, or the lack of it, is the real topic of conversation. It's not accurate to call their discussion an argument nor, for that matter, a discussion. Herman exhorts or laments while Frank listens with an inane smile.

Despite being named after St. Francis, Frank is another prominent Catholic who almost never attends church. The year of my search for the perfect example of The One True Faith, Frank suddenly appears at Christmas Eve Midnight Mass.

The building is so small that, even though there are only a few Catholic families in the area, it's strained to capacity when they all attend special services such as Easter or Christmas.

On some excuse or another, I arrive at the tiny church just before midnight. Later than the rest of my family. I find it packed with worshippers and barely make it in the door. Here I'm confronted with a wall of people forced to stand in the small narthex. I can hear Father MacGee but see nothing. My family is in there somewhere, but I can't make my way through to find them.

I wonder if this might be a good excuse to slip out, but my Ma will question me on the gist of the sermon and I'd better have the right answers. Besides, where would a fifteen-year-old go at midnight on a cold Christmas Eve?

Shortly after I arrive, the door bursts open behind me. In rushes Frank McCarthy. I don't have to turn around to know it's him. All the accompanying odors waft relentlessly over my right shoulder, magnified by Frank's heavy breathing. I had no idea that Frank was devout enough to attend Christmas Mass.

The door opens and again cold night air comes in. This time with Herman van der Berg. I don't know it's Herman until he starts to issue threats to Frank. I turn my head slightly to look at them without their noticing.

"You slimy cocksucker!" Herman says just above a whisper. "You think you can run in here and hide. Well, you got to come out when the Mass is over and I'll be waiting for you. You're dead, you fucking prick!"

Herman says all this as he makes the sign of the cross. Meanwhile, Father MacGee sermonizes about the visitor who arrived this day in our midst to bring a message of peace and good will to all mankind. The irony is lost on Herman.

When Frank notices the wine chalice, he bows his head at communion and joins the line. Herman twigs to the mission and follows. They ensure they're the last in line to sip from the cup, since they'll receive the biggest gulp. Father MacGee is not like those priests who want to save the holy blood for themselves.

At the end of Mass Frank manages to escape Herman's wrath by slipping out with the crowd. It's not necessary. Herman left after Communion and is asleep on the church steps.

Just as I am considering that perhaps the only model of the One True Faith is Father MacGee himself, he decides to talk about s-e-x at the next altar boys' workshop. I'm uncertain if any of the saints or other models of The Faith have ever heard the word, much less talked about it or indulged in it. I did, however, read in the library about some saints who had their own children. Unless they were Virgin Mary's, I had to presume s-e-x was part of their duty to God.

Although Father MacGee never says the word directly, he gives us to understand that we're going to learn a few tricks about how to avoid it.

"If you are ever tempted to touch yourself, boys..." he begins.

He uses both hands, folded in a prayer-like gesture, to point toward his crotch. Just in case we think he's referring to any other body part. Presumably touching anything other than one's penis is permitted. Briefly I wonder if Carla Baros's breast would qualify.

"Here is a gift for each of you that will both prevent sin and put you in the light of God."

He reaches under the lectern and withdraws a cloth bag that looks suspiciously like it once held a bottle of Crown Royal. From the bag he pulls a tangle of rosaries and distributes one to each of us.

"Once I bless these rosaries, boys, they will be your most trusted instruments for avoiding the sins of the flesh."

Father MacGee ensures that we each have a rosary in hand before he demonstrates its use. He holds up one hand in a half praying formation and nods at us to imitate him. Then he takes the other hand and wraps the rosary loosely around his left. We follow. Next, he slips the right hand into the rosary loop so both are captured in prayer.

"Now," he says ominously.

His voice shouts in exclamation, then whispers for emphasis.

"You will never give in to the temptations of the flesh. Instead you will be inspired to repeat the rosary as often as necessary!"

He whips his rosary heavenward, and his hands are suddenly free. A magic trick.

"Should the flesh be weaker than the mind, and should you feel that tingling down there..."

This time he dangles the rosary in the right direction. We all look down at his crotch where Jesus sways. I assume, were He alive, He'd be highly embarrassed.

"Take your precious rosary and wind it around that wicked instrument! Believe me, my dear lads, that will discourage further appearances."

I think of asking Father if the same rules must be applied to the process of rubbing yourself against the mattress of your bed. Hands are never involved. My wicked instrument is always hidden under the bedding. So I don't mention this method. Adding a prayer or two under my breath might suffice.

That year, I do notice a connection that seems to bind all the potential, prominent, living examples of The One True Faith in my town. One evening I am late getting home from Lorenzo Malpensa's house, so I cut through Bratus Park. Even though I have been told not to go there past dark, I am more afraid of the punishment I will receive if I miss dinner than of the ghostly shadows of trees.

I hear Herman's voice before I see anyone. He's lecturing again.

"Disraeli hisself said you Irish are a—and I quote word for word mind you—'wild, reckless, indolent, uncertain and superstitious race with no sympathy for the English character.' Or the Dutch character for that matter."

"I do have sympathy for the Dutch character, Herman, you in particular," Father MacGee replies from the shadows.

I stop behind an enormous tree trunk. From here I can see their silhouettes. Four sets of heads and shoulders. One is topped by a square hat with a tiny spare tire bun. On another the white-collar glints in the moonlight. I can vaguely see Frank's fedora. Herman's shadow bobs in time with his speech.

"Very funny, Father, and pass that over."

A shape that looks like Crown Royal still in its velvet bag floats across the darkness between them.

"Disraeli thought our religion was savage, filled with superstition and would never last," Father says. "Look now at nearly a billion or so faithful members."

"You're sure they're all faithful, Father?" Herman gives an amused and sarcastic chuckle.

"Present company not included," the priest answers. "Michael lad."

Mrs. O'Leary's voice makes me jump.

"You put my heart crossways before I figured out who y'ar. Get yourself home before I tell your Da where you were at night."

And so I do.

Years later, whenever I came home from college at a break, my mother related the latest gossip. Mostly people who'd passed away while I was gone. Some stories about crime and a few people who'd been locked up, including Frank McCarthy, Herman van der Berg, and my own brother.

The biggest news occurred when an unidentified body was found in an old shack by the railroad tracks along the Wadopika River. In those days, it was pretty difficult to identify a badly decomposed corpse. The owner of the shack, however, was positively identified as Frank McCarthy.

Herman van der Berg dropped dead on the sidewalk after what appeared to be a minor altercation with a neighbor. The poor neighbor swung one punch that toppled Herman like a tree. Of course this was after Herman spent several years in the local prison. My mother blamed his fatal reaction on a lack of nutrition. I would have thought many years of cheap booze might have had more to do with it.

Mrs. O'Leary made it to ninety-nine years old and only missed receiving a letter from the Queen by fourteen days.

As for Father MacGee, he was transferred to another parish and then shelved in a home for old priests.

"It's really a home for old drunks," my mother said.

Thus I shut the door on my quest to find living examples of The One True Faith. I decided that True Faith likely means something else entirely. Something that doesn't necessarily include an institution with rules.

Perhaps faith is friendship. Even the odd sort, where you gather under the trees to share a drink and argue a little. Or acceptance, even for those who don't conform or who struggle with life. Maybe it's forgiveness or courage or well-meant belief. Maybe it's all those things and more.

It was the stained-glass Jesus
that I loved best,
sitting in the choir loft,
his sad gentle eyes following me
as I sang the holy words
in my small girl voice.
He would have forgiven me the years,
the turns in the path,
the sins of choice.
Instead, they moved him,
piece by glittering piece,
melted him into something less gentle,
something more human.

Old Joe

Kathleen 1939
by Clare O'Sullivan Doyle

Joe was our first luxury item. Likely an ordinary draft horse, he was also a mundane color. A slight reddish tinge had become dull brown with what we supposed was age. The line of white down his nose darkened somewhat. No longer pure or striking. His brown mane was darker too. His squat legs ended in big hooves with dirty white cuffs that lined his hooves. He looked like every other old horse around.

We called him Old Joe right from the moment Farmer Knudson gave him to us. No one really knew Joe's age. He could have been ten or fifteen, which would mean he was only middle-aged. Most of the time, however, he behaved as though he were about thirty, which would make him truly old.

Until the birthmark was discovered, Joe's eyes were his only interesting feature. He kept them half-lidded, as though he didn't want anyone to know what he was thinking. Large, sloped, a tawny brown, Joe's binocular vision rapidly spied a potential call to work. If he wasn't leashed, he'd stroll casually in the opposite direction, as though he hadn't noticed my father or brothers coming to get him.

My father didn't use Old Joe in the fields. Farmer Reid supplied the horsepower or tractors. But Da or John did like to ride over to the mill when it rained, or to the market, or when they needed to check out a crop.

That's when Old Joe went into his routine. He leaned against the tree in the backyard. Snorted and moaned. Lumbered off as fast as he could lumber just as my father got close. He learned to untie a loosely fastened rope with his snout. He'd buckle or rear if the saddle came near, not enough to exert himself, just enough to make mounting him difficult.

Da could ride without a saddle and often did. Old Joe's sway back and broad sides made a great seat. Brigid and Liam were small, so both of them could loll together on his hairy surface. Lie down, roll, jump on and off. The only thing the horse did not do was speed.

If my father kicked his heels into the animal's sides, Old Joe looked around with a baleful, injured stare and refused to budge.

Da learned to cajole with an apple or a carrot. Once Old Joe got fat, he often turned up his nose at treats too. He only went on a trip if he felt like it and at the pace he decided upon. If it was hot, a journey out to the fields could take forever. If it was cold, the horse would move slightly faster. But only slightly.

Ma often watched from the kitchen as her husband or sometimes her eldest son struggled to mount the animal or get him to move. Fairly often she would open the window to shout suggestions, which Da and John mostly ignored. As did Old Joe. Ma shook her head and muttered.

The whole process was an ordeal for everyone. Daniel, for some reason, got especially annoyed. Perhaps because he himself was full of energy and had a determined work ethic. Many times he joined Ma at the window.

"I told Da I'd whip that old horse into action," he said. "But he won't let me."

"Don't be fooled, son," Ma answered, drying her hands on her apron. "Your Da loves that old horse. That's how they dance together."

From the look on Daniel's face, I could tell he thought our mother was slightly crazy.

As for Eddie, he tried kindness on Old Joe. The horse was smart enough to go along with this method to a certain extent. With sweet words and carrot bits, Eddie could entice the animal to pull a wagon for a short distance. He'd then feign exhaustion. Lowered head, hooded eyelids, a long shuddering snort of a sigh radiated self-pity. Joe pawed morosely at the ground as though attempting to summon the strength to pull that wagon even one foot further. He gazed at Eddie with what appeared to be tearful eyes.

I imagined that Old Joe could talk.

"I tried my best, Eddie. I really did. I just can't do it. I'm so, so sorry." Spoken in a tone of regret.

As for Corky, he loved Old Joe with a passion. The horse pretty much ignored the cat, which was in itself an act of affection. For most of the day, feline slept atop equine. Snoozed in the crook of the animal's huge bowed back.

The day we discovered the spot was no different. Joe leaned on the tree in the shade while Corky slept on his back. The horse's large appendage pointed to the ground as he leisurely peed on the grass.

When engorged, Joe's penis was the biggest thing I'd ever seen. Apparently, as Da solemnly pointed out to all of us, it was an average size for a horse. Everything Joe had and did was either average or far below that.

Still, Michael delighted in calling attention to the horse's member whenever Joe urinated or was perhaps fantasizing. The horse would turn his head and stare at his penis as though astonished by its appearance. It poked out from the brown shaft, a beige-reddish color. Like the rest of Joe, his penis pointed downward at the ground. A fifth leg that also did not move at speed.

That particular day was bright with October sunshine. Ma and I hung laundry on the line in the back yard. The older children were off working in the fields.

All around us, Brigid and Liam drove little stones up and down the grass as though they were toy cars. Made the appropriate sounds. Michael entertained them and kept Liam from wandering off while we did the laundry.

Liam toddled around after his sister, often landing hard on his butt. He never complained. Got up and repeated the action.

When I turned from the basket to hand Ma a thin bedsheet, I was met with her back. She was staring at Old Joe.

I put the sheet back in the basket and peered around her in the same direction. The horse's penis was thick and pointed, as usual, at the ground. The angle of the sun just happened to highlight the appendage.

"He's got a mark on his mickey," Ma said.

I was so shocked that my mother had loudly, in the middle of the day, uttered the euphemism for penis that I simply stood immobile as she wandered closer to the horse.

"It's in the shape of a heart. He's got a heart on his mickey."

I heard the wonder and amusement in her tone. Ma turned and caught my stunned expression. When she threw her head back and laughed, Michael, Brigid and Liam stopped to gaze in astonishment. Corky jumped off the horse in alarm at the strange sound.

Brigid clapped her hands in delight and laughed along. Michael zipped up close to Old Joe and pointed. In his excitement at the discovery, my brother did a few flips across the grass. Brigid tried to copy. Liam simply stared at his siblings and his mother, blond brows furrowed.

I crept slowly toward my mother and Old Joe. He blinked lazily as I bent down to look. Sure enough, on his still-erect penis, a brown spot was magnified in the direct light. A clear heart-shaped birthmark. As though bored by our attentions, Old Joe yawned hugely. His appendage became flaccid and withdrew.

By now my mother had tears rolling down her cheeks in merriment. None of us kids knew what was so funny. Neither did the horse.

I had no idea whether or not Ma told our father about the heart-shaped birthmark. If she did, it made no difference in Da's assessment. He eventually became more impatient with Old Joe. Began to talk about selling him. Ma countered with a reasonable response that we'd never be able to afford another one and that, once in a while, the horse was helpful.

Two things happened to push Da over the edge. First, somebody delivered a flyer advertising a livestock auction right here in Riverside. Second, Old Joe decided to unseat our father.

Though only Da witnessed the fall, we certainly saw the results. Mud-covered, furious, our father left Old Joe to saunter home on his own. As Da peeled off his wet and filthy clothing, he stomped and shouted in Gaelic. My mother's face told me she was glad we kids had never learned the language.

"I'm taking that useless old thing to the market on Saturday," Da hollered.

Sure enough, after chores, amid a riot of colorful leaves, Da, John, Daniel and Eddie headed for the market. The rest of us watched Old Joe slowly launch himself down the lane, guided by the boys, who took turns pulling on his lead or enticing him with treats. The horse looked back only once, as though to fix the little house in his memory, but only I was left to wave.

The sale went well, thanks to Da's quiet way of affirming the horse's qualities while not technically lying. The money was well spent on winter stocks, flour and sugar and knitting supplies.

We had an unusually small amount of snow that year, which meant that Da and my brothers and Peggy could work nearly every day at the mill.

It was a quiet, reflective time, a year in which I got used to a new body. A new perspective. There was plenty of work in the mill, food in our cupboard, and books in the local library.

Overseas, through 1939 into 1940, war raged. The violence reflected in dramatic words from our radio. At twenty and nineteen, John and Eddie itched to sign up. John brought his energy in favor of enlistment to arguments during dinner. Da was the only one who could stop the discussions.

"That's enough now, John," he would say. "I need you on the farm and in the mill."

And his son would sullenly obey. Until the next meal.

When March came around, the weather was cold and rainy. Slogging through mud and chilly wind in the fields was miserable. The new schoolhouse was completed. Michael and I began the trudge back and forth with Brigid in tow.

Despite the discomfort of wet and cool days, I was happy. I had Raeni, my first real friend, and I had book knowledge. Even Mr. Winter and I seemed to improve our relationship.

In May, John and Eddie ran off to join the army. John left a misspelled, badly written letter of good-bye with me. When I handed it over to Ma, she cried, but only briefly.

"They're in the good Lord's hands now," she said as she swiped at tears on her cheeks.

Daniel and Michael would follow, but that was a year and two years away.

Da was angry with his eldest sons, though I could only tell by the flash of lightning in his eyes. He said very little.

His work was now harder and longer, but Daniel, Michael and Peggy proved to be steadfast and reliable.

"Another auction is coming to town," Da announced one day. "We've got enough to buy a horse. One that works for a change. With John and Eddie off on their bloody crusade, we can use the help."

The horse that marched into our yard with a grinning Da and Peggy on his back was the same breed as Old Joe. Daniel trailed behind.

This horse's fur was shinier. His body sleeker. The white of his nose glowed clean and brushed. He held his head high. Eyes wide and alert.

They arrived in time for dinner. Da brought a heart-stopping treat for dessert: apple pie and ice cream. He gushed all through the meal.

"We got him for a great price, eh, Daniel?"

"Da was the perfect haggler," my brother agreed. "Kept waiting for someone else to bid, then would only bid a coupla cents more until we got that horse for practically nothing."

The days had become longer. That evening, we all went outside to pet our beautiful new horse, who waited beside the tree in the back yard. Brigid and Liam danced around the big animal. Da beamed with pride.

To our astonishment, Corky crawled up the tree trunk and settled on the horse's broad back.

"Just like he used to do with Old Joe," Daniel said.

The horse's middle sagged in a more relaxed stance so the cat could curl up. He leaned against the tree.

"Just like Old Joe," I said.

At that moment the horse's sheath opened and his penis emerged. In the waning sun, we could clearly see the heart-shaped birthmark. He looked around at us with half-lidded eyes as he urinated against the tree.

"You brought home the same horse, Séamus," Ma said.

My father sighed as he removed his hat in a toast. "Nicely done, Old Joe."

Something for the Dog

Kathleen 1940s
By Clare O'Sullivan Doyle

His eyes were huge blue orbs. Surrounded by dark smudges of fatigue and malnutrition, they sat on his brow like spotlights. Every part of him was thin. Even the blonde mop of hair on his head was wispy.

I stood awkwardly behind the cash. It was my first week of working for Mrs. Coulter in her grocery/butcher shop and the very first day I was in charge of the cash by myself.

"You're a fast learner, Kathleen," she had said, pleased with my progress. "You are absolutely ready to handle this. Besides, Raeni and Jakub will be in the back should you need any help."

Comfortable in her skin, Mrs. Coulter was large, imposing, yet kind and warm. She didn't behave like some of the other farmers' wives. She was more farmer than lady of the manor.

My friend Raeni was learning to be a butcher. She worked side-by-side with Mr. Kane, who himself was a large, red-faced but fair-minded person. He spoke with a thick Polish accent. Years later, I would discover that his real surname was Kania, gently changed for the English tongue.

To many, Raeni's choice of career was odd for a woman. Little did they know she had plans for a general store that would, eventually, transform into a chain of grocery shops across the province.

This position at Mrs. Coulter's General Store was a great summer job, both in pay and conditions. I could easily walk down the hill to work. As long as I earned enough money to assist with the family expenses, I was allowed to enroll in business college. That summer, I anxiously awaited a letter of acceptance or rejection. Whether or not I had earned a scholarship. To my delight, Miss Burton, who was now Mrs. Chilton, had written a beautiful letter of support.

Raeni had helped me get the job at Mrs. Coulton's. From my wages, I was allowed to keep fifty cents a week. The rest went to my mother. From my 'free' money, I was saving for a beautiful green tam and scarf I had seen in Beamish's front window.

When the little boy arrived, I was alone. The store was empty of customers. Jakub was giving Raeni a lesson in the back. For a while, I had tried to do busy work. Dusted. Ensured labels were front forward. Swept. Straightened. Finally, I stood behind the cash register, wishing up a customer. I received a be-careful-what-you-wish-for answer.

His head barely cleared the counter. Though his eyes looked older, he could have passed for six. He handed me a note written in shaky script.

Please a bottle of milk and something for the dog on our account. Helga

After I read the request, I shifted to the shoebox next to the cash register. Mrs. Reid had organized the customer accounts by last name.

"What's your name?" I asked.

"Willy," he answered.

"Sorry, I meant your last name."

"Nowak."

When I found the card, I realized Novak was spelled with a w. The boy's pronunciation and absence of an accent told me he was Canadian. The surname suggested Polish.

The card was filled with red marks. I glanced up at the boy, but his eyes were averted. A gentle pink flush snailed up from his neck to his cheeks. When he looked back at me, his eyes were wet, but no tears slid down his face.

"Please," he said. "The baby is crying and our uncle has come to visit again."

NoCredit-C! Mrs. Coulter had printed all across the card, several times. I had never seen this notation on any of the other files.

"Ummm…I'll be right back, Willy."

Inside the cold room, I found Raeni and Jakub examining a severed pig's head. I tried not to look as I held up the note.

"There's a little boy in the store named Willy who's trying to buy some stuff. But Mrs. Coulter marked their account with no credit."

They both looked up at me.

"Do you explain or I?" Jakub asked.

Raeni began to remove her blood-stained apron and rubber gloves. "I'll explain."

"I'll take care of the dog."

By now I was completely confused.

"Willy says the baby is crying and their uncle has come to visit again. Why do they have guests if they can't even feed their baby?"

Raeni drew me to the door where we could both see the young boy through the window. She tapped the card still clutched in my hand.

"Did you notice the extra C?"

I glanced down again, nodded when I saw it.

"That stands for charity. No credit. Charity. Mr. Coulter doesn't like Germans, so Mrs. Coulter used a code."

"Oh. I thought they were Polish."

Jakub's voice rumbled from behind us where he chopped up some fatty meat.

"Germans and Poles used to be neighbors in the real way," he said. "We could live happily only a few miles apart.

But sometimes that boundary makes all the difference in how you are treated."

"Mr. Coulter thinks Mr. Nowak is a spy for Germany. Pretending to be Polish but giving the enemy information about our soldiers. Mrs. Coulter disagrees. She asked him 'What could possibly be happening around here that would be of interest to the war?' He couldn't really say, but he ordered her to stop any credit."

"What about their uncle? Can't he help?"

"That's part of the code we've developed, this one with Willy. Their 'uncle' is actually the bailiff," Raeni said. "When he comes, he always stays for a few days if Mr. Nowak has a job. He doesn't want to evict them. He waits to see if Mr. Nowak will return with the rent money."

"The poor man can't get jobs around this area, so he goes off on the railroad and picks up whatever he can. If he is gone more than a couple of days, that means he has some work. He always comes back with the rent money."

"And sometimes a little to pay down his credit here and buy more food," Raeni added.

I stared at the little boy who stood solemn and still in front of the empty cash. He must have wanted to slobber over the various offerings in the glass display cabinet. Rashers, ground beef, steaks, chicken. On the other side, lettuce, potatoes, carrots. In the specialty area, chocolate, cakes, cookies. Willy did not turn to look around the store. He didn't appear to even blink. His thin shoulders were straight and stiff. His resolve was astounding.

"I give the missus pork hocks and some of the other ingredients for a good, hearty soup," Jakub said proudly. "Plus some of the meat a few people in this area give to their dogs."

"Things that wouldn't show up in an inventory should Mr. Coulter decide to look."

I met Raeni's eyes. Although children of poor immigrants, we were both better off than Willy.

"There's always someone richer but someone poorer, too," she said.

Raeni, Jakub and I split the cost of the milk. I knew this likely meant the green tam and scarf would be gone from Beamish's, but I consoled myself with the knowledge that a baby wouldn't go hungry today.

When we had loaded up a couple of bags of sustenance, we handed it over to the small boy. Stronger than he looked, he hoisted everything onto his shoulders, tipped his head in thanks, and left.

One morning on the way to work, I noticed a few bushes laden with strawberries tucked far from the usual fields on the Reid farm. I tucked my lunch sandwich into my purse and picked a bagful of the ripe fruit.

The Nowak house was a tiny wooden cottage built on an abandoned lot at the edge of town. When I came up the rickety steps, Willy stepped outside. I held out the bag.

"Strawberries," I said, as though he couldn't see the plump berries poking through the top.

Once again, that flush started at his neck and spread to his hairline. This time, though, he smiled gratefully. That's when I knew this boy was someone with a unique set of gifts. I dropped by as often as I could after that. He was the first to know that I had been accepted into business college with a full scholarship. The first to hear that Michael has joined the army.

Sometimes Mrs. Nowak would be outside hanging laundry. Other times, Mr. Nowak would be in the garden trying to coax their weak plants into producing food. Always, I would see Willy and be grateful for his smile.

In October of 1941, when I stopped by with a sack of potatoes, they were gone.

In August of the previous year, the Canadian government had enacted the War Measures Act, giving the Minister of Justice the authority to arrest anyone who was considered a public safety threat.

An 'anonymous source' reported that Mr. Nowak was a German spy. The entire family became enemy aliens, although none of the children nor Mrs. Nowak had ever set foot in Germany. According to the 'source', Mr. Nowak sent messages to the enemy through the Nazi Party of Canada.

Mr. Nowak denied being a member. Despite no proof of any treachery, he was interned in Petawawa for five years. Where his family went was a mystery unsolved. All we knew at the time was that they had disappeared.

Years later, in the late 1950s, Willy changed his name and became a famous actor in Hollywood. Known for his good looks and affable personality. Someone who made the world laugh. Someone who gave away most of his fortune to those in need. A fact which remained a secret until his death.

Once in a while, a rumor that our "famous son" was in town raced along the gossip line. Rejected and cast as an enemy by most of the population, Willy was suddenly an idol. Someone to greet with open arms and swoons.

In reality, Willy only came to visit at Raeni's large home in Toronto, where he had some anonymity. She had married my brother Michael, a surprise elopement that did not go unnoticed in Urbston. As a mixed-race couple, they were shunned by most of the population.

With their hard-earned wealth, Michael and Raeni lived in the larger city, pretty much anonymous. Both worked on their careers and did not seem interested in having children.

According to Raeni, Willy seemed unfazed by his past and his popularity. He would simply pop in for dinner, regale Michael and her with stories about Hollywood, and, while they lived, he'd visit Mr. Kania and Mrs. Coulter in their old age homes.

I was lucky to be there on one of his surprise visits. Tall, handsome, radiating confidence. When he turned to look at me, a welcome smile of recognition and gratitude, those huge blue eyes were the same. Captivating. Fathomless.

"Did you ever get that green tam and scarf?" he asked.

I blushed and shook my head. "I can't believe I told you that."

He reached into a bag and pulled out a beautiful green scarf. More shawl in size, it was soft as only hand threaded cotton can be.

"I got this in Istanbul," he said. "Turkey. It's called a pashmina, so it can serve as covering for your head and your shoulders. Even better than a tam and scarf."

I placed the beautiful shawl around my shoulders. Put my face down into its feathery folds. I shed a few tears of joy that the boy who had to beg for something for the dog could now afford to give a gift to a girl whom he knew years before.

Better still, he gifted me once again with that stunning smile.

The Potato

Auntie Beers 1961-1962

When Auntie Beers joined the family dinners, which she did most weeks, she ate several kinds of potatoes. They could be mashed or boiled or fried or covered in onions and cream. For dessert, she liked brown bread, milk and corn syrup.

Our families took turns hosting dinner. Except for Aunt Carol and Uncle John, whose house was too small. Our fathers had to lift Uncle John's wheelchair up porch steps and into bathrooms when he signaled. No one seemed to mind, especially as the evenings wore on and the drinks flowed.

The kids played outside. Weather didn't matter. We were outside until the streetlights went on in heat or cold and rain or snow. If the families stayed after dark we shifted to the basement, family room or garage depending on whose house we were in.

Each home had a basic television set. Ours was in the living room. We placed newspapers down to protect the carpet from food fights or defective whipping cream aerosol cans. Lying down in front of the television, we ate our dinners. On Sunday nights we watched Lassie and Disneyland. Fiona cried at the end of every Lassie episode. After cleanup the adults switched places with the kids to watch Ed Sullivan. Patrick, Grace, Mario and I often sat in the kitchen for the Auntie Beers show instead.

She was usually in fine form by now, full and soused and happy to have her audience tucked into her sphere. Sometimes she did the jig to whatever song she was teaching us. We pushed back kitchen tables and chairs and tried to mimic her steps.

It was during those moments that I saw the young girl behind the mask of wrinkles and disappointments. Instead of the austere, cold and critical blue eyes, there would shine an inner sea of joy. A glimpse of the younger Bairbre. Child of green hills and sea-kissed air. Red haired and freckled, full of energy and optimism. Life had not yet crushed her spirit. Painfully hard work and very few rewards had not yet darkened her perspective.

Auntie Beers had a beautiful voice. She could sing all the verses to the old Irish songs.

"My Grandda would sing and tell us stories every night," she said. "Yer Granny and me, we loved those times. In the dark, by the candle. Here is himself, doing the jig just like this."

When she mentioned her grandfather, I was thrilled with the thought that we were witness to the handing down of tales and thoughts from our ancestors. We lined up beside her, two on each side.

"Left foot in front of t'other," she said, and demonstrated. "Now point t'ord the right, bend up, jump, put it down behind your right, now you're ready to the same with it. Step. Step. Point. Jump. Here we go again."

Her long, graceful legs moved faster than we could think. We were serious, every time, though we never quite mastered the moves. Auntie Beers seemed not to notice our ineptitude as she became lost in the nimble, subconscious steps of her childhood.

When she got winded or wanted another beer, she sat in a kitchen chair. I tended to her needs. Brought her a bottle from the fridge. Ignored her attempts to criticize my efforts. All for the pleasure of her tales.

Some nights she sang and gave us her own version of a history lesson. For me, it was the best combination of music and story.

"I was born on a Dublin street where the royal drums did beat and the loving English feet, they went all over us and every single night when me dad would come home tight..."

Her voice was deep and melodious. The lyrics clear and striking. I was filled with longing. Or love. I'm not certain. I only know that I was in a state of awe.

"He'd invite the neighbors out with this chorus: Come out ye Black and Tans, come out and fight me like a man."

When she paused, Patrick was the one to seek the answers we all wanted.

"What are Black and Tans?"

This was the prompt to start Auntie Beers' version of events that happened before she was born. Herstory. Memories she gifted us that were as important to me as the blood I inherited from our Irish roots.

"Black and Tans were part of the Royal Irish Constabulary."

She used finger quotation marks for the word royal.

"Rotten bastards thought they were the English King's arse. They'd attack anyone who even whispered independence. Once they burned down our uncle's house for a bit of revenge."

"What's independence?" Patrick asked.

"The English thought they owned us." Auntie Beers nearly spat the words. "We're Irish, my pets, we're not bloody English. But the—quotation marks again—"royals" thought they could just take whatever they wanted.

"The Irish showed them, right, Auntie?"

Mario surprised me whenever he asked a question. He was normally silent. A cypher. Later I believed it was his Italian name and half Italian roots that kept him quiet. He was even more aware of Bairbre's inner prejudices than I was. But he was a scrappy boy, too, prone to temper and an automatic fist reflex. The idea of the Irish fighting off an enemy appealed to him.

"Oh we did so."

Auntie Beers looked as though she had planned and executed the rebellion herself.

"The Irish Republican Army fought and won. Southern Ireland became Eire in 1922."

My shy, fierce little cousin was proud. I swore his deep brown eyes looked a bit green.

"Not all the British soldiers were bad, though, right, Auntie?" Grace asked. "Daddy says one of them helped Gramma."

Auntie Beers grunted and ignored the suggestion that any British soldiers were human.

"That constabulary turned their wicked guns on people having a bit of fun at a football match. Shot them dead or wounded as they sat innocently in the stands."

She left out the murderous operations carried out by the Irish. We might have grown up believing the English were terrible and the Irish were perfect. The moderating influence of our loving non-Irish fathers or mothers taught us that all human beings could be wicked and all human beings could be good.

"When someone is desperate, starving, or made to feel inferior," my father often said, "a person can be driven to evil acts. Most of us just want a happy life."

I was never to know what Auntie Beers thought of my father's simple solution to uprisings and battles. As I studied the history of my ancestors' arrival in Canada, as I lived through the years of my own herstory of protests and riots, I remembered the stories she told of her grandfather.

Which always harkens back to the proud and mighty potato. Above ground the plant appears ragged and messy. Not symmetrical or stately. Instead, it presents like a weed that threatens to take over and choke the life out of everything else around it. Only underneath can you find the sturdy entwined roots and the delicious nourishing flesh. Filled with vitamin B, potassium, minerals, antioxidants, resistant starch and fibers. Rich in vitamin C to prevent scurvy. Weedy green, bumps and warts and dirt.

A lifesaving source hidden beneath a façade of ugliness.

Auntie Beers 1920s and 30s

Urbston: Orange Town 1962

Auntie Beers taught us poems from the 1920s, the Depression and World War II. We sang about Ireland, a place we'd never seen. We believed we would've joined the IRA. We dreamt of the wild Atlantic Ocean.

From the war songs we learned about Hitler's balls, gas masks and the White Cliffs of Dover. Our great-aunt had never set foot in a country other than Ireland when she arrived in Canada. After that, she never ventured out of Ontario, let alone the country. Nor had she been to war. Yet she had a huge repertoire of songs, which she belted out in a pure, alto voice that seemed to suit every tune.

Hitler has only got one ball; Goring has two but very small; Himmler has something sim'lar, but poor old Goebbels has no balls at all.

"Back then prejudice was much more open in Canada than it is now," she told us. "These days we hide it under a cloak of politeness. In my time it was an accepted thing that the only religion was the Protestant faith. That all faces were white and all eyes were blue. Anyone who wasn't Protestant or white was considered strange."

As though it were yesterday, I remember when my mother wandered into the kitchen while Auntie Beers ranted about prejudice. Kathleen was tall and beautiful and her laugh infectious. This time her chuckle was rueful.

"Very true, Auntie, it was a white, non-Catholic world back then," she said. "I was so desperate to fit in that I used to make up weird stories about our religion. When we had to go to church, I would tell the kids at school that the priest would beat us severely if we didn't go. I didn't want them to know that my family chose to go to the catholic church."

My cousins and I sat in shock. My mother, perfect Aunt Kate to my cousins, told lies when she was a kid. My mother, Aunt Kate, whom the entire family adored for her intelligent, outgoing, witty nature, had been desperate to fit in.

At many family gatherings, Auntie Beers didn't tell stories. Her hand and mind were often too preoccupied with the sudsy alcohol in her glass. Our parents petted and abetted her. Buzzed around her as though she were a delicate vase that, if tipped over, would immediately shatter and release shards of glass to pierce us all.

Summer parades in Urbston were a family tradition. We watched every street event from Uncle John and Aunt Carol's house.

"Why do we have to go to their house again?" I whined at my mother before we left.

"They have no kids and they're on the parade route," my mother explained.

I complained that I didn't like Auntie Carol.

My mother continued fighting my little sisters into their shirts.

"You should be nicer to poor Auntie Carol. She wanted kids badly but was not blessed with them."

My mother sweated after her struggle with a squirming two-year-old and a five-year-old who liked to remain naked.

By the way Aunt Carol treated us during our visits, I had my doubts about her desire to procreate. Maybe it was the idea of kids that she liked but she certainly wasn't fond of the reality.

I picture us all now, as though it is a home movie.

All the kids lined up along the roadside. Our parents and Auntie Beers sat in lawn chairs or sprawled on the grass. No alcohol past the property line; therefore, no adults either.

We grinned at the clowns and scrambled for the candy flung our way. Aunts and uncles and cousins crowded the lawn. The adults slowly got louder. A bottomless fridge inside supplied beer to a cooler stationed on the driveway, handy to the side door. Auntie Beers presided in her chair on the porch. Matriarch. Queen for the day.

Uncle John danced in his wheelchair. The stump of his leg thrummed alongside the whole limb. His face was seared with scars, but he was still handsome. Those piercing blue eyes and dark black hair had miraculously not been spoiled by war.

Grace, Patrick, Mario and I took breaks from the parade to run after each other. Tumbled on the grass. Laughed and teased. Our families were from different ancestries but only by a few miles. European. White. Catholic. A couple of Protestants married in but had sworn to raise the children in the One True Church.

The parade stomped by all afternoon. We waved little flags on sticks, smaller versions of the big ones carried on two poles by younger marchers. Bright orange with a purple star, the flags were as coveted as a lollipop.

Bands hollered at us. Someone played a little black instrument that looked like a flute. Others tapped the drums strapped around their necks in time with the march, march, march of the men's boots.

The paraders were dressed in black with bright orange collarettes. Sashes formed an X on their chests. Little round hats sat atop their heads like curled kittens.

A big fellow with a round florid face and a neatly trimmed beard marched past distributing a flashy handout. I became aware that the sheet he offered was blank on the other side. To me, this empty page represented many lines of stories.

I reached out eagerly as he paused nearby. His eyes, round and cracked with red lines, gave me a strange sensation when he glared down at me. I was not used to pity and distaste. I was a beloved daughter.

He didn't touch me or say a word. Perhaps the way he shook his head as he reluctantly handed me a flyer communicated his disgust to Auntie Beers. Somehow, she knew.

Suddenly Auntie Beers was by my side, shoving me behind her. My cousins stepped back in alarm.

She was on him in a flash. Arms flailed. Fists punched. No choreography in this fight. An awkward beat. The tall thin woman a broomstick at his side. He easily swatted her away, laughing. Auntie Beers fell backward, landing hard on her rump. She screamed obscenities at him.

"Feckin' orangie," she yelled. "Go back to the ole country with yer proddywhoddy shite."

The man laughed louder. His fellow paraders laughed with him.

"Another drunken mackerel snapper," he sneered.

I was still right behind her, trying unsuccessfully to help her stand again, staring over her head at the man. When they both paused in a moment of frozen shock, I could see their faces. Tracks of memory snaked across their widened eyes. Mouths opened in a fruitless attempt to speak.

Although I was young, it was obvious from the body language, up this close to these two people, that they recognized each other.

Auntie Beers tried to get up but slipped back down in a sloppy heap. Spittle flew from her mouth. She spun around like a rabid dog.

Our dads, Steven and Marco, out-laws both, non-Irish, non-religious pacifists, hurried into the street. The two men picked Bairbre up by her armpits.

For a moment I saw her as the men in the parade did. Undignified. Sloppily drunk. A rubbie. Her mouth opened and closed exactly like a fish. I was astonished at the transformation from the person I knew.

Bairbre shook off her in-laws' help and straightened her slim, tall, glorious frame. Her wide shoulders and long neck. Once again, she was woman. Storyteller. Historian. Leader. Critic.

With great ceremony and grace, she settled back into her throne upon the porch. She smirked.

"I guess I told him," she said. "You can't let the proddies away with their shite. Get me a drink."

Uncle Michael handed her a fresh beer.

When Steven Doyle, my father, turned away from Bairbre to look toward me once more, I saw pity in his eyes. I felt dread and astonishment again. That anyone would dare to pity Auntie Beers.

"Stay back on the lawn, kiddos," he said to my cousins and me.

The next week, Auntie Beers taught us a new rhyme.

Up the long ladder and down the short rope,
To hell with King Billie,
Three cheers for the Pope!
Here's a needle, here's a thread,
To sew a pig's tail to an Orangeman's head.

When I recited the poem at dinner, my father looked sharply at my mother, pointing his fork for emphasis.

"I told you that woman is a bad influence."

"Aunt Bairbre is lonely, and she adores the kids," my mother said. "Besides, she's only laying out the history. This is an Orange town. Many Protestants have always felt hatred for Catholics."

My father shook his head, as though at a loss for an appropriate response.

"It's not our fault our parents picked this area to move into," she added as though to soothe him.

I noticed his brow unwrinkled somewhat.

"Why do we go to that Orange Parade if they hate us?" I asked.

My parents looked at one another. Shrugged.

"It's a parade. We like them," my father said. "And not all people have those feelings of hatred."

Which of course was no answer at all.

My mother shoved more food into my sister's mouth then used the spoon to mimic my father's method of drawing attention.

"However, Clare, there are some things we don't repeat in polite society."

Polite society? I looked around at my little sisters. My father in his sleeveless undershirt. My mother with baby food stuck to her lip. She seemed to read my mind.

"We don't spread hate. No matter who they are or who we think we are. And those poems are hateful."

I wasn't so sure that my mother was right. Hate spread even as you stood happily waving your flag at a parade.

Auntie Beers wasn't right either. People weren't so politely hiding their prejudice these days.

Not-A-Nine-Feet-High-Featherbed

Auntie Beers 1930s-1960s
By Clare O'Sullivan Doyle

Before Séamus and Maggie died and Auntie Beers moved to the Queen's Hotel, she lived with our grandparents in a two-story brick house on McManis Street. It was by far the largest home in which the family resided and the one that I remembered.

When they first arrived in Canada, Maggie, with five children in tow, assisted by Bairbre to cross the ocean, there were only shacks. Overcrowded tiny houses often without running water. An outhouse. A well.

Bairbre was often forced to room with strangers, on the same or a nearby farm. Sometimes as far as in town. Later, when they were able to get jobs in factories or the army, the family was able to move to McManis. At that age, I had no idea about Farmer Reid and the tragic illness that forced him to sell his business and property. I considered McManis a step up.

I was so young that these particular memories only play around the edges of my mind. At times dreamy and cloudy. At other times vivid and real.

The song 'Gramma's Featherbed' always conjures up the excitement of piling onto our grandparents' old bed that was neither nine feet high nor six feet wide but did have feathers in the mattress and upon which we could fit six or seven little cousins. We'd lie in rows heads-to-feet to save room. Talked about nothing. Teased. Giggled.

Downstairs the party roared. Our parents had survived the Depression as children for whom poverty was their skin. They hadn't known a different way of being. Suddenly the 50s and 60s brought them a level of wealth that, to them, was stunning. They celebrated for years until their middle-aged selves either cracked at the seams or they adopted a healthier lifestyle just in time.

For their children these years were a rollercoaster. The peaks were high and exhilarating but when the track turned downward, it was often frightening and dangerous.

My grandmother Maggie is one of those cloudy memories because she passed away when I was seven. Grandpa Séamus followed shortly afterward when I was ten. My Mom believed that her mother died of a broken heart over Liam's transgressions.

Yet behind my eyes the weeping willow clearly leans silver-green. Spreads its thick arms and thin branches all over the lawn. Sends ants to tickle my back and arms. Rectangular and narrow, the backyard is laden with crops. Tall lacey tomato plants and hairy cornstalks. Red stems of rhubarb. Of course, scraggly rows of potatoes. Afternoons and evenings of races up and down the adjacent lane. Nights cuddled face-to-face in the deep featherbed. These memories are all vivid.

Perhaps the responsibility of remembering a person is too important. Whereas a scene or an object can withstand the changes wrought by imagination. Perhaps for me the words from Auntie Beers have withstood the erosion of years better than the pictures.

Once she left the house for the Queen's Hotel, Auntie Beers told us endless McManis Street tales.

"We grew the sort of beefsteak tomatoes that you could make into a whole meal," she said. "Just add some salt and vinegar and you got yourself an awful good supper."

The old stove stood in the centre of the kitchen, unused in my childhood except as a holder for dirty dishes and washcloths.

"Sometimes we'd make a meal out of beets and butter," Auntie Beers told us.

She'd lick her lips as though the thought of real butter had sent her over the edge of memory and into desire.

Our older cousins told us stories of the best French fries. They came out hot, crisp and dripping with reused lard from an ancient frying pan heated by that very stove.

Picturing Auntie Beers stoking the fire to boil rhubarb and fry potatoes was not difficult. She loved to eat, and nothing would prevent her from making something, anything, into food.

"There were days when everything was arseways. No work on the farms because everything dried up. As long as the farmhands paid their rent, they could get a job somewhere else. Séamus got one on the railway," she told us. "It was simple grunt work. Men—of course only men in the nineteen forties—were hired by the dozens to travel on freight rail cars. They were each given a blanket and a small pillow."

The train would stop at places where weaknesses had been found in the railway line. These weaknesses usually were the deterioration of the wooden supports that the rails were laid on. Steel rails lasted almost forever. The wooden supports that they rested on had a much shorter life span. When these reached a certain point of deterioration, they had to be replaced. This involved lifting the rail off the track in order to fix any that had reached that stage. Each rail was six to ten meters long and weighed hundreds of pounds. Lifting them was the job of the grunt workers. Thirty or so men were required to move each one.

Workers ate and slept on the rail cars and were gone from home for two to four weeks. Bathroom facilities were non-existent.

"The jacks were the woods or a field of crops," Auntie Beers said to hoots from the boys and gasps from us girls.

The pay per grunt worker was about twenty dollars a week with the additional bonus of free meals. Séamus had never earned more than fifteen dollars a week, so twenty plus meals was a dream job.

"The catch…and remember, there's always a catch; nothing is ever free," Auntie Beers said, repeating her mantra as though we'd never heard it before. "Grunts didn't get paid until the end of the journey. This meant that at home, we were reduced to starvation levels until the men returned home with the abundance. John and Eddie signed up for the army in the late 1930s. Michael and Daniel in the early '40s. They were able to send us money, but it was never regular and wasn't enough. Peggy got a job in a munitions factory, but she moved to Toronto and didn't send much money home."

Often, our great-aunt would sit in her rocking chair and wave her cigarette around, as though smudging the air. Hers wasn't sacred tobacco, however; it was dark and oily and always made Grace cough.

"Kathleen went to college, but she worked part-time and full-time in the summer to help out. Food was expensive. Bread was nearly ten cents a loaf. Eggs eighteen cents a dozen and hamburger thirteen cents a pound. Maggie supplemented our food supply by hunting in the area for mushrooms. Sometimes I helped her. Someone told her that she had to be careful because many poisonous toadstools looked like mushrooms. Maggie was willing to take the risk. Dying from poisonous toadstools didn't seem any worse than dying of starvation."

She looked around to make sure we were paying attention.

"Once we discovered a crop of rhubarb close to the river. Those plants never seemed to stop producing stalks. There were times when we had nothing but rhubarb to eat."

A couple of my cousins took this as an exaggeration. A way to explain the difference between her life and ours. Perhaps it was, but I know from my mother that there were many months when all their money went to pay the rent. When the corn withered or potatoes weren't ready, the hardy rhubarb spread its green palms and red legs over the dry earth regardless.

"Have you ever eaten rhubarb without sugar?"

It was a measure of our easy childhood that we could imagine no greater pain than the vinegar taste of sugarless rhubarb.

"I had to get creative about how to cook that rhubarb for three meals a day."

"Tell us about the kids," I said to distract her from the days of near starvation.

This wasn't unusual. I often begged Auntie Beers to retell the stories of her nieces and nephews when they were just a little older than we were then. In adulthood, our uncles and aunts seemed so stiff and staid. We couldn't imagine them as they were in Auntie Beers' stories.

"Oh but Maggie's kids were wild in those days."

She always complied, always began with that same sentence.

What would follow sometimes differed in the details, but they were tales of daring do and excitement. Adventures and foolish deeds that were so outlandish I often wondered if they were true. Mario, Patrick, Grace and I could scarcely imagine our parents disobeying the rules in such ways. Or being cruel or thoughtless or foolish.

Although our mothers and fathers had a lot of fun, they had a rigid, very clear set of rights and wrongs for us kids. A strict system of reward and punishment ensured that usually we did what we were told and didn't question the rules at all. Most often we just learned to be sneaky and cover our tracks.

For me, Auntie Beers' stories, like all her tales, appeared as word pictures in my head. I didn't much care if they were true or not. I enjoyed them and replayed them endlessly.

Two-legged young John drives a jalopy. His light brown hair flows in the wind through missing windows. Sun darkens the freckles all over his nose. His mouth is wide open in an expression of fear mixed with bravado. Down the rickety wooden boards placed across the trestle bridge, he steers wildly. Crooked and barely under control. John's whole body jumps and trembles as the heap rumbles over the uneven logs and giant bolts. When he gets to the end, he turns sharply. Crashes along a dirt path until he reaches the top of the dam. Weaves in and out of hydro wires that droop so low they almost touch the roof of his car. His face is flushed red with excitement and the adrenaline rush of danger.

Peggy races after a chicken in the fenced-up coop yard. Dust and feathers fly in the air. Although she doesn't know this until someone discovers old family pictures, Peggy is built like her paternal grandmother who was born in France. Short and thin, Peggy is a little wisp of a thing physically but the opposite in personality. She's strong and stubborn and self-centered. Until she hears the song "Peggy O'Neill," she insists on being called Margaret.

"She kept demanding how on earth you could get Peggy from Maghread or Margaret," Auntie

*Beers said, pursing her lips in disapproval of Peggy's
lack of respect for a family moniker. "Your Grandda
told her it was the same with William and Bill.
People kept saying names like Maggie and Mag and
Willy and Will until they got twisted into Peggy and
Bill. Changed her mind when she heard that song.
Probably helped that a handsome lad from one of the
farms sang it and changed the lyrics to suit."*

*If her eyes are blue as skies, that's Peggy my girl.
If she's smiling all the while, that's Peggy my girl.
If she walks like a sly little rogue,
If she talks with a cute little brogue,
Sweet personality full of rascality,
That's Peggy my girl.*

"Peggy wasn't only full of rascality, she could be as
mean as she thought necessary to accomplish a task," said
Auntie Beers.

*The chicken continues to escape until Peggy
loses her temper. She throws the ax in its direction
and catches it square in the side with the blunt end.
Just as it scrambles back to its feet, she slices off its
head. Blood spurts everywhere. The chicken races
around the coop three more times before it falls, dead
weight, into the dust.*

*Peggy picks it up by the feet, triumphant.
"Supper!" she announces.*

Often, as my cousins and I slept in the big feather bed
at the McManis Street house, the voices downstairs would
awaken us in the dark. A change in tenor, a rise in volume.
Indistinguishable words that gave off waves of angry intent.

We'd snuggle in tighter together. Know in our hearts
that Uncle Daniel had plunged into his nightmares again.

Whereas John had left a leg behind in the war, Daniel had brought some extra burdens home with him. As far as I knew, the adults didn't seem to connect his experiences in battle and the amount he drank with the hallucinations that reverberated through his mind. Years later, his condition would be labelled post-traumatic stress disorder, which could be dealt with through therapy or pharmaceuticals.

When I was a child, however, our family simply accepted that this was Daniel and there was nothing to be done about him or his occasional tirades.

As I approached adulthood, I discovered that my cousins felt the same way I did. Afraid, ashamed. Bewildered. Add to that my very healthy imagination and those nights were terrifying.

Murmurs crescendoed into shouts. Unexplained sounds. Sometimes the muddy thud that may have been a punch landing on plasterboard. A shudder would move through me. Terrorized by the violence that made my body quiver with fear and indecision.

Very often during these fights, my mother would come upstairs to fetch us. She'd quietly and calmly direct us to put on our shoes and socks, grab our clothes and stuffed animals, pillows and anything else that belonged to us.

"Silent as mice," she said, though I didn't think mice were silent.

My cousins and I slipped down the stairs behind her, clutching our belongings, barely breathing. Whenever a step squeaked or someone sneezed, my heart would pound fiercely in my ears. Never once did Daniel stop us on the staircase, but the sounds of his tortured anger and madness increased with every downward movement. We remained in terror of those advances in the dark.

On each occasion, when my mother hustled us out onto the front porch, I marvelled at how a change in atmosphere could alter the landscape. This porch, often that very evening, was the site of much laughter and energy.

"Look at the stars and hear the cars!" we would yell.

Silently we'd stare up at the sky, searching for stars that could hide behind moonlight or clouds or appear like a blanket of twinkling dots. If we heard a car approach on the road, off we ran to scramble together on the porch, duck behind the wooden wall before the headlights touched us.

When Uncle Daniel shouted and raved, when he threatened and bullied, the porch looked small and incapable of hiding us from the torch of his madness. My mother and one of the aunts or uncles would usually get us to our respective vehicles. We would huddle in the back seats and wait for the storm to pass. Wait for our parents to either wrestle Daniel's demons to a manageable level or sneak out to join us.

We'd often peek through the windshield into the living room where the struggle ensued. Once in a while, Daniel would hover in the doorway, screaming obscenities at his siblings. On those occasions we scrunched down on the car floor, holding our breath.

I never really knew how Daniel's children felt. Aunt Colleen always kept her eyes straight ahead and impassive. Her children copied her.

Once, as adults and very close to the same age, my cousin Mary spoke about her now deceased parents.

"They tried their best," she said, "with the tools they had and the baggage they inherited."

Grace, the cousin to whom I am closest, and the one to whom everyone told their secrets, never said a word about whether or not Mary revealed their trauma to her.

Feisty and blunt, Grace was similar in personality to Mario's mother, our Aunt Peg, as a girl. At least the one Auntie Beers related to us. Grace did have some of the temperament of her father, Eddie, who was always kind and supportive.

My cousin became a clinical psychologist. Worked in wards with people who had forgotten how to cooperate or relate or adopt any of the behaviors that community required. Perhaps this was a way for her to control or prevent what happened to our uncle.

Most of the time when Daniel had his outbursts, the only person who could unruffle him was Auntie Beers. Creeping down those stairs, I would almost always glance into the living room on my left.

Auntie Beers sat in her old rocking chair, long slim legs crossed, dangling a cigarette from between her yellowed fingers. She spoke in low calm tones to Daniel while he whirled around in circles. Shaking his fist at one or the other of his siblings until they all had left the room.

Through the windshields of our vehicles, John, Michael, Eddie, Peg, Kathleen, Brigid and families would wait until they knew Daniel and Auntie Beers—and before they died, Séamus and Maggie—were safe from the threat of violence. Only then would we all drive across town to our own homes.

Like a drive-in movie theatre without sound, the action played out in predictable ways.

> *Daniel: mouth opens in a torturous rerun of witnessed and experienced horror.*
>
> *Auntie Beers: placid, chain smoking; head nods in implicit understanding without judgment.*
>
> *Daniel: shoulders fold over in defeat; tears take the place of shouts.*
>
> *Auntie Beers: stands up. Places her hands on those overwhelmed shoulders.*

Daniel: turns toward her. A man vanquished by the power of the harm that men can do to other men.

Auntie Beers: takes him in her arms as she once did when he was a little boy, defeated by the things that boys can do to other boys.

Prison Visit

Lorenzo 1959
Urbston 1950s-60s:
by Clare O'Sullivan Doyle

Lorenzo Malpensa flips the snaps on his lunch pail with a resounding pop. The sound gives him a sense of satisfaction. Determination. A signal that he is ready to face this day with energy and motivation.

He tiptoes into the bedroom and kisses Carla's soft sleeping face. She is the reason he gets up every morning and goes to work. Nowadays the second reason sleeps in the crib beside their bed. Lorenzo leans down to smooth the blanket over his baby son and stares at the little miracle.

At least at this moment he is. His eyelashes splash over his cheek. His little chest rises and falls in fast sleep. Last night as the infant turned purple with rage and screamed into their frustrated ears, he was not such a miracle.

Normally Carla gets up and has a coffee with Lorenzo, but today she needs the extra rest. Their little apartment is stuffy with sweat and baby puke. Lorenzo is happy to open the door and breathe in the fresh air.

Other than a few people rushing toward the train station to work in Toronto, Urbston is dead asleep. Most of the residents work in town, either for the Robus Estate or the Civitas Federal Prison. Most often known as the Urbston Jail.

Lorenzo never imagined he would remain in the town of his birth. Become a prison cop. Get married. Be a father. Every day he is amazed to wake up beside someone as beautiful and glamorous as Carla Baros.

Although he knows he is good-looking, there are lots of other lads who are downright handsome. Like Lorenzo's friend Michael O'Sullivan for instance. The bastard went off to college on top of having those smoky blue eyes and thick hair. A war medal and one small, easily hidden scar to prove his bravery.

Lorenzo always imagines that if Michael had stayed in town, Carla would have married him instead. Michael disagrees.

"You're the ladies' man," Michael has often told Lorenzo. "I'm the nerd. I'll never get married. You'll have a nice family and be happy ever after."

Up until recently, Michael was right. Suddenly, the guy up and married Raeni, his childhood sweetheart, and moved to Toronto. They were a highly successful career couple.

And up until recently, Lorenzo had been very happy.

Robberies and a few break-ins, an occasional fire set at the school, some domestic problems. These are—were—the most common crimes and misdemeanors around the small town. Most of the time, these crimes are handled by the local police, which consists of a rather portly chief and his slow-witted deputy. Then along came Urbston's biggest crime spree ever.

From what the cops can tell so far, robbery is the prime motive. They mostly go for cash and booze. Any accompanying violence or destruction appears to be purely entertainment. Lorenzo believes he knows who the culprits are. Or at least one of them.

In his opinion, Lorenzo's family shines over Michael O'Sullivan's for one reason. Siblings. There are only two Malpensa children, Lorenzo and his sister Fiorella. (A dearth of offspring being more proof that they are one of a minority of non-Catholic Italians, which is a huge plus in this particular neck of the woods.)

Despite being rather plain and plump, Fiorella has a solid marriage to a Robus son. Lorenzo figures it's a good match since David is plain and plump too.

Robus Estates has taken the focus off a sordid and unsavory history when the town agreed to allow the stink of a federal prison in its midst.

For all those of English descent—and they were the majority—the name of the appointed Warden does not help generate respect. Glen Luckinbill is a huge man, both in body and voice. He reminds the many Yorkshire transplants, for better or for worse, that they might have descended from the Vikings. Some of them even know that he was born in Giggleswick, a fact that has provided years' worth of jokes. As for the rest of the English who are one or no generation away from the old country, they are amused that a "Bill" could be endowed with luck.

Over time, acres of greenhouses transformed Urbston's down market status into "the flower town of Canada" and currently employs hundreds of people.

Fiorella is the head of several ladies' groups and has enormous social influence. They even play cards with the mayor and his wife. Lorenzo and Carla often bask in her glow.

Meanwhile, the O'Sullivans may have a war hero, but they also have Liam. Although Lorenzo would never say so out loud, Liam O'Sullivan makes him feel proud and superior. The youngest of eight kids, Catholics all, Liam is wild. By the age of sixteen, he'd been carted home by the police more times than Lorenzo can count.

The O'Sullivans live in Riverside, in a house on the Reid farm. Their father, Séamus, is well respected by the farmers in the region. Therefore Liam commits all his crimes in Urbston.

"The lure of the big city," Police Chief O'Malley has been heard to say, as though the little town were a hotbed of sin and misbehavior.

In Lorenzo's opinion, Liam O'Sullivan has a calling card: wanton destruction. The kind that many of the prisoners in Urbston Jail exhibit before they escalate into murder. When Liam is away, living elsewhere or perhaps in someone else's prison, the robberies are normal.

The thieves don't bother to leave a trail of shit or break family photos or smash mirrors. Instead, they politely go in and out. Wipe their feet on the mats. Take possession only of those items the owners might not miss too much or would provide quick cash.

One day, however, Liam returns and so do the malicious crimes. Lorenzo happens to meet up with the kid, who is now in his early twenties, in front of the Queen's Hotel.

"Got yourself a suck bag, eh, 'Renzo?"

Lorenzo turns to look at the tall, thin young man who smokes and leans languidly against the wall.

Liam O'Sullivan is movie star handsome. Even better looking than his older brother Michael. Blond hair dusted with darker strands of brown. Freckles that give him an innocent, sweet look. Eyes the color of a sky lit by soft sunlight.

Most people would think him angelic if they judged from his exterior. Many women have wanted to take care of him. Often too late, they realize that you need to look deeply into those eyes to see the hints of cruelty underneath.

Liam, tall and broad-shouldered, is so fit that Lorenzo has no trouble picturing him vaulting over a neighbor's fence to break in through the back door.

Lorenzo gives him his guard's quizzical glance. A raised eyebrow and silence.

Liam points to the lunch pail.

"Working stiff suck bag," he says, as though Lorenzo has asked the question.

When he responds, Lorenzo uses a flat, quiet tone that implies a simple statement of fact.

"Better than a jail mate's suck."

Most cons turn purple with anger when he uses this technique on them, but it doesn't work with Liam. He simply tosses his cigarette butt on the sidewalk. He chortles dismissively. Walks away.

That very day Lorenzo's boss tells them about the sudden crime spree and the help the federal guards are to provide.

"This unsavory and shocking crisis of violent crimes," Warden Luckinbill announces, "has forced Chief O'Malley to ask the feds for help. Which of course means us. Any of youse who want extra work, you're welcome to sign up."

Lorenzo nudges Brian Cottreau, his shift partner.

"What do you think, partner? Can we catch these thieving bastards?"

Brian nods happily, so Lorenzo signs them up. Carla isn't exactly happy, but he convinces her by adding up the extra money. Lorenzo knows exactly who is spiking the crime stats. Not only does he like a boost in salary he also secretly envisions capturing Liam in the act. Being the hero.

Brian and Lorenzo spend several fruitless double shifts chasing the thieves whenever they strike. The problem is the cops are always after the fact and there are no clues left behind. The robberies don't require a great deal of skill. Small town residents aren't in the habit of locking up. Unlocked or open windows are common. People go off to work and leave the door unlatched.

Most often missing are the contents of piggy banks or money from under a mattress. Several bottles of whiskey or beer or homemade hootch. Once in a while a necklace that had been handed down a couple of generations.

"They must have to take the bus to Hogtown to hawk that stuff," Lorenzo theorizes when they first discover a theft of jewelry.

Which isn't exactly brilliant deduction, though Brian, with his half English, half French vocabulary, tends to misunderstand most directions. Which leads him to do whatever Lorenzo tells him to do. This suits Lorenzo just fine and, in his opinion, makes them a good team. His leadership, Brian's heft.

The first time Lorenzo notices Liam's calling card, he confidently points it out to his partner.

"Look here, Brian," he says in what he considers his most officious tone. "Human excrement."

"What?" Brian asks, staring down at what appears to be a small pile of dried-up mud.

"Shit."

There's still a hesitation as Brian leans over to sniff.

"Crap. Caca. Merde."

"Doesn't have the *odeur* of *merde*," Brian says doubtfully.

"It's been there a while. And I know exactly who did this."

His partner gapes in what Lorenzo believes is admiration.

"You do?"

"Yup. Not saying just now, mind you, but remember this moment. Remember to mark my words."

Lorenzo knows exactly why he doesn't mention his theory to the Warden or the Chief. He plans to take the glory for himself, with a side dish for Brian. Most men don't like Lorenzo, he realizes, for reasons he can't comprehend. Carla says they are jealous, and she is usually right.

After all, she is right when she lectures him about being so obsessed with Liam O'Sullivan that he has begun ignoring her and the baby.

Their shift is normally 7 a.m. to 3 p.m. Lorenzo and Brian decide to take a 7 p.m. to midnight shift too. At first only two days a week; then suddenly it's more like five. Lorenzo doesn't tell Carla that a couple of those shifts aren't Luckinbill authorized.

They patrol the streets on foot and sometimes in Brian's car. Urbston shuts down around 9 p.m. most nights.

"You could make a piste de bowling in the Main rue," Brian says.

He repeats the joke many times because initially Lorenzo completely misinterprets the phrasing. Brian now thinks of himself as hilarious and witty.

It is quite true, though, that the main street, creatively called Main Street, is normally devoid of traffic of any kind, vehicle, horse, or people. You really could throw a bowling ball down the street and not hit any person or object. Yet somehow the thieves manage to break into streets where not only homes are vacant, but the cops and the feds are not on patrol.

Lorenzo decides they must be spying from the Queen's Hotel. He and Brian march up and down the halls but of course the doors are all shut once someone shouts, "po-lice" from a stairwell. When they're called to a break-in, they search the homes as though the victims are the perpetrators. Ask intrusive questions as they comb areas that aren't even touched by the thieves.

Warden Luckinbill gets a few complaints, but not many.

"Go a bit easy, boys," he says with a wink.

After a while Lorenzo believes that Liam is leaving messages for him. A toy police badge is broken in half and left on a side table. A red stripe painted down a wall. Once, a ham hock left out on the kitchen table with a neatly printed note in red crayon: "For the pigs." A hunting rifle sits on a chair pointing at the front door. "Bang, I got you" says the note, this time printed in pencil. Lorenzo can almost hear Liam's laughter.

A copious amount of booze goes missing. Many victims don't officially report this to the police. Urbston remains, ironically, a dry town, though you wouldn't know it from the amount of drinking that goes on. If they just want a pint or a glass of whiskey, they visit people at the Queen's Hotel. Everyone is forced to drive to Flavio Fumagalli's Pub in Riverside if they want a substantial amount.

Loosely translated as "blow smoke at chickens," Fumagalli mostly blows smoke at the law by selling beer, wine and liquor from behind the bar. To preserve some propriety, Flavio has a gents' entry and a ladies-with-gents' entrance. He used to have a sign that said, "Irish Catholics not permitted," but he quickly learned that this was bad for business.

The townspeople are quite honest with Lorenzo about the alcohol they are missing. They trust a man who has grown up in the town and has such a prestigious job. Plus, Lorenzo knows he can be very charming, and he uses it well.

"Seventeen bottles, Paddy?" he asks, ensuring that his tone is not pejorative.

"Aye," the older man replies.

His face is wrinkled with remorse and anger.

"Jesus, Mary and Joseph, we'll be having nothing for the holidays."

"Any idea who…?"

"Haven't a baldy notion."

Along with the booze, cash and jewelry are the items most commonly stolen. The Montreal Bank has never been so popular. Despite the fact that accounts cost a few pennies, the bank is suddenly a lot more trustworthy than a mattress or a freezer.

No one has any ideas to offer about the transgressors until a couple of serendipitous incidents.

One particular night, the moon is especially dazzling. A giant spotlight on the town. Tim Doyle steps right into it by sheer coincidence. Not only that, but Chief O'Malley calls the Warden for assistance, meaning this shift is Luckinbill sanctioned.

Brian and Lorenzo meet Tim in his driveway. Skinny with a fair height on him, the man literally shakes all over. He reminds Lorenzo of a twig tossed in a whirlwind breeze.

"I was coming back from my mate's, you know him, 'Renzo, Johnny O'Connor, right?"

Lorenzo nods and stays silent so Tim will keep the tale going.

"And by god, out of my own front door saunters Frank McCarthy. As though he owns the place. Two bottles of my finest whiskey in his arms, one of which he's suckin' on like it's his mother's teat."

Tim takes a deep, shuddering breath as though the sight of Frank gulping down that whiskey is the worst thing he's ever seen. Lorenzo would bet the whole of his overtime salary that that bottle didn't come from Johnny O'Connor's homemade still at the Queen's Hotel but from behind the bar at Fumagalli's. Flavio imports some fine whiskey.

"Good thing Verna and the kiddies are spending a couple of days at her mother's."

"Though if they had been home, you would not have had the pillage," Brian says.

Tim is about to be sidetracked by this obscure and irrelevant comment.

"What did you do?" Lorenzo prompts.

"Well, I give him chase, didn't I?"

Tim gapes as though this course of action should have been obvious and he's gob-smacked that Lorenzo doesn't know it. He points to the back yard.

"They took off out back and into the woods."

"They?"

"Yah, there was three of the buggers. Two of them left by the back door so Frank was the only one I recognized."

"How long ago was this?"

Tim scratches his head.

"Fifteen, twenty minutes. Soon as they crashed into the woods, I gave it up. Luckily, they left the one full bottle behind, so..."

He holds the whiskey up like a prize.

Brian and Lorenzo look at each other briefly. Grab their flashlights and take off into the trees. Tim sputters and spins but doesn't follow them. They crash into the bush in a haphazard fashion.

Lorenzo streaks off ahead of Brian, his heart pumping with adrenalin. Instead of seeing dark branches that reach out to scratch his face and hands, Lorenzo pictures tackling Liam O'Sullivan. Shoving the bastard's face in the rotten detritus of the forest floor.

Anger and hatred fuel his zigzag through the woods. He's running so fast that he almost trips over Frank McCarthy.

Small and thin, huddled in a fetal position, the man is nearly invisible in the dark brush. If not for Frank's loud sobs, Lorenzo might have stepped right on him. When he pulls the guy out of the bush by the collar, Frank cradles the half empty whiskey bottle as though it were a child. Lorenzo lets go and Frank curls up on Tim's lawn.

At that moment Brian stumbles out of the forest with Herman van der Berg. The prison guard is able to hang onto the taller man because of the handcuffs that yank his arms backward. Herman falls flat on his face.

"I broke my neck! I broke my neck!" he hollers into the grass.

"Dagnabit, Frank, why'd you have to drink my best whiskey, you pisser?" Tim snarls. "You stupid git. Berk. Arsehole."

Tim continues to relentlessly bark obscenities at the man. Each word becomes progressively harsher. Frank sobs even louder.

Lorenzo has finally had enough.

"Go on, Tim, get back into yer house."

Points as though the man may have forgotten where he lives.

"We'll take the arseholes to the jail."

Frank wails uncontrollably at this and curls up tighter. Despite his broken neck, Herman allows Brian to help him stand.

"Where's Liam?" Lorenzo snaps at the two prisoners.

Herman just shakes his head, but Frank sputters through his tears. Doesn't bother to deny Liam's involvement. Though his words are harsh, he says them like a cry of self-pity.

"Off in them woods. Kid's a sprinter. Bastard."

Lorenzo has a moment of indecision. He badly wants to go after Liam, despite the dark and the odds against. He believes the two in hand don't equal the one in the bush, but he knows the Chief and the Warden won't agree.

Both men are disappointed that O'Malley isn't on duty when they file Herman and Frank into their holding cells.

"He didn't deny that Liam's involved," Lorenzo says as he and Brian start the trek home.

"You said this," Brian replies.

Lorenzo takes it as a compliment, an acknowledgement of his premonition about Liam all along.

"He's still out there."

Lorenzo says this in an aggrieved tone, as though Liam's getaway is a personal affront.

Carla and Lorenzo have another row when he gets home. Where he expects admiration and applause, he receives a bollocking instead. The quarrel is all the more insidious as it's conducted in whispers to avoid awakening Junior.

The baby has been fussy all day. Carla hasn't had a break. All Lorenzo does is work, take extra shifts. He is obsessed with O'Sullivan, she hisses, more than he cares about his wife and son.

Over the next three weeks, Lorenzo toes the line. He goes to work and comes right home afterward. Helps with the baby, even once changing a diaper. Urine only, thank you, son.

He doesn't offer to join the extra forces who comb the forest and search for Liam amid the acres of glass greenhouses. Some sections of the woods, Brian tells him later, aren't searched properly in his opinion.

"Those hills, they go down into the re-ven and I hear the boys don't want to fall in the water."

It takes Lorenzo a moment to realize that re-ven is the French pronunciation for ravine. Not that he blames the buggers for avoiding those steep ditches. He's more and more convinced that Liam has found himself a sweet hiding place.

When the judge takes Frank to trial, he spills everything. Still sobbing. Herman has no choice but to plead guilty too. They are sentenced to two years in jail, which Lorenzo thinks is unfair. They'll probably get conditional releases in one.

Initially Herman and Frank are placed in the same section of the prison, but their loud arguments force the guards to separate them. Whenever Lorenzo has the chance, he continues to ask the two men where they think Liam could be. He encourages them to give up the mastermind of the crimes, but they consistently claim they don't know anything about a hiding spot.

"It's getting colder," Frank says. "I don't know how he can still be out there."

"Unless you know about a cozy little hideaway tucked into those woods," Lorenzo says.

Something flashes in Frank's eyes but it's so fleeting that Lorenzo can't pinpoint what it means. The little man refuses to speak again.

Despite Lorenzo's efforts at coming home on time, Carla's moods worsen. The baby cries constantly. Finally, Doctor Webster dispenses some kind of liquid and a daily pill, for Junior and his mother respectively. He also instructs Carla to switch to formula, which the doctor swears is much healthier for infants. As well, Lorenzo can feed his son for bonding purposes. Of course, Lorenzo does not argue with any of this.

Almost immediately, Carla floats happily around the house. Junior smiles and gets fatter. Lorenzo becomes confused and resentful. Not only does he bring home the bacon he gets to cook it too, he thinks.

A few times, Carla hands him the baby the moment he arrives home from work. She floats out the door.

"Need to pick up some things at Loman's," his wife says as she glides past him and down the street to the grocers.

Lorenzo discovers that the bonding thing is kind of fun. He bounces Junior on his knee. Sings to him when they're alone.

Nearly forty days after Liam disappeared, Lorenzo doesn't even notice that Carla gets home late from the grocers. On the afternoon shift this week, he has to scramble to get ready for work. He can only hope Brian gets there on time to relieve the other guards, or there will be hell to pay.

Sure enough, when Lorenzo reaches the prison gates, Brian stands there grinning at him.

"Have a late *partie rapide* with the wife?" he smirks.

Lorenzo translates this into a reference to quick sex. He grimaces.

"Not *rapide—rien*," he answers with one of the words he has learned from his partner, though his pronunciation leaves Brian extremely uncertain about the meaning.

"I punched you," he says.

This means, presumably, that Brian has punched Lorenzo's timecard into the clock, which means he won't lose any hours.

"Thanks, Buddy."

Lorenzo puts his lunch pail on the bench. He gazes into the prison yard, which is suffused in sunshine, but deserted. This is the end of afternoon visiting hours, but it seems that no one has left yet.

"All quiet today?"

Brian nods and checks a list.

"Not many visitors," he answers. "No combat. All bien."

They are silent for a moment. Cherish the infrequent calm of the prison.

"Here is something *interessant*," Brian finally says. "Frank and Herman have a visitor."

"They do? Herman's father?"

Brian shakes his head.

"A lawyer?"

"Non. Some guy. Tall bugger. Beard and a wool cap on his head. *Un ami?*"

"Didn't know they had any friends," Lorenzo says. "Except…"

At that moment, the visitors' door opens and a couple of women saunter out. Seconds later they are followed by a tall thin man with a wool cap and a straggly blond beard.

"Hello, Liam," Lorenzo says pleasantly.

The kid looks like he might try to run, but one glance at Brian Cottreau's bulk blocking the exit convinces him otherwise. He settles comfortably onto a bench and holds his hands out to be cuffed. Smiles pleasantly.

"What the hell were you thinking, O'Sullivan?"

"Figured the boys deserved a prison visit." Liam smiles. "Besides, it was starting to get cold in the…out there."

Lorenzo wants to be happy he has his man, but this is not the hero capture he'd envisioned.

Liam looks around affably and eyes Lorenzo's lunch pail.

"Still got the suck bag, I see," he says amiably.

Lorenzo pulls the kid to his feet and marches him into a holding cell. There is no one around to see.

The next day, and all the days after that, Lorenzo brings his dinner in a paper bag.

Twisted Sister

Urbston 1961
by Clare O'Sullivan Doyle

I've heard a lot of people say they would kill for a drink. Or a cigarette. Or a cup of tea. I've never heard one say they'd kill for a sibling.

My sister Fiona was quintessentially beautiful for our era and place. Marilyn Monroe of the future. Blond hair, blue eyes, full lips, a perfectly shaped nose. She could act, too. Those eyes filled with tears at any minor tease.

"You're a stupid pig," for instance, brought rivers of water down her perfect cheeks. Not that I, the often thoughtless, cold-hearted older sibling, cared.

When we were kids, there was no talk of sexual harassment. At least I never heard those words. Male attention was something females had to suffer through. My sister's beauty, even as a very young girl, brought her nothing but attention from boys and men. Jealousy and hatred from the girls.

Even Auntie Beers made drunken reference to her loveliness. In a suspicious sort of way. I remember the comment clearly, as I sat on the floor looking up at her. Perched on the side of her bed in the Queen's Hotel, she smoked and talked.

On this occasion, one of the few when I was there with my parents and not my cousins, Auntie Beers applied her deep critical look with practiced skill. It was in the narrowing of the eyes. The toss of that luxurious main of greying red hair like a lid over a box of opinions written by people much wiser than we. The slight sneer of an upturned lip. The confident way she held her head. She knew she was right.

"These lasses," she said, as though being a girl meant trouble just by the fact of our genitals. "They look so innocent with their blond hair and big blue eyes. But they're probably trouble. You be on the watch, Kathleen." She shook her head at my mother. "They could be acting the maggot. Getting into big trouble. Innocence is only skin deep."

Auntie Beers' pronouncement was both a curse and a prediction.

Though trouble is not always hidden. Sometimes it's very obvious.

Samuel Beasley suited his name. He was a beast. Tall, lumbering, wide-shouldered. A slack mouth and thick lips. He used his size and his swagger to bully everyone in the yard at Mary of the Angels Elementary. Through the fence, he'd taunt the kids in the public-school next door.

"Catholics, Catholics, ring the bell, Protestants, Protestants, go to hell," he'd holler.

Over and over like a virus until it caught everyone else in its grip. Until we all chanted. Became a mob. Even me in my tentative, frightened whisper.

He'd entice some poor sucker to put his face close enough to the fence for a good punch. More often than not, blood spurted. Protestants never learned not to confront Sam Beasley.

We Catholics did, though. We were always on the alert as we walked to and from school. Sam Beasley stood on one corner or another to confront the unlucky bastards who crossed his line of sight.

My friend Debbie mentioned the short cut through the ravine when I complained that we got home so late I missed certain television shows. Cutting diagonally from the schoolyard, alongside the river, to the street that led home would save a lot of time. None of the school kids took that route. Not even Samuel Beasley.

The culvert had been created to divert floodwaters away from the city's downtown area. Hence its name, The Diversion, which had become synonymous with forbidden.

Sculpted concrete slanted down to the river. On the school side, trees blocked the view of homes. A weedy pathway, trampled by feet of the past, curved around this edge of the forest. On the other side, the slope spread upward toward more clumps of trees that hid the city dump.

Though the Wadopika River only flooded once every hundred years, it had happened during our lifetime and was therefore always a threatening possibility.

The air was always different by the creek. Musty. Earthy. Human voices were absent, leaving room for cicadas to rattle their tails. For frogs to grumble and Canada geese to complain and shit.

Part of the fear of The Diversion was the water: it had swallowed many a school child according to the teachers at Mary of the Angels. Sometimes slow and shallow and benign, it could rise without notice into a roaring menace.

The other part of the fear was that it was forbidden territory. We'd all been warned on numerous occasions to stay away from the diversion. Both the school authorities and our parents constantly lectured about the danger. If we got caught, we faced punishment both at school and at home.

For me, once I was down there, I found the walk relaxing and peaceful. I had to watch my sister even more carefully of course, but we saved so much time that I didn't mind her ambling saunter. When we'd reach the hill that led to the street toward our house, I often had to half-carry, half-drag Fiona with me in my hurry. Reaching that hill caused me to be terrified by my own transgression. It was here that someone might see us emerge and tattle on me.

After several journeys through the shortcut I had the feeling that we were being watched. It took me a while to notice Sam. Despite his size, he was clever at hiding in the trees. Moved only when we moved. Stayed just far enough behind.

Sam Beasley had never, as far as I knew, used the path. No one to torment down here but frogs and geese. It was like seeing the priest or a teacher in a swimsuit. I didn't recognize him at first. No longer a pop-up toy, a scary clown or a weasel. He was a coiled and hidden reptile.

There was one thing I thought I knew about Sam Beasley, however. Not once had he taunted a girl. I had never noticed the same voraciousness in him that the other boys exhibited toward Fiona. For that reason and others I never defined, I did not stop using the shortcut despite the first sighting of the beast. I began to think of the path as mine. A place that was quiet and deserted and water kissed. My secret. My Diversion. A way to put Fiona in a little bit of danger without really taking much of a chance that she'd get hurt.

Samuel Beasley stalked us for weeks. Never jumped out to scare us. Never shook his fist. I began to wonder what this meant. Was he more dangerous than I thought? Would a bully try to tease and torture a couple of young girls without an audience? I doubted it. Perhaps that's what he was waiting for: an audience. He wouldn't find one down here.

Fiona obliviously followed my tracks. Gazed around with her big innocent eyes and muttered.

We shouldn't be here. We're not supposed to be here. Mom said.

Tell Mom and I will kill you.

Her long fair hair trailed in wind and shone in sunshine. Her face was guileless and pure. Lovely. Her body soft and innocently inviting.

The walks through that ravine became a test of will. I would protect my right to be here. I would protect my sister if Sam tried to bully us. I would march along without fear. I would not let him see me even flinch.

On the day he attacked, we were almost at the street. Halfway up the hill to safety. From all those days of defiance, I had built up a momentum that filled my chest. Pumped up my arms and legs. Made me a machine with a mission and no hesitation. I was ready for him.

I didn't count on the difference in strength. I was tall and lean but had nothing of the muscle mass that was Samuel Beasley. He moved like a freight train toward us, grinning all the way.

I had also misjudged his intentions. When I saw his eyes up close, I knew. I had made a terrible mistake. I also knew I was not the object of his intent.

Ripe, that look told me. Delicious.

He swept Fiona into his arms. Threw her over his shoulder firefighter style and slammed me with his right arm. I fell flat on my butt. The landing reverberated through my bones.

He stood over me and laughed while Fiona screamed and struggled.

Neither of us had counted on my sister's strength, however. She bit down on his ear until he shrugged her off, howling in pain. Fiona rolled down the hill to the grass, sobbing. Blood poured from the side of his face and clung to her lips.

I scrambled to my feet. Threw myself at his back. Kicked and scratched. He twisted his body and grasped my feet. Yanked me to the ground. Samuel crashed down on top of me, pinning me with his weight. Laughed in my face.

Stupid little girl.

As he raised his head to laugh with delight, perform for a non-existent audience, he began to pull down his zipper. Both actions put him off balance and one-armed.

I wormed up, hard. Head butted him on the chin. He rolled over instinctively.

Next thing I knew, Fiona was there. Splayed on the ground and wide open, Sam was vulnerable. She kicked him squarely between his legs. Her little feet became weapons in her rubber-soled boots. He screeched in fury and pain. Staggered to his feet.

I got my balance before he did and shoved him. Hard. Arms windmilling, he stumbled backward. Further down the hill.

I shoved him again.

Samuel Beasley, carried by the weight of imbalance and his stocky body, somersaulted over the embankment.

Fiona and I ran to the edge.

Over and over he tumbled. Blood poured from his head as he hit the concrete sides of the diversion. He sank into the water without a word. The only sound a splash that echoed along the deserted path. The Wadopika River swallowed another student.

Fiona sobbed and wiped at the blood on her lip. I took a tissue from my pocket and removed it with a little spittle. We stared at one another for a while.

I didn't have to threaten her with death about not telling Mom. I didn't have to say a thing.

They searched for Samuel Beasley for days. No one could guess where he'd gone.

Someone told the principal that Sam had been taking the shortcut. Debbie mentioned to the teacher that I had been down there, too. With Fiona.

Auntie Beers was right. Innocence is only skin deep. Big blue eyes can hide, deep down, big trouble. After questioning Fiona and me, no one suspected our involvement at all. I had talked about taking the shortcut, I admitted, but I obeyed the rule. Fiona said she didn't understand the questions. What was The Diversion?

When they found Sam's body downstream a couple of weeks later, they assumed he'd been the victim of his own tomfoolery. Taking the power of the water for granted.

Which was the truth. He had certainly engaged in foolish behavior.

Announcements were made over the school public address system to reiterate that the shortcut along the river was forbidden. Dangerous. Even to someone like Samuel Beasley. Students were warned never to walk that way to or from school.

Fiona and I never did. Again.

Death in the Yard

Urbston 1963
By Clare O'Sullivan Doyle

Lorenzo is late again. Fortunately, despite years of doing so, his partner Brian hasn't tired of covering his friend's ass.

Brian Cottreau is thirteen years younger than Lorenzo Malpensa, but they have a great deal in common. They were both raised in Urbston. They both love to watch hockey and television. They are both interested in their jobs, not simply as a job, but as a career. They study the prisoners and attempt to guide those who are open to therapy or chànging their behavior on their own.

Brian continues to be grateful to his pal for the kind, patient training that he provided a Quebec-born young guard who had difficulty adapting to English. Brian was shunned and teased by most of the other guards because he was French, so Lorenzo's kindness gave Brian a lifelong devotion to the older man. When Lorenzo Junior was born, Brian instantly adored the baby, and nowadays, the motherless little boy.

These days, morning shifts are the worst for Lorenzo. He has to get Lorenzo Junior to school, a process that includes cajoling, pleading, tricking, and scolding. Threats to take away television privileges usually work, though Lorenzo hesitates to use this technique. He actually enjoys the relaxation and laughter they share in front of the small screen after dinner. Sometimes during dinner, if truth be told. Often with Brian.

Ever since Carla left them, LJ has been moody and unpredictable. Lorenzo finds this surprising, since his mother barely paid attention to him even as an infant. There is something to be said about carrying them around as part of your own body, he thinks. A father cannot replace that no matter what they do.

Lorenzo sweeps through the prison doors and pats Brian on the shoulder. They grin at one another.

"LJ is giving trouble this morning?" Brian asks.

Even after years in Ontario, he has retained his Quebec accent, which makes everything he says charming. At least to Lorenzo and LJ.

"He was really ornery today," Lorenzo confirms. "The teacher says she'll try to impress upon him the importance of being on time. I told her that if he doesn't do it for himself, he should do it for me. And you. I told him that if it weren't for Uncle Brian, Daddy might have been fired by now."

Brian has never married. Nor as far as Lorenzo knows, even dated anyone. He seems to be a-sexual, rarely making an off-color joke, though he sometimes laughs when someone else tells one. He makes an excellent uncle for LJ and the best friend Lorenzo has ever had.

The prison is quiet this morning. All the usual routines, checking the rooms, filing in and out for breakfast, proceed smoothly. No contraband or homemade weapons. The men appear subdued by the summer heat. They do their jobs with few complaints. In the exercise yard, they lean against the walls in the shade, smoking. Play a restrained game of basketball. Even their conversations are low key.

Lorenzo stands in the sun, his face shaded by the peak of his hat. Turns this way and that to keep an eye on as many of the men as he can. Brian is on his break. Above them, in the tower, sentries with guns watch their every move. Including the prison guards.

Lorenzo loves outdoor time as much as the prisoners. He's a sun worshipper. However, unlike most of the pale men who avoid the rays as though they are infused with mustard gas, Lorenzo knows how to tan his skin to a golden brown without burning. It's all about timing and lotion.

He thinks about the inmates who grew up in Urbston in the shadow of the prison only to end up on the other side of these scary, intimidating walls. You'd think the daily sight of a giant, unforgiving cage would frighten all the residents to follow the rules.

Not so for Herman and Frank.

Not to mention Liam O'Sullivan.

Herman van der Berg spent a total of five years in jail, two years here and three years there. When he was released the last time, he got into an altercation with a neighbor. One punch from the other man had felled Herman as though he were a broken tree branch. According to witnesses, he was stiff and straight when he landed on the pavement. Opened his head like a raw egg.

Frank McCarthy did his required two years, quiet and contrite. When he was released, he disappeared into the woods where rumor had it there was a shack previously owned by his parents. Last year his shriveled body was discovered by some hunters. Dead for a long time. Alone and sad. Not surprising, nor undeserved, but Lorenzo still thought it was a waste of a life.

There is one Urbston related prisoner that continues to both frustrate and fascinate Lorenzo. Liam O'Sullivan spent five years in the prison for his part in a bank robbery where a guard was killed. A member of The Lads, a notorious gang of robbers. Probably its leader, Lorenzo thought.

Almost instantly, Liam gathered a group of followers in the prison. They mimicked a band of merry men who enjoyed being cooped up in jail. They played cards, basketball, and watched television together. Mostly, they had fun teasing the men (and occasionally, a woman) in uniform. Lorenzo and Brian in particular.

Those five years were tough. The guards had to watch for flying shit. Listen to comments about their sexuality or manhood. Hear things that were never spoken aloud outside these walls.

Sometimes Lorenzo imagines his sister, Fiorella, walking in on the shouts and innuendoes. She would surely faint from the shock. Married to the son of the Robus Estates fortune, she hobnobs with the mayor and his wife, keeps a beautiful, orderly home, and has kids who obey their parents' every word. In contrast, Lorenzo's life is a bit of a shambles to say the least.

Without Carla, he is no longer invited to any dinners or cocktail parties. Fiorella now and then has her brother and his son over for dinner, but it's always only family. No jewelry roped necks or arms, no flowing skirts nor silky ties. A table with plenty to eat but no longer matching the banquets with the mayor and other muckety mucks. A single man whose wife has run off with an insurance salesman is persona non grata.

At the family dinners, Fiorella and David spend most of the time frowning at LJ's behavior. His sister provides advice for Lorenzo on how to raise her nephew better. David says nothing. His plump face now and then grimaces toward Lorenzo with a smile that he imagines is meant to be supportive, but David would never question his wife's wisdom.

LJ's after-school babysitter, Polly, is a source of consternation for Aunt Fiorella too—not enough discipline in that disorganized household, too many kids—but Fiorella never offers to take her nephew. In fact, LJ likes Polly. Her relaxed style suits him just fine.

Lorenzo spent years in a constant state of stress and worry. Liam O'Sullivan drove him nuts, though he never allowed his face to show the depth of his hatred.

Lorenzo was good at giving quips back to that gang of idiots. He discovered ways to secretly retaliate for slights and pranks. Salt instead of sugar in the coffee. Too much pepper on the mystery meat. Cereal bits spread inside a cell or two, so they'd crunch underfoot. Forgetting to open his cage, leaving Liam to languish all morning inside.

Sorry, sorry, the lock must have stuck…

Nothing made a difference to Liam O'Sullivan, however. He never seemed to care about anything. He responded to life as though he were watching an extremely boring television program. No reaction. Never angry. Always a smiling, relaxed, disconnected look on his face. Ready for a laugh perhaps, but never ready to show any other emotion.

"O'Sullivan is insensible," Brian says, "…*un psychopathe*. He does not feel what normal people feel."

Lorenzo recognizes some of Liam's traits in himself and his wife. Until Lorenzo Junior, he didn't really care about others. His feelings for Carla were more about pride. This gorgeous, sexy woman had chosen him. Carla herself was a mean, self-centered person without empathy for others. Even her own child.

LJ is surrounded by adults who are socially awkward and selfish. Lorenzo is amazed that he is a loving child who likes to hug and kiss. He's well-liked by other kids. By his teachers and caregiver. Although he's struggling right now, Lorenzo is certain this rough patch will pass.

Occasionally he catches the sweetness behind the sad, confused face of a motherless boy. Although the school staff try very hard, most people look down upon a child whose mother would leave him behind. Assume there must be something terribly wrong with him.

"There's something terribly wrong with his mother," Lorenzo wants to say, but his own shame keeps his head down and his mouth shut.

When he is alone with LJ, that freckled face and thick, wrinkle-frown eyebrows looking up at him with troubled brown eyes, Lorenzo talks.

"I love you, LJ," he says. "Your mom loves you. She doesn't like me very much and she couldn't take you with her. It's nothing to do with you, son."

LJ simply nods. Lorenzo wishes he would talk, but he sits silently. Contemplating? Figuring it out? His father can only hope so. He doesn't have the skills to help his son explore those feelings.

Brian seems to accept LJ's silence with ease. When he comes to watch a show with them, he's quiet yet quick to laugh when something is funny. He's a great companion because he gives off an air of comfort and acceptance without even trying.

I Love Lucy can reduce them all to tears of laughter, though LJ has been reticent lately. The three of them love The Roy Rogers Show, too. Lorenzo notices, however, that his boy hasn't commented on a plot or a good shoot-out in a long time.

Goodnight, Gracie, Brian would sometimes say as he left the house. Which was the only statement that could still elicit a loud laugh from LJ.

When Lorenzo and LJ have dinner at Fiorella's, they sometimes watch The Ed Sullivan Show together. No one speaks. Lorenzo's niece and nephew sit with their hands in their laps. His sister and brother-in-law sip water, while Lorenzo has a beer. Despite the disapproval in the air, Lorenzo figures that since he brought the beer, he would drink it. Plus it's the only way he can get through the evening.

LJ fidgets with whatever he can get his hands on. Picks at the carpet. Twirls a dime he found under the couch (your housekeeper missed that one, Sis). Sticks his hands down the cushions and tries to lift his father's butt. Pulls—gently mind you—on his cousin's long curls. She smiles flirtatiously, though her mother frowns and tells LJ to keep his hands to himself. Fiorella says it with a smile and in a stage whisper, as though this manner will make up for the fact that she is disciplining his child.

"Why do you go?" Brian asks him.

"She's got a really good cook," Lorenzo answers, though he knows that's not all it is.

He refuses to allow Fiorella to win.

He wonders idly about where Liam O'Sullivan is now. There's an aunt who lives in the Queen's Hotel. Would she be charmed enough by her nephew to allow him to stay with her? Crime has been almost non-existent, and the prison has been manageable. Though if Liam were in Urbston, surely someone would have spotted him by now.

Later, Lorenzo wonders if his thoughts jinxed everything. He moves his face out of the sun to follow a sound that echoes across the yard. One of the prisoners lies on the ground. Someone else is doing the hollering.

He blows on his whistle and grabs his walky-talky, trying very hard to do both things at once as he runs toward the gathering circle of men.

Padre Benedict Collins lies on the ground, curled up in a fetal position. The stillness of his body tells Lorenzo everything he needs to know. A grey shade to the man's face. The droopiness of his limbs. Urine leaks through the fabric of his prison jumper.

Fortunately on site already, Urbston's doctor is there quickly. Lorenzo helps Brian get the men back into their cells. A temporary measure he tells them, just let Doc do his thing first. Once again, they are quiet, subdued by the death or baked by the sun or a combination of the two.

When the two guards return to the yard, there isn't much for them to do. Paramedics and the doctor swarm over the dead man. Warden Luckinbill does his dancing and politicking. Brian and Lorenzo lean against the wall, watching along with three others on shift.

"Do you know the stories about Benedict?" Lorenzo asks his friend.

Brian shakes his head. "Not too much."

"He was a Catholic priest. His real name was James, but the Church gave him Benedict when he got ordained. The story is that he was an Irish freedom fighter who got away with a lot because he was dressed in a holy frock."

"*Je suis surpris*. I did not think he was *Catholique*."

Lorenzo shakes his head. "He was not, for the last part of his life. The two sides of the Irish are like French with the English."

Brian smiles in understanding.

"You know that in the prison Benedict is called Padre by all the men, right? He leads both sides."

"*Oui*, I have noticed this. He has the respect to do it," Brian says.

He pronounces respect in a lilting French.

"He was a priest, then he was an Orangie. He had sway over both sides. That's why they've been a quiet bunch lately," Lorenzo observes. "I wonder what the Padre's death will do to that balance."

"He is a cousin to O'Sullivan."

Brian says this as though it's an ordinary statement, not the shock that hits Lorenzo like a punch.

"What the fuck?" he bursts out, even though he knows Brian doesn't like swearing. "I was nice to that bastard this whole time and he's related to Liam?"

Lorenzo feels like kicking something but there's only the brick wall and he doesn't want to break a toe.

Luckinbill waves them over just as the paramedics lift the body and walk toward a gate where the ambulance waits.

The Warden towers over all the guards and the doctor. It's as though a tree has been placed in the circle of men. One that waves back and forth with sound, threatening to crush them if they don't listen and obey. Lorenzo wants to step back but he doesn't dare.

When Luckinbill speaks, however, there is no anger or blame in his voice. The volume is merely a result of the vastness of his lungs.

"Doc here says Padre's heart gave out. He thinks it was a defect from birth. But the fella's in his early seventies though...so pretty old."

Words that can only come from someone in their late thirties for whom the life expectancy of sixty-three or so seems very far away.

"Does anyone know his kin?"

Lorenzo is determined not to get involved. To mention Liam O'Sullivan's name is to bring the man back into his life.

I have enough to handle, he tells himself, though work has been easy enough lately, but...

"O'Sullivan is a cousin," Brian says. "He was the only *visiteur* to the Padre that we ever saw."

Lorenzo cringes.

"They're related?" Luckinbill booms, sounding incredulous. "But the Padre's a Proddie. One of the Orangemen."

"*Le plus probable mariage,*" Brian says, slipping into French in his nervousness. "The man or the woman would choose if they wanted to marry outside the faith. Maybe his mother or father chose. Some of the converts were more ferocious in the belief than the *originales*."

Luckinbill harrumphed. "That was Benedict. Outside the prison he was always fighting some Catholic or other. It's the reason he was here. Manslaughter."

"The man he killed was an O'Sullivan cousin, too," Brian says. "They are keeping the murders *en famille* at least."

The group laughs, but there is a nervousness around the edge of the sound. Luckinbill gives Brian a strange look. He is not used to this man speaking up. Or knowing anything.

"Inside, the Padre was a calming influence for all the prisoners," Brian adds. "No matter what their religion."

Luckinbill pauses, obviously thinking about what to do from here.

"Give the men another hour in the yard," the Warden finally says, startling the guards with the generosity of time. "Up until lunch, then hopefully it will be a quiet afternoon."

Although the men are pleasantly surprised when they are released into the yard again, they play basketball or dice or bathe in the sunlight in a subdued manner. Many of them talk about the Padre, praising him. Grieving him in a way they would not normally mourn anyone.

Lorenzo can't help himself. He continues to talk about the Padre too. Even if Liam O'Sullivan's specter creeps back into his head. Brian listens intently.

"The Padre was born James Collins," Lorenzo begins. "But like I said, the Church gave him the name of Benedict when he became a priest. According to some of the Irish who knew him back then, the Father was very popular in his town. He encouraged some of the wealthier Catholics to aid the peasants. Soup kitchens and the like at his parish. Of course by then things were not so difficult. Farming was revived and imports increased. The problem in Ireland was the rebellion. Father Benedict's big mistake was Paddy O'Brien."

"Who was he?" Brian asks.

"He was an Irish freedom fighter. IRA or Sinn Fein, one of those. He lived with the Collins family until the house was burned to the ground. He disappeared after that. Father Benedict was crushed."

"You think he was queer?"

Lorenzo nods. "I do. Many other people think so too. When the Church discovered the connection between Benedict and Paddy, they gave him a one-way ticket to Canada and no help when he got here. But the priest found Paddy again. They lived together until Paddy died."

"Did the Father have a parish around here? I only remember him as a prisoner."

"No, he left the church and joined the Orange Order."

Brian stops in his tracks. "*Sérieusement?* That is such a big change."

"When Paddy first got here, he was starving and abandoned. The Orange Order helped him. And he helped them. When Benedict got here, that's where he went. Anything for Paddy."

Lorenzo turns around in a slow circle, eyeing the men in the yard. They slump against the walls, sit on patches of grass, lean on benches. Very few play ball or exercise or let off any kind of energy. A dark pall clouds the yard. Mourning? Fear? The great Padre, leader of men, arbiter of disputes, is gone.

"How did Paddy help the Orangemen?" Brian asks.

"Think about it, *mon ami*," Lorenzo replies, using one of the few French phrases he knows. "Local elections. The Grand Master of the Orange Order becomes the Mayor of Urbston by acclamation. All other candidates drop out of the race around the same time. None of them will say why. All the councilors are Orangemen too."

Brian stops walking and stares at Lorenzo.

"This is true?"

"There's no real proof, but it all adds up. Paddy, an Irish freedom fighter. Used to tactics of fear and threats of death. Willing to carry out the warnings if need be. Paddy O'Brien and his smooth-talking priest. A perfect combination."

"Bien entendu, there came a time when O'Brien met someone who fought back. Not a surprise—an O'Sullivan cousin. He fatally stabbed Paddy," Brian says.

Brian and Lorenzo turn to walk the opposite way through the preternaturally quiet yard. The sun tips past the roof of the prison to suddenly cool down the pavement. Still, the men slump and remain immobile.

"How did you know about that? And how did you find out that Benedict was related to the O'Sullivans?"

"It was my first patrol here in Urbston as a police officer," Brian says. "I had not transferred to the prison, and I had not met you. LJ was not even here yet; can you think of that?"

Lorenzo shakes his head, smiling. His friend's support and love are gifts he has trouble acknowledging without a rush of uncontrollable emotion and gratitude that prized tears from his eyes. He avoids thinking about this for too long.

"Father Benedict, in turn, killed the O'Sullivan cousin with the same knife. Sliced his throat open so his head was hanging like it would fall off. The blood..."

Brian shakes his head, the memory a thick cloud across his eyes.

"Mon dieu, the blood was everywhere. I had a very difficult time to hold my stomach together. In the middle of the blood was Father Benedict, holding Paddy in his arms. Crying. He sobbed like a baby. Rocked back and forth. We had four of us to make him let go and come to the police station."

"My gawd," Lorenzo breathes. "I remember all the rumors and the town being obsessed with the story. I think I was too head in the clouds with Carla. I didn't pay a lot of attention."

Brian rests his hand briefly on his friend's shoulder.

"*Naturellement.* I would not know this story if I had not been there when Paddy O'Brien died. I am amazed that Father Benedict became such a leader in the yard. I guess he knew both sides of the religious wars."

"Yes, he had a way with all the men. I wonder who will take his place."

They both gaze around the yard, seeing only defeated prisoners. No one stands out as having a vision or a passion for leadership.

"Why do men carry their old feuds with them into new places? Why not start over? Some of these men were born here, not there. They could have decent lives. Free from all that hate."

Brian studies his friend as though he has never heard him speak so eloquently. Perhaps he hasn't. Lorenzo's obsession with Carla clogged his brain for years.

"I think the hate is inside them. In their bodies. Passed down by generations. They are like cats who hate dogs, *simplement* by their scent and their sound. It has become an instinct. Not in the brain. In the blood."

Lorenzo thinks of his obsessions. Carla. Liam. For LJ's sake, these cannot become part of him. Flowing in his blood. For the first time, he begins to truly let go of the past.

The bell rings for lunch and the men file in, still quiet and stunned. Lorenzo, Brian and the other guards wait and watch all afternoon. Activities are normal. Cards and books and tasks all take place with a low murmur of acceptance. The local priest and a minister stay in the chapel to hear the men's expressions of grief. They are both young and compassionate and believe they are offering essentially the same service. Under the same god.

It takes eighteen months for the men to erupt. The riot is short but fierce. Two prisoners and one guard are murdered. Fortunately for Brian and Lorenzo, it happens when they are not on shift. They join the police and the army on outside patrol. It's tense and frightening, but at least they are not imprisoned inside. Several prisoners are transferred to different prisons around Canada.

Six months later, the murder at the Queen's Hotel takes place and both Lorenzo and Brian there to handle it.

On the day that Benedict died, Lorenzo picks up LJ at Polly's. The little boy runs into his father's arms. Delighted with a picture he has drawn and colored, he babbles on about how he got the idea and how Polly said he was amazing at coloring inside the lines.

"Especially for my age," he says, very grown up and wise.

Lorenzo looks down at his son's long eyelashes, lowered as he gazes at his masterpiece. A rush of love so fierce it hurts runs through his body. This kind of emotion is the one he will keep, Lorenzo thinks.

He vows that he will be obsessed with the present. With each moment as his son grows up. Grounded in love. No longer waste precious time wondering what Liam or Carla are up to. Or what his sister thinks of him. He is here. Now and forever.

LJ looks up at his father as they enter their small but cozy apartment. His eyes are a deep brown with fathoms of spirit, intelligence and free emotion.

"I love you, Daddy," he says.

Lorenzo wraps his arms around the small boy and hugs him tightly. He carries him into the living room.

"I love you too, LJ," he says.

Lorenzo cannot remember a purer moment of joy.

"Now let's see where we can hang that picture so everyone can see it whenever they come to visit."

Murder at the Queen's Hotel

Urbston 1965
By Clare O'Sullivan Doyle

Grace and I enter the front doors as usual. The hotel has passed its glory days, the way some of its current residents have. The porch sags a bit. Paint fades or peels from its walls and trims. For some reason, we never give the balcony above us a second thought. We have never stood upon it, nor do we know anyone who has. Perhaps it's ready to crash upon a visitor's head, but we're oblivious.

At fifteen, three months apart, we are best friends. We have grown up together. We never have trouble with conversation or laughter. Even tears sometimes. Our world is small but full. Despite some family issues, we know we're loved.

We continue to visit our great-aunt. We truly love her. She's grumpy and smelly and her smoking makes Grace cough. But she's also smart and garrulous. Often without meaning to be, she's funny. We learn about family history and myths. For vastly different reasons, we love hearing her tales.

Today we've brought food from my mother. Sandwiches for all of us, carrots, celery, a few oranges and several apple crisp tarts.

The staircase was once grand. My mother calls them Scarlett O'Hara stairs, after a heroine in a movie she watched and loved. Auntie Beers lives on the second floor of the hotel.

When our great-aunt lived there, it was no longer a "nice hotel," but had deteriorated into a rooming house. Original hotel rooms were divided in two, with cheap dry wall in between. Sound above a whisper was for anyone to hear. Inexpensive paint peeled long before a brush touched it again.

The hallways at the Queen's Hotel creaked and echoed like an old wooden ship. I've always wondered why the original owners chose to construct and decorate the hotel in the Italianate style. Perhaps they were from Italy, like the Malpensas.

The outside walls were red brick from the city of Brampton nearby, cleverly named Brampton Brick, which seemed to provide most of the facades in Urbston. All the windows had ornate, molded caps painted white to stand out from the dark red. Lots of two-by-two windows and decorative woodwork all around the decks.

The staircase is wide and welcoming. Shiny with the imprint of many shoes and boots. I could always imagine the big parties held in the heydays of the hotel. Perhaps 1890s dresses swept across these railings. Instead of the stench of poverty and unwashed bodies, I imagined the scent of perfume wafting through the halls.

Inside, the builders appeared to have run out of money. There was nothing grand about the lodgings. Cheap wallboard and thin carpets ensured the décor did not last. As a hotel, it was considered luxurious in its first few years. The furnishings made it seem deluxe. As long as the clients only stayed one or two nights, they judged it opulent.

If only the Queen's Hotel had retained its royal status, and the men in our family had chosen differently Auntie Beers always declared, she might have been rich instead of beautiful. I think she would have been both. I could picture her in a lovely gown, her long red hair a frame around her aristocratic face. Maybe waving a fan so she could appear shy and coquettish.

"Men are eejits," she had often told Grace and me. "So easily drawn into whatever shite you want them in."

I very much doubted that Bairbre was right. I supposed it depended on the man. And the woman. Sometimes it appeared to me that either there was a firm partnership or one person in the couple was in charge. Didn't seem to matter if the leader was the male or the female. From what I knew, never in her life had Auntie Beers been in control of a man.

My mother told us that Bairbre had had a sweetheart in Ireland. Family lore said that he'd gone off to fight for the rebels and never returned. Presumably, he's in an unmarked grave near Dublin, though no one ever clarified.

"Can you imagine if Auntie Beers had been alive when the hotel was really a hotel?" Grace asks, reading my mind.

"What do you think she would have done?"

"She would have done a roll down the staircase in her froufrou gown making sure her frilly panties showed."

We both laugh loudly. When we stop, we hear a throat clear behind us.

We turn to find our great-aunt standing at the bottom of the steps, grasping a paper bag, a cigarette dangling from her lips.

Grace and I burst out laughing again. We run to her side, take her bag for her (heavy as it is with beer) and tuck our other arms through hers. Over the years, as the boys stopped coming, Auntie Beers has allowed our outward signs of affection. Though she never smiles when we embrace her, we notice that she stiffens less and less at our touch. Today, perhaps in her glee to have a beer or two and tell us some tales, she leans into us as comfortably as she ever has.

"Would you really do such a thing, Auntie?" Grace asks, ever the excavator of people's behavior.

"Go on with ya. I'm Irish and Catholic. You can find my name in the dictionary next to the word guilt."

We chuckle and prance her up the stairs. At the top landing, I turn us around and raise my arms toward the ceiling.

"We're the O'Sullivans, don't you know! May the roof above us never fall in. And may the friends gathered below it never fall out."

This time Auntie Beers laughs.

"Where'd ya hear that one, ya rascal?" she asks.

"Mama said it was an Irish family blessing."

She shakes her head, miraculously still chuckling.

"Ahh, Caitlin," she says, pronouncing Kathleen in the Gaelic way.

When we reach her room, Auntie Beers is quite out of breath. She sits in her rocker and puts her head back, eyes shut for a moment. We sit cross-legged at her feet, as we have done for years.

Grace opens the food basket. I open a beer, which I hand to our great-aunt when I see her piercing blue eyes looking down at me. Auntie Beers has bought us two cokes.

"Slainté," we all toast, looking into each other's eyes for a moment, as we have been taught.

Wishing one another good health. In retrospect, ironic on that particular day.

We sit amiably in silence for a while. First, we eat the tarts, following Auntie Beers' edict to always have dessert first. Next, we begin to share the sandwiches and veggies. We sip our drinks slowly.

"I've been warned I might be getting a visitor soon," Auntie Beers announces after a few minutes of munching. "I'll ask you weans to leave if that should come to pass today."

Grace and I give each other a look of utter astonishment.

"Who, Auntie? Tell us!"

"Your uncle Liam."

"He's out of jail?"

Bairbre nods. "As far as I know, he hasn't been a guest of Her Majesty for two or three years. Last week, I was told that he's in Urbston. I think he'll come here."

"Why?" I ask.

"Because I have something he wants."

"What's that, Auntie?" Grace asks. "A place to stay?"

There is a beat of silence.

"No, there isn't room here and he knows it. I have something of his. He gave it to me years ago for safe keeping."

"We hardly know anything about our uncle Liam," I finally say. "Only that he's been in jail, and we should never talk to him in the street."

"Jesus Christ," Auntie Beers says. "That to be sure comes from your fathers. No faith in their daughters. Or maybe because they know what goes on in a man's mind."

By fifteen, Grace and I are well aware of what goes on in the male psyche. To be honest, the same thing goes on in ours, too, but we're not allowed to speak about that out loud. We're good Catholic girls, after all. We scarcely know anything about our own sexual pleasure, other than the tingling sensation that happens now and then during some fantasy or the other. I am still in love with Marlon Brando, for instance.

"But why will you ask us to leave if he comes? We're not pushovers," Grace points out.

"Not enough space in this room for too many visitors, is there?"

"Tell us about him, Auntie," I say, with enough sincerity and lacking in prurient interest that I convince her. Or perhaps she simply wants to talk about him.

She takes a long sip of her beer and lights a cigarette.

"When Liam was born, Maggie was seriously depressed. She didn't want him. We had a difficult time getting her to hold him or feed him. Maybe that explains everything or maybe he was always missing something in his brain."

Grace sits up at this observation. She has already read up on the latest brain research, although in the 1960s it was not always correct. She's keenly interested in psychopathology. She tells me all about the traits of people who can be violent or cruel toward others. Lack of remorse. An emotional void. Egocentricity.

She has noted some of these characteristics in our cousin Peter. Though ultimately his violence is turned inward. It's difficult to tell with Uncle Daniel, because his doctors assumed he had shellshock from the war. His violence could be outward, against his parents, siblings, wife. Never his children, according to his daughter Mary. In the end he too turned the anger on himself.

Grace wants to study families like Daniel's. Perhaps she thinks she could have prevented his and Peter's suicides.

As a budding mystery and crime writer, I was fascinated by the things that people do to one another. Perpetrated by bad guys as well as good.

What we both didn't know back then is just how beautiful evil or mental illness can appear on the outside.

"Kathleen, how she loved that boy. Twelve years old when he was born, she was more of a mother to him than Maggie was. He was a lovely wean in the southwestern Irish tradition. Blond, blue eyes, freckles all across his perfect nose."

I am surprised that my mother loved her little brother so much. I can count on one hand the number of times she has mentioned him. Not once have I heard her speak positively about him. Usually it's a warning or a whispered piece of information to my father. Her cheeks are often red when she talks about him. From the flash of anger in her eyes, I assume the blush is fury. But perhaps it's more complicated than that.

"In her heart Maggie might have known Liam was missing something. She let his wickedness gnaw at her. I believe she died of a broken heart. Ashamed and sad that her child could be so sinful."

"What did he do that was so evil?" I ask.

At first, I'm afraid I've pushed too far, but Auntie Beers accepts another bottle and drags on another cigarette. Grace coughs quietly.

"He most likely killed the pet cat. It was called Corky. Corky's body was found hanging in the shed. The one that John slept in before he went off to war."

My cousin and I are silent with shock. It's easy to banter words around. To try to describe evil with adjectives and different nouns. It's the factual recitation of deeds that opens your mind and scares you with its ferocity.

"Lots of animals died around the farmhouse from the time Liam was three. He threw things at his mother and siblings. He dug in the coal cellar and used the bits to write on the walls inside the house. By the 1940s, we were all in better shape money-wise. Maggie and Séamus extended the shack. Made it into a real house. Even an indoor toilet."

Auntie Beers took another gulp.

"Liam never starved the way his brothers and sisters did. Farmer Reid appreciated Séamus's hard work. Things were quite good during those years. Reid and Séamus sort of became partners for a few years until Reid became ill. Sold up and moved to town. Séamus and Maggie followed, but they had no stake in the land, so they were back to scraping by. Little did I know they didn't own the house on McManus either."

She waved around her small room.

"If anything, Liam got worse once they were in the city. There were lots of complaints about his mistreatment of younger kids."

It was only as an adult that I translated "mistreatment" to "abuse" and realized that my understanding of Liam as a bully was an underestimation. Sexual. Physical. Verbal. Our uncle indulged in any behavior he could get away with.

"He was thrown out of school so often they finally put him to work on a farm. He didn't last long anywhere. The farmers found smashed eggs. Strangled hens. Tortured cows. Cigarette burns on horses. Séamus knew it was Liam. But no one knew what to do."

Tears roll down Grace's cheeks. It's a wretched and tragic story, but I'm not sad. I'm angry. At that moment, I hate my Uncle Liam.

"Finally, he was placed in the Ontario Reformatory when he hit another child so hard the boy was mentally retarded the rest of his life."

We both draw in a breath, despite the smoke swirling above our heads.

"Sine é! Done! My sister thought Liam would learn from the discipline offered there."

She paused to sip some beer and draw in a puff of smoke.

"Being in that place simply made him worse. He came out with a posse of thugs behind him. A gang of thieves who decided to rob banks."

"He learned even worse ways to live, eh, Auntie?" I asked.

She gave me a short smile.

"Depends on what you think of as worse, mo daor. The money was covered by insurance and, at first, they didn't hurt anyone."

I could understand Auntie Beers' point of view. Better to steal than to beat little children.

"They didn't get caught for a long time. Called themselves The Lads. Some wee prick at a newspaper in Toronto caught wind of the name and made a big deal out of the gang. Handsome men cloud everyone's judgement. Turn people into admirers of a criminal. Turns gobshites into gods."

"And Uncle Liam is very handsome, so I've heard," Grace says.

"Yes, if you like that sort. Blond and blue eyed like I said. Even these days, a young face. One that says I need taking care of. I'm misunderstood."

"Reminds me of West Side Story," I say, thinking of my favorite movie. "The song to Officer Krupke. We're misunderstood, underneath there is good."

"What happens if there isn't good underneath? Ye cut a few of the bad bits off the potato and all you see are more bad bits. By the time you're done, there's only a tiny bit to eat."

"I think after a while you'd be hungry and go somewhere else," I say, liking Auntie Beers' analogy but thinking with my head.

"But what if that bit is as sweet as the sweetest pie you ever tasted? What if you start to ignore the bad bits just to get to the prize in the middle? What if you get so you think you can't live without that bit of pie?"

"That's addiction," Grace says, quoting from her most recent reading. "You believe you can't live without that drug and then you get physically hooked."

Auntie Beers nods in agreement.

"Yes, I suppose there are people who feel as though there are some things and even some people they can't do without."

She lifts her bottle of beer, gulps, then puffs on her cigarette. Grace and I stare at her for a moment. When she meets our eyes, she understands. We all burst out laughing.

"I'm the shitehawk calling a fella a culchie," she says.

We laugh again, trained as we are that culchies are Irish lowlife. From the country, ill dressed and smelly. Auntie Beers' family in fact.

I think about how we have changed over the years. No longer the little kids sitting at our great-aunt's feet, mesmerized by her tales. Now we are young women, with greater understanding of the female experience. We can relate to Auntie Beers now. She to us, as well. She's mellowed. Become less unhappy with her life. Perhaps a little more at peace with her past.

"We never used to use fancy words like addiction. We're just old drunks."

We ate a bit more food. Drank some Coke and beer respectively.

"Your Uncle Liam can tell people to eat shite and they ask where they can find more. He's got an air about him. So good-looking. Confident. Funny. Charming."

"What happened to The Lads?" I ask.

"Eventually they crossed the line from Robin Hood to Dillinger. They weren't giving any money to the poor, so. Got more and more violent as they went. The public started to turn against them. Then during one robbery, they killed a guard. He was a young man, had two little babies, and hadn't even pulled out his gun. They gathered up all the money and left him lying in a puddle of blood. People in the bank said they begged to help him, but The Lads ignored them, didn't they? Poor fella died on the way to the hospital. That turned the tide against them."

"Did they go to prison?"

Auntie Beers nodded. "Ended up right here in Urbston Prison. Of course, our Liam got the lightest sentence because he was in the getaway car when the shooting happened. Five years he spent in jail. For being part of an armed robbery and murder. Proof that deadly flahs are treated differently."

"What's a flah?" I ask.

"Someone who's very good-looking. You ought to be in movies level. Stop in the street to stare level."

Like Fiona, I think. Deadly beautiful.

"He looks and sounds like the best fella you've ever come across, when he's what we'd call a langer. Bad news. An eejit and a user."

"Telling stories about me, are you, Auntie?"

He leans in the doorway, filling the space with his presence. Immediately I think of a cat. Sleek. Comfortable in his body. Oozing the kind of confidence that comes from only caring about the next catch. He emits a seductive sound the way a cat chirps at a bird. Soft and welcoming.

Yet, those claws. Deadly.

His blond hair slips nonchalantly over his forehead. The color of his eyes is startling. A blue that holds swirling depths that spark of mystery and challenge. When he smiles, his impossibly white teeth show an endearing suggestion of a crooked one here and there. Freckles still dot his nose. His face crinkles in all the right places. Like an adorable child.

He's tall and lanky. Muscular but not too much so. A narrow waist. Hips and ass that conform to a symmetrical circle and slip into long, well-formed legs.

Auntie Beers is right. He is beautiful. Stop in the street, movie star beautiful.

I knew nothing about pheromones back then, but Liam O'Sullivan must have been the definition of sexual chemistry.

I look over at Grace and see that she's blushing. It's difficult to physically remove ourselves from the atmosphere that swirls around our uncle. The heat is both annoying and irresistible.

"Are you sure you're related to us?" Liam asks Grace and me. "These beautiful young ladies are from O'Sullivan stock? Hard to bloody believe."

He sits down on our great-aunt's ancient ottoman and helps himself to a beer from her little fridge.

"I hear you've been telling stories to these lovelies since they were kiddies, Auntie. Are you sure that's the right thing to do? Telling all the secrets of the past to fragile minds."

"Fragile minds?" I demand. "What the hell do you mean by that?"

Liam laughs. Even his voice, his chuckle, can make anyone quiver or cuddle up.

"Oh, here's a feisty one, eh, Auntie?"

Still Auntie Beers says nothing. Her face is a mask. Stoney. Closed. She's angry. Or perhaps sad. It's difficult to tell.

"Maybe the wrong word to use, sweetheart," he says to me. "Just meaning innocent. Easily influenced."

"We make up our own minds," I tell him. "We aren't stupid."

"Or easily influenced," says Grace.

It's amazing how he tries to direct all the energy in the room toward himself. For the most part, successfully. Like a kitten desperate to monopolize the mother's teats. No instinct to share. No inner mechanism that gives him a conscience. Liam is all about Liam.

"Girls, it's time to go now," Auntie Beers says.

Grace and I look at each other and back at our great-aunt. Her face is pinched tight. Although I am anxious about leaving her alone with Liam, I can tell by her eyes that she will brook no opposition. Steady, cold, focused on her nephew.

Little did we know what lay hidden in her dress pocket. The item she believes Liam has come for.

I also know that Grace's and my parents would be extremely angry with Auntie Beers if she allowed us in Liam's sphere. We must leave her, both protected and unprotected.

We gather up my mother's basket and a few other things. Reluctantly we sidle toward the door. Liam stays exactly where he is, essentially at the feet of his aunt. He sips nonchalantly on the beer.

"Bye, independent girls," he says. "O'Sullivans all. Go forth and speak your minds."

He laughs as though his words are ridiculous and therefore funny.

We purposely leave the door open. As we move into the hallway and make our way toward the stairs, we hear a scuffle from another room. Thinking in unison, we stop in the exit to the steps and look back.

A red-faced, shirtless man faces two men dressed in the official uniform of prison guards. The officers have their backs to us, but I can tell that one is Lorenzo Malpensa, a friend of our Uncle Michael's. I've often seen the other man with Lorenzo. I think his name is Brian Cottreau.

Although the man's words are loud, they are muddied with anger. Marred by the illogic of fury.

We pick up "bastard," and "bitch" very clearly. "Mackerel snapper" dislodges a memory but I can't quite place where I've heard the phrase. Soon after the argument begins, the shirtless man, his belly hanging below his belt, flies out past us toward Auntie Beers' doorway.

"Come out and face the music, O'Sullivan! I called the cops and looky here—Lorenzo and Brian, your usual keepers. They're ready to cart you off to the prison where you belong."

Bairbre steps out from her room, Liam right behind her. He leans in the doorway.

"He hasn't done a single thing but visit his auntie, has he, Robert? And ye're already on the blower to the cops. Still pissed off that the Orange Order got defeated and your wife kicked you out, eh?"

When the fat man turns his head toward the guards, Grace and I have a clear sight of his face. Suddenly I recognize the half-undressed man. He's the one from the parade so long ago when Auntie Beers decided to attack him. It's astonishing how hatred can continue to fester if left unchecked over time.

"They're a pack of liars and criminals. Take them both to jail. They deserve it."

Even more astonishing is the weapon that Robert Foster withdraws from his pocket. He waves the gun in Liam's direction.

"Arrest him, Lorenzo."

Lorenzo steps toward Foster, arms up and hands spread wide.

"Put the gun down, Robert," Lorenzo says calmly. "We're not here to arrest Liam. We have some questions for him is all."

That's when Bairbre decides to reveal the gun inside her dress pocket. The item Liam was there to retrieve.

"I'll kill you, Robert Foster, if ye don't stop getting in my way."

"No, Auntie," Liam says calmly. "Put that away."

Auntie Beers has consumed too much alcohol and very little food. She's unfocused and disbelieving. Angry. Bitter.

She waves the gun above her head. Points it at Robert Foster.

The fat man fires just as Liam steps completely out of Bairbre's doorway into the hall.

At the same moment, I hear Liam say, "Auntie, that gun's not even..."

The bullet hits Auntie Beers and spins her around. Her nephew grabs her. Holds her gently in his arms. Is in the act of carefully lowering her to the floor when a second bullet catches him in the neck.

This one fired by the gun in Brian Cottreau's hand.

Grace and I are frozen in the cloud of noise that reverberates through our ears and into our heads. Just down the hall, blood spurts everywhere. Thick and black-red.

Liam and Auntie Beers fall in a heap. Their limbs jerk and flail. A sound like a wolf in distress fills the air.

Lorenzo and Brian kneel beside our great-aunt and our uncle. Foster stands stock still. As do Grace and I, though I wish I could go to Auntie Beers.

Instead, I slink down to my haunches, shaking. Cold outside and in with shock. I am ashamed that I can't move. Tears cascade down my face. Grace huddles in my arms.

I'm not certain who makes the calls, but all at once there are emergency workers everywhere. Sirens wail out front. Stretchers.

I hold Grace as she vomits into a garbage pail.

Kind, worried eyes suddenly appear. My mother. My Aunt Jenny, Grace's mom.

I am in our family car, then through the front door of our house before I can focus properly. I lie in my bed, shaking despite being covered by three or four blankets. My mother gives me a sip of something vile, but it puts me right to sleep.

My memories of the immediate aftereffects are sketchy. No one seemed to know why Lorenzo and Brian were at the Queen's Hotel. Perhaps they wanted to question Liam about a series of robberies that had occurred in Urbston. That really wasn't the job of a prison guard, so I suppose they insisted it was Robert Foster's call that took them there.

No one appeared to consider their actions odd or unprofessional, though I was always certain that they were. Brian insisted he fired because he thought Auntie Beers was about to shoot at them.

Years later, Grace discovered through her practice that Brian Cottreau was one of Liam's abuse victims. That bullet had meant far more than stopping a woman from firing a gun.

There is one moment, a day later, that will always be clear and memorable.

Grace and I stand on either side of the hospital bed. Our great-aunt is still and white. We cry silently, our hands gentle on her cold arms.

Her eyelids flutter. Blue eyes suddenly stare out at us. She clears her throat.

"By the look on yer faces, I suppose I won't be winning a beauty contest any time soon," she says.

We laugh. Cry. Insist on hugs.

Liam died on that hallway floor. I told my mother that his last act had been one of kindness. He was lowering his aunt to the floor. Protecting her.

She lost three fingers on her right hand. He lost his life.

The weapon Liam gave to Auntie Beers turned out to be a replica. This fact went unexplored. Our great-aunt refused to provide any details such as whether or not she knew it was a fake. About why she was certain that retrieving the gun was the only reason Liam had come to see her. We've had to fill in the blanks ourselves.

I've always thought she believed it was real. That Liam needed it for protection. At any rate, she was determined to give it to him, or it would never have been in her pocket.

Brian Cottreau was exonerated. He had used proper force in the belief that Bairbre's gun was real. No one knew about his past with Liam. Not even his best friend.

The first bullet had been fired by Robert Foster. A reaction to Liam O'Sullivan's appearance. The fear that the younger man could have grabbed the gun and used it more effectively than his aunt.

How could anyone know hers was a replica?

Since Foster was on parole, however, possessing his own gun sent him right back into Urbston Prison. Firing it and nearly killing someone ensured he would be there for the rest of his life.

No one charged our great-aunt with anything. Somehow the fact that she waved a fake gun in the direction of another human being went unquestioned.

Auntie Beers never returned to the Queen's Hotel. She went to live with Grace, Uncle Eddie and Aunt Jenny, plus Tim and Joan. She was never an easy roomie, but she had her own space above the garage. Joan, preparing to be a nurse, came twice a day to massage her hand.

Grace and I continued to sit with and listen to Auntie Beers weekly. Mario and Patrick never seemed to find the time. Gone were the chocolate bars and pop; we continued to bring the treats instead. Carrots, celery, cheese and crackers. Food that our mothers sent because they worried Bairbre wasn't eating properly.

Certainly, our great-aunt became a bit thinner. At seventy-one, though, she was still beautiful. Her skin was virtually unlined. The creases she did have simply added to her mystique, curling lazily around her mouth or fiercely wrinkling in disgust. Her eyes were beacons of inquiry, always pinning you down with her inquisitive and judgmental gaze. Her long wavy hair was filtered with white, grey and red, as though she had deliberately streaked it.

When she told her stories, her long legs crossed at delicate ankles. Her fingertips were yellowish from holding hundreds of cigarettes, but she managed to look glamorous anyway.

"My grandfather—he was also called Michael; you'd think we had a shortage of names in Ireland— travelled to the United States in 1847 with the bulk of the Famine Irish. I can't even imagine the state of those ships. Mind you, I've since read a great deal about the overcrowding and the lack of food and water. They had nowhere to put their waste and very little room to sleep. Hundreds died on the way; their bodies dumped unceremoniously overboard. But reading about something is nothing like going through it, as you know, girls. Not that I recommend experiencing everything. Experience is a good school, but its fees are high."

Which is why, I think, the murder looms so large on my list of life traumas. Direct experience truly is far more costly, as the saying warns.

"Even when he got to the United States, my grandfather suffered. He couldn't find a job. Signs were all over the place stating that Irish Catholics need not apply. The only way he got employment was when a ringleader saw him doing tricks for the kids in the street. Grandda had lost his bottom teeth on the journey from Ireland, so he could twist his lower lips up and over his upper jaw. He could distort his eyes and nose into grotesque shapes that made kids and adults laugh or scream. So he went to work for the circus as a gurner."

"What's a gurner?" I asked.

"Someone who can do what my grandfather did. Put one jaw up over the other and make a grotesque face."

We couldn't help bursting into giggles. Even Auntie Beers laughed along.

"He entered a few gurning contests and won them. He'd put his face through a horse collar and twist it this way and that. He made a few quid from those competitions. Between that and the circus job, he eventually had enough to return to Ireland. He married Mary—another name that runs all through the family trees back home—and had a bunch of kids. Stayed there, he did. Some work in travelling circuses and county fairs, a few gurner competitions, and his family had enough to eat. Made his living proving he had the ugliest face in the region."

We all laughed again. Her stories were sometimes historical and often hysterical. We listened. Laughed or cried. I wrote the fictionalized forms and Grace excavated the reasons why.

Bairbre had so many guests that she tried to shout them all away. Family dinners. Parades. Christmas events. She was a part of them all. Hard as nails. Funny without meaning to be. We loved her in spite and because of who she was.

What A Fool Believes

The Old Country 1973
By Clare O'Sullivan Doyle

Stones are the markers here that interrupt an undulating sea of green. Rocks thrown about by a violent earth. Red sandstone shaped by a need for shelter or security rise from the land to peer toward the ocean. Always toward the water, in fear or hunger. At once savior and harbinger of invasion.

We climb to sit on a rock fence that has stood for centuries. Hunched mounds of ancient intrusions lined up to keep animals in or people out. The wind whips our hair skyward as we breathe in the beauty of this vista.

We are, ourselves, intruders. Tied to the land only by the smallest thread of blood cells. Above us the sky is robin's egg blue while the sun skirts shyly around large misty clouds. Unused to making its appearance at this time of day.

We make shapes with our bodies and faces for the camera. Balance on the sturdy wall left by our ancestors.

Ireland. The "old country." Home of our Irish ancestors. The hills above Bantry Bay.

Cemeteries have little appeal to any of us, though we stop by the graves that our Great Aunt Grace mapped out for us. Our great-grandparents and some great-uncles have tombstones that are polished and free of weeds. Someone still cares for them.

The woman at the farm next to our relative's place, where we stop by mistake, tells us he's not "fit for company." Her face is unwelcoming and fierce. Perhaps she is disgruntled by the interruption or perhaps confused by our Canadian sound. We, on the other hand, have no trouble understanding the Irish accent.

"Just another sign we are descended from here," Grace declares, as delighted as I am with the broad connections.

Our sisters, Fiona and Theresa, aren't as enthralled. Perhaps being younger, they have not yet been bitten by the ancestry bug. They are, however, reveling in the sights and sounds of our adventure.

Aidan is an O'Sullivan, descended from a brother of our great-grandfather. A cousin of our grandmother and our great-aunts. I wonder if they are related to the man who made his living as a circus entertainer.

We are undeterred by the neighbor's attitude and ignore her advice. Great Aunt Grace, Bairbre's younger sister, has told us this cousin still resides in the original homestead. She texts, in response to our inquiry:

"Ye should go take a look, since you're interested in the genealogy side of things."

Grace and her husband Brendan are at their townhouse in the city. Since we are flying out of Dublin, we decide to visit the south first, followed by the city.

We are determined to see the original O'Sullivan homestead. Excited to make this connection, bridging the past to the present.

Great-Aunt Grace fuels our fire when she writes. Cousin Aidan stays in the original O'Sullivan homestead. The one our great grandparents built. That would be several greats to you young 'uns.

When we meet Aidan, however, we understand the neighbor's caution. He has a face carved by need. The way he devours my sister Fiona's beauty with his eyes as though he has been starved of any skin and bone that measure up to the splendor of the land.

Aidan has an awkward speech, cut short by long silences. No sense of social graces or the scent of his own body. If we had met this man on the street in our city, we would have been frightened.

Here, in the vast hilly land, bewilderingly, we are not afraid. There are four of us, tall strong well-fed women, while he is one small painfully thin man, so we carelessly consider him no threat.

We snap our pictures when he meets us at a wooden door that sits awkwardly in its frame. Thrilled to see a traditional Irish homestead, with its raggedy roof and plaster-covered rock walls, we ooh and ahh as though it's a castle.

"I'd invite yeez in," Aidan says, "but it's a might messy. Didn't know I was having grand company, did I?"

His eyes are mean. There is no other way to describe them. They glint with a malevolent attitude toward the world. Or, at least, toward my sister, my cousins and me. They trail up and down our bodies. Stare at our chests. His conclusions lace his glare with disapproval.

"This was the new house," he says. "Built in 1860 by one of our grands. Hung onto it through the famine, so Grandda did."

I slide my hand over the rough plaster and stone, walls of our direct ancestors. Built somewhere in the distant past by strong determined hands. Were they excited by possibilities, driven by fear, or practical workers? A bit of all three?

"We don't care about your housekeeping," Fiona says. "We just like the history of the place."

Aidan can't resist Fiona. He opens the wooden door and leads us in. Tall, nourished Canadians that we are, we are forced to duck under the frame.

As I step inside, I try to imagine living here in cold, heat, wet, dry. Any condition at all. It's dark and damp. The floor feels like hard cement but is mud stamped down by years of tired feet. I run my fingers along a stone in the wall, rounded by wind and decades. As though I can feel the roughness of assiduous, callused skin. The tracks of their dreams, goals, mistakes and accomplishments.

"Just put yerself in the place of our oul wans, would ye?" Aidan cackles, as though he has caught our dismay and revels in our discomfort. "Imagine if ye were a bhean back then, so? Life would not be quite as grand."

I'm not exactly certain about what he's said, though Grace tells me later that "bhean" is a woman or a lady. When I look at Aidan's face, I see disdain. He thinks we're uppity; that we believe we're superior.

The cavernous fireplace is a pile of stones and rock with a yawning face. Like a child who has smeared its mouth in dark chocolate, the frame is black with ancient soot around the edges. From a sturdy iron hanger, an enormous pot displays its rusted belly with sagging fatigue. Wooden benches and once-weaved seats lean against the wall.

"Try sitting down on one of these."

He picks up a chair with legs that have splayed like a four-footed spider. His laughter mocks us.

Suddenly the dank air feels like a blanket. I duck back under the doorframe and raise my face to the sun. Out here, I smell and feel the land, the green.

I can only imagine sitting around that crooked table on uncomfortable seats, eating oatmeal and potatoes. Shivering in the cold dampness even in summer. Perhaps they spent most of their time outdoors. I hope so, but I can imagine that outside wasn't terribly welcoming either. In the fields meant work. Close to the walls of the house meant scrubbing clothes or peeling potatoes.

Auntie Beers' words have meaning here. Her bitterness has roots. I suppose even the beauty of the land could not overcome the stink of death and poverty.

I lift my shoulders and walk back in. Determined to shed the cloak of fear and disappointment. I will not be my great-aunt.

Aidan is in the middle of climbing a rickety ladder to point out the loft above the cottage.

"This here's where they slept in the winter," he says. "The cattle would be down where yeez are."

He turns his head and looks down on us. At that moment I think I have misjudged him. He looks benevolent. Perhaps he is simply nervous with all this company. Perhaps I have been unkind.

"Let's take a dooter around," he says.

When we figure out that he means to take us on a walk, we follow him to a hill that spreads over the horizon. From up here the sea is vast as it rocks and rolls along the shore in the distance. Feisty and busy, it's deep blue with streaks of turquoise. Now and then we can spy a head or two, as small as peppercorns from here, poking through the waves.

"Seals," our cousin explains. "Loads of them like to fish and play around here."

We're surprised by small palm trees and bushes that look as though they belong in the Caribbean. Aidan tells us that the winters are so mild that lots of tropical plants survive here.

"Sure, the Gulf Stream brings warm water," he says.

We spend long minutes staring at the scenery. Rather than taking my breath, the view fills me with wonder. I breathe it in. I am reminded of other moments filled with awe. Times when beauty and magnificence are no longer simply words.

Silver green and light blue. Sun plays golden fingers over the sea. Hills that look soft with clover crouch along the land.

Aidan leans over and picks a bunch of greenery.

"Shamrocks," he says.

He hands them to Fiona. A blush races from his cheeks to his ears.

"Said to bring good luck, aren't they? Ward off the evil spirits."

Fiona flashes him a smile that could have restarted a long dead car engine.

"That's magical," she says.

He nods. "Aye, truly magical."

A shout makes us turn our heads.

"Yes, I know who tha' tis," Aidan says, as though announcing a sudden death. "What're ye doing here, ya ronnie?"

At first, I expect a man whose name is Ronnie. The visitor who appears, vertebra by vertebra, is very tall. Broad, and, as the term implies, typically mannish. Except she is female with enormous breasts that fill up her sweater. A sprinkle of freckles on a round face. Piercing blue eyes and unruly light brown hair, she is an arresting creature. Wide shoulders and hips, she climbs the hill with a stride that speaks of confidence in her physicality.

She lifts her hand in greeting and swipes at her hair. The wind instantly whips it back over her forehead.

"The word has spread," she announces. "The beautiful lasses from Canada have come to visit."

She grins wickedly.

"And I see the rumor is true. Yeez have hooked up with this eejit here. Are yeez brave or stupid?"

"This is my sister Aoife," Aidan says mournfully.

I hear Ay-fah and don't see the Gaelic spelling until much later.

"Half-sister," Aoife corrects in a tone that is almost a growl. "Siblings from different mothers but the same sower.

Except the seeds were getting poorly by the time they met up with this one's ma."

She looks over at Aidan and roars laughing, her head bent backwards. Her mouth open as though she were determined to be heard over the hills.

"Right high-larious, you are, Aoife."

"Did he take yeez to the oul homestead?"

"He did! We were very excited to see our ancestral roots," Grace answers.

"If ye ever want to invest a few hundred thousand, feel free," Aoife says, but her tone is light and humorous. "Just sits there and rots. No one would buy it and no one but the eejit here could live in it without major renos."

"We'd never sell our land," Aidan retorts.

His voice reflects the instant anger that comes from an ongoing and frequent argument.

"Unlikely to get a buyer anyway."

"If we ever win a lottery…" Theresa offers.

Aoife laughs again.

"Same odds," she chuckles.

"Come to take the tour with us, Aoife?" Aidan asks.

His tone suggests he would rather she doesn't.

"Sure listen, I would if I could, but duty takes me away. I thought I'd invite yeez all out to the pub tonight. Me mates are playing down at The Snug. Starts at 8. We'll have a whale of a time."

Within three seconds, all four of us say yes, enticed not only by the magnetism of Aoife but by the prospect of a night in a real Irish pub with authentic Irish music.

"Sure and our tourist hearts have no shame at all," was how Grace put it, in our hotel room later on, doing her best impression of the local accent.

When Aoife disappears, Aidan takes us on a long winding walk. Past crumbling ruins. Pink heather rings the remnants of a church. Large stones, grey and chipped, stand looking over a patchwork of green and yellow fields. Narrow or wide, up to our shoulders in height, the rocks form a small tight circle with worn grass inside.

We snap pictures. Our cousin refuses to stand in the center with us.

Aidan shrugs when we ask what the stone circle means.

"They don't really know, do they? Though they're good at the craic; always telling stories of dug up bones, like."

We're not sure what he means by "craic" and we're unsure about "they," but he invites no further questions. When Grace finds the signpost with the explanations, Aidan drifts away.

"Estimated to have been built between 1400 and 80 BC," Grace reads aloud. "Probably used for religious rituals which may have included observations of the sun and the moon."

Fiona and Theresa have drifted away now, too.

"Lots of estimates, probably's and may's," I say as we continue to read. "I guess Aidan is right. They're just havin' the craic."

"Having a good time with us. Spreading the gossip," Grace translates as we both laugh.

We soon follow the others as Aidan silently leads us down the hill toward the cottage.

When we say goodbye and thank Aidan for his time, he gives us the same nonchalant lift of his shoulders.

"Will you be there at the pub tonight?" I ask him.

"Don't know, do I? Bit wrecked at the moment."

He disappears through that crooked wooden door and shuts it firmly. I surmise that if Fiona had asked him to come out with us there might have been a different answer.

We return to our hotel, cleverly called the Bantry Hotel. Our rooms are very tiny. When Grace and I lie down, we are almost nose to nose. The bathroom is down the hall, containing both toilets and showers with very little privacy. We're used to a different level of luxury but we're enjoying every minute.

We set out for the pub with an expectation of fun.

From the street, The Snug looks tiny. Squished between a general store and an undertaker's office. From her guidebook, Grace relates that, a few years ago, most pubs were built as a one-stop shop. Buy your groceries, have a few drinks and exchange the gossip, and arrange your burial all in the same place.

By the time we make it inside, it's jammed. The low ceilings and dark lighting make it look like a cave. Wooden beams. Stone flag floor. Down a step or two, the small entry gives way to a very large room.

Filtered with the haze of smoke and dust, the place is standing room only. Luckily Aoife has saved places for us, close to the circle of musicians. Rings of people surround them, and now, so do we.

A round faced woman with the muscular arms of someone used to lifting weights shoves huge glasses of ice-cold beer into our hands. When I grasp mine, I know what weights she lifts.

"I keep a good pint here, don't I?" she says, but we know it's not a question. "All in the creamy top it is."

We smile and nod our agreement and toast her as we drink. It's cold and smooth and delicious.

Even most of the musicians stand, balancing their instruments on bellies and shoulders. A fiddle, a banjo, a guitar. Our cousin is one of the few who sits. We can easily see why. She plays a Uilleann Pipe, which looks to me like a smaller version of a bagpipe. Though later, I think the sounds it creates are much sweeter.

Aoife cradles the bellows under her elbow and the pipes in her lap and on her leg. A couple of others play flutes or whistles. One holds a mandolin.

Aoife introduces us.

"And these lovely ladies are all the way from Canada, so they are," she says to a round of hoots and welcomes. "They're family and I'll eat the head off anyone thinking they can act the maggot."

Everyone laughs and raises their glasses.

"Sure you're the one to give us a pain in the bollocks," someone shouts.

"C'mere ta me for a minute and I'll demonstrate," Aoife says, shaking her finger at the speaker.

When the laughter dies down, the musicians break into a song that sounds so perfectly synchronized it's as though they have practised for days. And perhaps they have. Perhaps it's one they repeat weekly.

> *Can anybody tell me where the Blarney Roses grow?*
> *It may be down in Limerick Town or over in Mayo.*
> *It's somewhere in the Emerald Isle but this I want to know,*
> *Can anybody tell me where the Blarney Roses grow?*

They play sad and slow, fast and joyful. Despite the laughter and often humorous lyrics, the harmony is infused with centuries of pain. Their voices have been fashioned from grief and loss. Strengthened by hope and redemption.

We find ourselves singing with wide mouthed enthusiasm once we learn the choruses. We're never without a cold beer in our hands, though sometimes I'm not sure how it arrived there.

Sound bounces back from the tin plate ceiling, where lost and found items hang and sway with the vibration. One boot from a pair of Wellingtons. A large serving spoon. A hat. A carved wooden cane. A shirt adorned with Cork City FC on it.

In the resettling of breath when this round of songs halts, a voice shouts out.

"In the oul days no ladies would be caught drinkin' in a pub. I guess there's no ladies anymore."

There's no return laughter. Instead, a wave of dismissal and annoyance mutters through the crowd.

I recognize the voice. It seems no one thinks Aidan is "fit for company."

Our bartender, however, feels obliged to respond. Perhaps she takes it as a teachable moment for the Canadian guests as well as the misogynists in the crowd.

"Why'd ya think we're called The Snug, ya feckin eejit? We pay our tribute to those matchmakers who stood in little booths with their ladies and pointed out the good, available gents in the pub. Too bad those matchmakers aren't around today, fella. Though they might not tag you as a gentleman, so."

Now there is a round of laughter.

I glance over my shoulder and catch Aidan's eye. He flinches as though I have thrown something at him. But it doesn't stop him.

"You wouldn't recognize a gent yourself, Mary."

"As the saying goes, Aidan, you gotta go up in your arse to know who you are. Nobody's even glimpsed your arse for years."

This time I join in the laughter. Aoife tunes up the pipes and we're back to shout-singing.

> *Dirty old town, it's a dirty old town.*
> *I am a bold jobber, both youthful and airy.*
> *I know where I'm goin' and I know who's goin' with me.*
> *I know who I love, but the dear Lord knows who I'll*
>   *marry.*

Later, when the pub is less crowded, the band breaks off into little groups for a break and a chat with their family and friends. Grace and I end up leaning on the bar with Aoife and Mary, the bartender. Fiona and Theresa wander through the crowd, talking to the locals. There is no sign of Aidan.

"This is so much fun," Grace says. "I wish we had pubs like this at home."

She sways a bit, happy drunk, elated by the atmosphere.

"Aye, the local tends to be a comfortable place to be," Aoife says.

"Sure it's a bit of a confession box at times," Mary says. "People come to try and work out their problems, don't they? Sometimes just saying it out loud gives them the solution."

Aoife puts her empty glass on the bar and gestures for us to do the same.

"People used to bring their jam jars to the pub because there wasn't enough glass around, isn't that right, Mary?"

The big woman grins. Her face is round and pink cheeked. I can imagine telling her all my troubles.

"That your way of saying give me a jar, Aoife?"

We all chuckle as Mary refills our beer from a big tap.

"Yeez come here to have a chat, meet with your neighbors. Relax. Slow your thoughts for a while."

"We Irish like to enjoy life. Live for now. Probably because of our past right enough," Aoife adds.

"Likely true that. Our oul ones never had a restful time at all. Always fighting in the streets. Begging for freedom."

"Sometimes begging for the food that they grew in the first place."

The two women exchange a look that Grace and I can't fully understand and certainly can't feel. A path we haven't travelled runs through their veins. Muscle memory.

Instinct. Trauma caused by abuse, poverty and violence. Protection, a warning, passed down several generations before healing can begin.

"My father would relate the stories of the Black and Tans," Mary says, "banging down that very door."

She points to the solid wood entrance, propped open just now for the breeze.

"You can still see the marks from their battering rams. He never wanted to change it up. Wanted everyone to remember."

She swivels and points along the rear hallway.

"If any lights were spied past curfew time, they'd bash their way through and chase the culprits out that back door."

We are silent for a moment. Each of us contemplates the past.

Just then a thin, short man stumbles into the pub. He has a wide smile. The kind of face that endears all to whom he gives that grin. His body betrays his age in its crooked caution as he steps lightly into the room. Otherwise, his eyes shine youth. Mischief. That very joy-of-the-moment Mary had mentioned previously.

"There is himself at last," she says now. "I was beginning to think ya'd skipped the Snug, Old Tom."

She pours a pint into a wooden mug from the shelf behind her. Old Tom takes three steps to grasp it. He turns his gaze on Grace and me, his smile even wider.

"I see ye've brought me an audience this fine evening, Mary," he says.

"They're my family, mind," Aoife cautions. "These are my cousins, Grace and Clare. Over there is Fiona and Theresa."

Old Tom captures my heart. He has a magnetism that's difficult to explain. Especially since, up close, he has a neglected, musty smell. His teeth are yellow with some gaps here and there.

Yet when he smiles, I am reminded of the song. His Irish eyes are smiling. I feel as though I have been warmed by the sun.

Any of the band members left in the pub turn away from their conversations and fire up their instruments. Soon everyone has formed a circle around Old Tom. He jigs and free dances to enthusiastic applause and toe-tapping music. The atmosphere is light, frenetic, dizzying.

> *The first thing I spied was a long-legged goat:*
> *Bedad, and says I, for a trifle of dealing,*
> *This long, nosey puckawn is worth a pound*
> *note!*

I'm more than slightly drunk. For this reason, I don't hear the ruckus at first. I sway and sing and lose myself in euphoria. Fiona's voice, strung high with anger and fear, breaks into my reverie.

The band stops playing. Old Tom continues to whirl as he mutters the words to The Dingle Puck Goat.

The rest of the crowd swings toward my sister's strident notes.

"I said no, Aidan" are the words I hear. A couple of the tall burly men in the band place their instruments on a table. In an instant they stand between her and Aidan. Our cousin radiates the kind of malevolence that's threaded with desire. A need to control, to own.

Instantly I feel sober. I race to Fiona's side and hold her. She trembles. Folds herself into my arms. I can tell she refuses to cry, though tears fill her eyes.

"Christ Almighty, I was just tryin' to be friendly," Aidan screeches as he's carried out the door.

A month after we return, Fiona receives a small package in the mail. Inside, the carefully wrapped shamrocks have all withered and died.

Annually, for five years, the dead shamrocks arrive as failed apologies.

Amazing Grace

The Old Country 1973
By Clare O'Sullivan Doyle

When I drift off to sleep on the plane, I dream about our visit to Dublin. The city dances in my head.

When we first arrived, we sat in Grace and Brendan's cottage, gathered around their wooden table in the large kitchen. We decided to call our great-aunt GG, due to our confusion with two Graces in the room. Great-aunt Grace loved it.

She is Bairbre without the rough edges. Tall, slim. Red and grey hair. Six years younger than her sister, who this year will turn eighty, Grace is full of good humor, energy and warmth.

"We tried to convince Bairbre to come with us," I told her. "But she wouldn't even consider it."

GG's laugh was a tinkle of delight.

"I talk to her once a week on the telephone," she said. "But it never lasts more than a few minutes. Hello, how are ye and good-bye are her favorite words."

We all laughed in recognition. I was a bit surprised that Auntie Beers never mentioned those calls, though. Allowed this connection with her sister to remain unacknowledged. Especially since Maggie has been gone a long time.

From the outside of the Murphy's townhouse, we see that their home is a hybrid of old and new. They built two modern additions on either side of an old stone cottage.

Inside, antique furniture blends with modern conveniences such as a fridge that makes ice, and a dishwasher.

The décor might be called cottage. I was a fan whatever the term. Muted colors with a splash of red or dark blue here and there. Sculpted curtains. Little wooden signs displayed in various places, stating rules of the house, such as, If I get to drinking on Sunday and ask you to stay until Tuesday, remember, I don't mean it.

The cottage is tucked away in a street just a short walk from the River Liffey, surrounded by houses that have either been modernized, removed and replaced, or refurbished. If we made the short walk to the river, the city of Dublin would roar around us.

In this little enclave, I expected to hear the hooves of horses pulling a carriage. Little did I know that was exactly the form of transportation we'd use that day.

Next door, we learned, is a large old house that has been updated as well. It belongs to Anne, their eldest child, and her husband, Colin. Anne is a professor at Trinity College. Colin works in the tech industry, which always defies my understanding. They have two children, whom Grace and Brendan adore, naturally.

Their son Sean lives in France, again employed in the mysterious tech industry, with his wife Michelle and three children. GG tells us all about them.

How they visit often. How Michelle works on their large property, growing fresh vegetables, making wine. They have built a tiny home on the land for guests to stay in. Right now, Anne and her family are visiting Sean and family. We have GG and Brendan to ourselves.

I'm happy that their life in Ireland has turned out to be a good one. Their children are successful and have solid marriages. I think about Auntie Beers and wonder if she should have stayed here. Perhaps our granny Maggie too.

Brendan poured us each an enormous amount of Irish whiskey, which I had more trouble sipping than my sister and cousins did. Luckily, we were traveling by bus and staying a couple of nights in a hotel. No one had to drive or fly home with whiskey in our bellies.

"Sure I'm sorry ye didn't get to see our farm," GG said. "We spend a great deal of our time there, though we do love the city too. I'm delighted that you were able to see the old homestead. I would have difficulty living the way Aidan does, but he wants to keep it as it was in the old days. Which is grand for the family history, isn't it?"

"He's a dosser," Brendan said. "Too lazy to change things up."

The way he phrased it and the smile he gave us took the sting out of the comment.

"Ara, he's just happy out. And it's brilliant for being able to understand how they lived in the past," GG said.

"We did learn a lot," I offered, grateful for their help in mining our family history. "It's a tribute to our great greats' strength and determination that they could live like that and survive."

"It was particularly brutal during the famine," Brendan said. "They—and ultimately, we—were fortunate that one of our greats, mine and yours, bid for those lots and purchased them at some stage in our combined history. Otherwise, they would likely have been thrown out. Owning the land meant they could scrape out an existence."

"Sure it was a bold and intelligent move," GG agreed. "And a miracle they could hold onto it when the British began giving away the land to loyal soldiers after the world wars. Even the ones that the Irish owned."

Brendan gave a rueful chuckle.

"True that. But nobody wanted those small bits of land above the ocean. Out in the middle of nowhere. It looked like scrap. Even eejit soldiers didn't fancy it. It stayed with us instead."

"My husband is a miracle worker," GG said, patting his hand affectionately. "He had so many ideas and turned our farm into a money-making machine."

Theresa and Fiona nodded politely, while Grace looked pensive.

"Do you think Maggie and Bairbre would have been happier if they had stayed in Ireland?" she suddenly asked.

I looked over at my cousin. Once again, she had read my mind.

Perhaps the whiskey made her feel comfortable enough to pose the question. Her study of psychotherapy has led her to be curious about motives even amid the family history. Perhaps especially amid the family history, given our connection to Auntie Beers and the trauma of Liam's death.

"Uncle Michael said that Maggie was given jars of phenobarbital by her doctor. He believes that's how she died."

Now I was shocked and nearly choked on my sip of the Jameson. I sat up straight, trying to think straight as well.

GG didn't look surprised. Nor was she reticent about answering. Even Fiona and Theresa listened. This revelation was astounding.

"Yes, Maggie allowed her troubles to overcome her and unfortunately, she had a doctor who simply wanted her to go away and not bother him. So he supplied her with drugs to keep her calm. Bairbre and I talked about the situation from time to time, but there seemed little we could do about it."

"My mother thought she was brokenhearted over Liam," I said, astonishing myself with the ease of my admission. "She felt such embarrassment over his actions. As though it was a mark against the family."

Our great-aunt nodded, sipped her whiskey and closed her eyes for a moment.

"Maggie took after our mother, so she did. Even though she wanted the opposite. The two of them always worried about what other people said or thought."

"Uncle Michael told me she was very proud. Wouldn't accept charity even when they needed the gifts of food or clothing. When Séamus became a sort of partner with the farmer Reid, she thought they had finally reached their station in life. Then Mr. Reid became ill and everything fell apart again."

Michael was always open about his experiences. Grace went to him occasionally as her primary source for family history.

When I write the story of my family during the War of Independence, I'd have no better source than GG and Brendan. That meant I'd have to return to this city of passion.

"Poor Maggie seemed to have more ups and downs in her life than any of us, didn't she? Except perhaps our mother, Fiona. Our Ma won and lost and won and lost. Ma would turn scarlet if anyone, even family, made a comment about the state of things. Sure herself was very like her daughter after her."

I cast my mind back to the fleeting memories I had of Granny Maggie. Her hands were as soft as our kitten's fur. I remembered looking into her light blue eyes where a crinkling smile would be given to me in turn. She stroked my cheek affectionately and whispered in Gaelic. "Is tú mo stóirín." You are my sweetheart.

Her voice was low and raspy, giving her words an intimate sound. Most visits, she would cut each of us a giant piece of what we called chocolate roll. Mainly because it was chocolate cake rolled up with cream inside. In my memory, Granny was kind and loving to her grandchildren.

"Ireland was a rough place to live in the late 1800s and early 1900s," Brendan said. "More so than most countries. We were kept under the thumbs of the British crown for so long we forgot we were class. Many people lost the will, so they did. They're saying now that the famine was a form of genocide."

"It took bold people to fight for freedom," GG added. "When Maggie and Séamus lived in Dublin, they were in the thick of it. Irish fighting Irish, Irish fighting British, Catholics against Protestants, Pro-Treaty versus Anti-Treaty."

"It was a different world from ours," Brendan said. "We were culchies. People from the country. Each day was a struggle to feed everyone. Both our families. Ourselves. We spent every hour from when the sun came up to when it set again, working in the fields, the bog. On the sea."

He sipped his whiskey and looked around, as though he still couldn't believe his surroundings.

"Here in the city, they were struggling for our independence," he continued. "For Ireland. They'd a different life. Every day their thoughts were of a political nature. A violent way of living. Who would have to be sacrificed today to move their way forward?"

GG had been nodding while her husband spoke.

"Here in Dublin there were always skirmishes. Even shootings. People were tossed into prison just for being part of a discussion group. The cruelty and bullying on the part of the British created harsh retaliation from the Irish. The Crown wanted to repress the people they considered their subjects and keep the country under their rule."

Brendan took up the tale.

"For hundreds of years most people wanted to be free from Britain. To be an independent country and own our land once more. After centuries of repression, people had very different ideas about what an independent Ireland looked like. There were even disputes among the freedom fighters," Brendan said. "When they weren't fighting the British, they were fighting each other."

"But Séamus and Maggie were so in love. They couldn't get enough of one another."

"Almost as fierce as Grace and meself."

Our great-aunt smiled fondly over at her husband.

"In those days, that fierceness meant lots of children if you were strong enough to bear them. Which Maggie turned out to be."

"Maggie wasn't able to stay in Ireland anyway," Brendan said. "Not after Séamus had to flee."

Once again, I nearly choked on my whiskey. Which had, miraculously, almost disappeared from my glass.

"He had to leave Ireland?" Grace asked.

For once, she didn't know this piece of family history either.

GG and Brendan looked at one another, a silent signal passing between them. The grandchildren didn't know. Should we be the ones to tell them?

GG made the decision.

"Séamus got involved with the Irish Republican Army. Something he didn't share with Maggie at the time. We haven't got the details, but he was advised to remove himself from the country and given passage to do so."

"Someone discovered they could work on the farms in Canada. Sure they believed that would lead to ownership of land. Free housing on top. Of course, none of that was true," Brendan continued.

"Bairbre loved Maggie's weans so much," GG said. "There was no question that she'd separate from them. Life in the new country was not easy. Séamus had to work as a farmhand to pay off the entire family's passage before he received any compensation. They were terribly poor even before the Depression destroyed the world balance."

Brendan stood up suddenly.

"Sure, listen, enough of the past," he said. "Let's take these weans off to see our city as it is now. Not completely stable, mind, but filled with the joy of life. Come see how we'll trot to the city in style."

When we tumbled out onto the cobblestone road, there was the horse and buggy I'd imagined. The driver smiled and helped us climb in. Over the bridge across the Liffy. Into the wide street of O'Connell. From here, we walked.

The city buzzed around us. Buildings that were very old, refurbished. Bulletin-ridden columns in front of the impressive General Post Office.

By bus, we travelled across the city for a tour of the Kilmainham prison with its shameful past. Cells tiny, oppressive. Frightening.

We took another bus to the Guinness Factory. Not only did we have fun, but we learned a lot about beer and received certificates stating that we poured a beautiful pint. From the top floor of the building, we gazed over the roofs of the city. From here it was quiet and lovely.

We sampled the night life in the Temple Bar district, joining the tourists and the residents in music and laughter. And whiskey and beer.

Over the next couple of days, I took notes in earnest. Determined that someday, I would return and write that book.

On the airplane home, Grace and I leaned against one another. Half sad and half thrilled to be going home.

"Judging by Aidan's performance in the pub…" I said at long last, having mulled these thoughts around in my head. Feeling a sense of betrayal at ruining the beautiful image we'd formed of our Irish relatives. "There's a lot more to the drinking than Mary or Aoife would admit. I read that alcoholism is a huge problem in Ireland overall. About three people a day die of it."

Grace snuggled closer.

Whispered with that same sense of disloyalty.

"People are people," she said. "Doesn't matter where you live. We just have to do the best we can. At least with a pub on every corner, they must cut down on drunk driving."

I chuckled. "Good point."

Grace began to recite a Celtic poem we found in a book in our hotel's library. Soon I joined her. Softly. Reverently. Wishing we'd all live in the present.

I arise today
through the strength of heaven, light of sun,
radiance of moon,
splendor of fire,
speed of lightning,
swiftness of wind,
depth of sea,
stability of earth,
firmness of rock.

Leaving Urbston

By Clare O'Sullivan Doyle

Nearly sixty years later, the murder at the Queen's Hotel is still the worst thing that ever happened to me.

Despite the times that lay ahead. The losses. The choices in the path of life that led to heartache in various ways.

At fifteen, I planned to join a volunteer group to help build homes in third world countries. I would do that when I was sixteen.

I did not.

In the 60s and 70s, I went to school and marched. Got involved in social justice groups. Vowed we would be the generation that would change things.

We did not.

From Auntie Beers, I learned to struggle past any regrets. I didn't see the point of allowing life to get me down. I was lucky to have an optimistic disposition that drove me uphill every time I fell into a valley.

I write mystery books, almost always with a crime, and always containing puzzles to be solved. Perhaps in this way, I retain control over life. I can solve anything with fiction.

To my surprise, a top agent picked me up and my novels sold well. The 70s were flush with government grants in the arts field. I was able to travel. Network. I had Margaret Laurence and Al Purdy on my list of pen pals.

During those years I was a hippie of sorts, though never did I suffer from want. My career in journalism and publishing allowed me to travel. Be quirky. Take chances. Never rich, but never poor either.

I did get to perform some of those charitable acts that I dreamt about in my youth. Speaking gigs that supported people in need. Donations. Enticing wealthy people to pay to have their name in my book and other creative fund-raising ideas that came from those who did this for a living.

I haven't found a relationship that lasted through my wild adventures. It doesn't help that I disappear for months at a time to either write or research or both. Promo tours take me away for weeks at a time, too.

Now that I am older, I don't even want a relationship. In this way, I am like Auntie Beers. Never settling for one man. Always interested in what a physical romp with this one or that one would be like. Thus breaking the trust of the current lover.

Unlike my great-aunt, I am happy.

I left small town Urbston behind and it grew in my absence. The prison became a huge, ugly sore at the edges of the city. Its fetid breath spread along with its giant walls. Turned that side of town into dark alleys and empty lots for drug deals. People slumped against fences. Houses were abandoned and left to rot.

On the other side of Urbston, the one that brushed up against Robus Estates, even the air was different. Perfumed with the scent of roses and other plants. Canada's Flower Town. Awards hung inside the glass. Green opaque walls and rooftops sat primly along the river.

People were either employed by the Robus Flower Estates or they worked in the Civitas Federal Prison. In the 1950s and 60s, at least everyone was employed.

No one spoke out loud about the differences in status, but it was a blanket that fell over prison guards or administrators. Only Warden Luckinbill escaped the condescension, though people still joked about his name and his birth town of Giggleswick.

Uncle Michael's friend, Lorenzo Malpensa, worked as a prison guard for forty years. He saw the youngest of the

CATHERINE ASTOLFO

O'Sullivans, Liam, go through the jail. He survived the great riot of 1964. The murder at the Queen's Hotel.

Eventually, he replaced Warden Luckinbill. Warden Malpensa, roughly translated from the Italian to "bad thinking," was arguably worse than Luckinbill, but most people had no idea what the name really meant.

Lorenzo's son, LJ, became a well-known lawyer in Toronto, he too leaving Urbston behind. Yet he cared for his father and never let a day pass by when they didn't speak, or a weekend go where they didn't meet. Lorenzo was, by all accounts, a wonderful grandfather. He lived until he was ninety.

Brian Cottreau remained a good friend of Lorenzo's after retirement. They were both frequent visitors at the Legion even in their eighties. Brian died at seventy-nine. Some people believed he couldn't live without Lorenzo.

Auntie Beers' heart silently gave up beating somewhere in the middle of the night when she was ninety-three.

I believe the murder haunted all of us. The sight of the endless spray of blood throughout that dour hallway could never leave any one of us.

Sometimes I can still hear my great-aunt's voice. The lilt of her accent that made her words sound soft even if she had something nasty to say. The lustiness of rare laughter that filled a room. Her way of stating an opinion as though it were fact.

From Auntie Beers, I learned to be strong. To follow my own path. To make my words count. I learned from what she did as well as what she said. I learned from the mistakes she made.

I learned that violence could sear a heart. Can leave a scar that awakens the nightmare every time I picture a tall, lanky blond man with a beautiful face.

Violence can also turn fear into words and stories that are controlled by the hand of the writer. Can be a world where love and respect always win.

> *As easily as that,*
> *the rock turns*
> *in my hand,*
> *displaces soil,*
> *the lives beneath.*
> *I am a glacier.*
> *Move mountains*
> *on whim*
> *change histories*
> *on impulse.*

Acknowledgements

Thank you, Carrick Publishing, for your support of Canadian authors and, always, of me and my efforts.

Thanks to my editors, Mary Jo Wiley Dwyer, Wendy Gill, Patricia Goodfellow,

Kristen Henderson, Cynthia Straw, Helen Duplassie, Maire Kearns and Vincent Astolfo.

Special thanks to my Personal Assistant, Catherine Soehner, who helped with everything from edits to marketing to keeping me going.

Immense thanks and love to my husband, who not only goes through the worst aspects of my illness, but who doesn't complain that I sit at my desk for hours ignoring him. To my children, Kristen and James, for absolutely everything.

Thank you to Ma Belle-Fille, actress/producer/writer Meredith Henderson, who was my caregiver for seven months and who kept listening and telling me I'd finish this book, dammit! Watch for the audio version of Auntie Beers in Meredith's lilting, captivating voice.

To my sisters, Cindy Straw, Chris Asquith and Kim Atkinson, who kept listening and encouraging me through good times and bad, and who are my "three sisters." To my sister Candace, who, if she were still here, would have been on this like a kid to…well, Candy.

Huge appreciation for my Uncle Thomas Sullivan, who gives me his stories, shares his memories, and encourages a wicked sense of humour in all of us. We love you.

Thanks to Leslie Smith, Lynn Patterson, and Jennifer Kerr, who went with me to Ireland in October 2022 so I could cement my memories from trips of long ago. To Scott

Hummel and Kristen Henderson for continuing to listen when we all went to Portugal.

Thank you, critique group, the Deadly Dames: Melodie Campbell, Janet Bolin, Joan Callaghan, Alison Bruce, and Nancy O'Neill.

Thanks to Bruce Bolin for the cover picture and other promo pix.

To all of you who have Multiple Myeloma or other forms of the disease, I hope you have care as exceptional as mine at the Juravinski Cancer Centre in Hamilton. I hope you have a John Kearns, too, who safely gets me there and back.

Any errors, of course, are mine, Clare's, or belong to Auntie Beers when she tells the history, and all poems and songs are old enough to have lost the copyright or are quoted in small (legal) doses.

About the Author

Catherine Astolfo is an award-winning author of mystery short stories and novels. She is a Derrick Murdoch award winner for service to Crime Writers of Canada and a Past President.

Catherine's a member of Crime Writers of Canada, Sisters in Crime and The Mesdames of Mayhem.

Auntie Beers is an amalgam of tales her mother told her as well as a mystery that she couldn't resist.

For updates, check amazon.com/author/catherineastolfo.

Printed in the USA
CPSIA information can be obtained
at www.ICGtesting.com
LVHW090243220424
778057LV00002B/228